WESTOVER

WESTOVER

by

RICHMAL CROMPTON

HUTCHINSON & CO. (Publishers) LTD.

LONDON : NEW YORK : MELBOURNE : SYDNEY

Made and Printed in Great Britain by
Cheltenham Press Ltd., Cheltenham and London.

WESTOVER

WESTOVER stood a mile or so beyond the village of Pakenham, a small eighteenth-century manor house, built in rather a pretentious Renaissance style, its long uniform façade broken by the inevitable pediment and portico. Actually it was neither as picturesque nor as commodious as it appeared when glimpsed through the trees from the main road, for, on a closer inspection, the stucco was broken and discoloured, and the breadth of the building was too narrow in proportion to its length. It lacked even the glamour of tradition that can redeem the ugliest buildings, for no one interesting or distinguished had ever lived in it, and it had never been in the possession of the same family for longer than two generations.

Its last owner had been a Lieutenant-Colonel Gideon, who had been killed in the second year of the war, leaving his widow with five children and insufficient means for the maintenance of the house, even if she had wished to live in it. She had left it soon after the outbreak of war, as it had been commandeered by the military authorities for use in connection with a neighbouring aerodrome. They had restored it to her shortly after the armistice in not too bad a condition considering that it had formed part of the "front line" during the Battle of Britain, and that a flying bomb had fallen within three hundred feet of it in 1944. The pediment over the front door was broken and a portion only of the parapet that ran along the top of the house remained, but ceilings and windows had been repaired, and the building had been made habitable.

Mrs. Gideon, now comfortably settled with her children in a small modern house, a mile or so distant, was faced with the problem of its disposal. The post-war scarcity of servants made it difficult to sell or let such properties, and an idealized description of it in the columns of the daily press drew forth no response.

It was her brother James, a London solicitor, as practical and business-like as she herself was vague and unbusiness-like, who had suggested turning it into flats, and Mrs. Gideon had allowed herself to be persuaded half against her will. She had been dismayed by the cost of the necessary alterations, but her brother had insisted that there must be nothing makeshift about them, and the house now contained three fair-sized flats, each newly decorated, with kitchen, bathroom and the usual offices. Very little had been done to the outside of the house, and the broken pediment and parapet had not been repaired.

"We can see to that when the rents begin to roll in," said her brother.

One of the flats had been let to a widowed aunt of Mrs. Gideon's. A notice in *The Times* advertising the others had brought such a spate of answers that Mrs. Gideon despaired of ever sorting them out, but her brother had taken charge of the situation and selected the two tenants whom he considered most suitable. One flat was now let to a widow and her daughter, the other to two brothers, recently demobilized, and their wives. The brothers and one of the wives were coming this afternoon to look over the flat and take measurements for curtains and furniture.

"Well, I think I've fixed on tenants who won't give any trouble," said James with a self-congratulatory air.

"Oh, James," said Mrs. Gideon, "I wonder if you can really have so many people enclosed in such a small space and be sure there won't be any trouble."

"Of course there won't," said James shortly. He was the sort of man who never had any doubts about anything. His sister, five years his junior, had always stood slightly in awe of him.

"I barred children from the beginning," he added.

"I'm rather sorry you did that," said Mrs. Gideon. "I think I'd have liked children here. They'd have been friends for Richard and Rachel. Besides—" she considered the house, her head on one side, "it needs children. They take away that bare look—prams and babies on the lawn and little boys climbing trees."

"It has—associations for you, of course," said her brother indulgently. "I realize that the whole business must be rather distressing."

"Not in the way you think," she said slowly. "I came here when I married and all my children were born here, but I was never fond of the house. I think I disliked it for trying to look more important than it really was."

He laughed—shortly and a little impatiently.

"That, my dear, is an asset in the eyes of sensible people."

"I'm afraid I'm not very sensible," she said apologetically. "I'm grateful to you for seeing to all this for me, James."

"You're certainly not very sensible, my dear, but you must try to be as sensible as you can. About these tenants, I mean. Don't have anything to do with the business side of it. The agreements are all cut and dried and everything's in Monk's hands in Nettleford. Don't let them expect you to see to repairs or leaking pipes or anything like that. Just say 'It's nothing to do with me. It's in Monk's hands in Nettleford'."

Her grey eyes twinkled.

"I see. Just like that. 'It has nothing to do with me. It's in Monk's hands in Nettleford'."

There was the faintest imitation of his preciseness in her manner. He accorded her a wintry smile.

"You'll find I'm right, my dear. The less you have to do with your tenants either socially or in the way of business, the better."

"Oh, but—socially!" She sounded like a disappointed child. "I like people, and I was looking forward to having some new neighbours."

He shrugged.

"Well, don't blame me if——" He took out his watch. "I hope they aren't going to be late."

"No, I'm sure they won't be," she said soothingly.

"My dear Julia, how can you be sure? You know nothing whatever about them. You've never even met them, have you?"

"No, I suppose I haven't." She wondered why she always seemed more foolish with James than with anyone else, and went on hastily, "We hoped you'd come and have dinner with us afterwards."

" 'Fraid I can't manage it. Got a dinner engagement in town. . . . How are the children?"

"Very well. Colin seems to like his work."

"Greig's a good man," said James approvingly.

It was James who had advised that Colin, Julia's eldest son, should be articled to Nettleford's leading solicitor, even suggesting that later on he might take him into partnership himself.

In spite of his hard-headedness, James was generous, and one of his few weaknesses was a fondness for his only sister. That he considered her utterly lacking in commonsense and devoid of the faintest gleam of intelligence increased rather than diminished his affection. He had always considered commonsense and intelligence a male prerogative.

He was a thin stooping desiccated-looking man in the early forties, with keen humourless eyes and long straight lips generally slightly compressed as if in judicial consideration. His old-fashioned style of dress—wing collar, cravat-like tie, narrow trousers—made him seem older than he was. His smile was rare and reluctant. He inspired confidence in his clients, though few were on familiar terms with him.

"And Roger?" he said.

His sister's manner became a little nervous and apologetic. Roger was sixteen, and since her husband's death James had paid his school fees. Roger, unduly sensitive, resented being under an obligation to his uncle, and put down James' patronising manner (which happened to be his normal manner) to the fact that he was paying two hundred pounds a year for his education. When the two met, anyone who knew Roger well could have sensed the resentment beneath his politeness. Fortunately James did not know Roger well.

Mrs. Gideon was conscious of a feeling of relief that James would not be able to come to dinner with them. Just as well that he and Roger should not see too much of each other. . . .

"He won several prizes for running at the sports," she said.

"Running's not everything," said James.

"He had a poem in the school magazine last term."

"Hope he's not going in for writing poetry," said James, disapprovingly. "That won't get him anywhere."

"I know, but it's nice for him to do it. I mean——" she searched for words to express the pride and joy that Roger's poem had given her, and ended lamely, "it was a very nice poem."

"Waste of time, waste of time," said James.

"Do you think so?" she said wistfully. "Anyway, I'll send you his report."

Oh dear, she thought, I wish I hadn't promised to do that. Roger had been furious when he discovered last term that she had sent his report to James, and she knew that he would do his best to prevent her sending the next one.

"Fantastic prices these places charge," went on James, adding, "I don't mean I grudge it . . . I'm speaking quite impersonally."

"Yes, of course," said Mrs. Gideon meekly. "When the rents begin to come in I can pay it myself, can't I?"

"Well, well," said James, "We'll see . . . we'll see."

He was a man who cherished his grievances and the grievance of Roger's school fees was his favourite one. He grumbled about them to his clients, his friends, his acquaintances, even his employees. It was a grievance he would have sorely missed, had it been removed.

"Laura's left school, I think you said."

"Yes . . . she's helping at a crêche in Nettleford. It was started during the war for the children of war workers, you know, and it still seems useful so they're going on with it . . . she enjoys the work."

He nodded approvingly. He liked a woman, if she worked, to do womanly work, and crêches were essentially womanly. He had always approved of Laura—a quiet flower-like slip of a girl, with brown hair and soft brown eyes.

"And the others?" he said.

"Richard and Rachel? They're all right, bless them." Richard ought to be going to a prep. school, she thought. Perhaps I shall be able to send him now we've let the flats, though I suppose it will take some time to make up for all the money we've spent on them. I wish I understood better about money. I never needed to when Humphrey was alive . . . And I'd miss Richard terribly.

"You spoil 'em, you know," growled James. "No discipline in the home."

"No," agreed Mrs. Gideon deprecatingly, "there really isn't much, is there?"

James derived a certain satisfaction from the position he had lately assumed as protector of the fatherless household, though, fortunately perhaps, he saw little of its members.

In spite of his affection for his sister, he had never been very intimate with her family. He had always felt ill at ease with Humphrey and the two had by mutual consent avoided each other.

They had reached the house now and Mrs. Gideon stood, looking up at it.

"No," she said slowly, "I don't like it, even now. I'm not even sorry for it. It doesn't care. It's probably quite pleased with itself. It's a selfish sort of house. It never cared what happened to us."

"Don't talk such nonsense, Julia," said James impatiently.

"It isn't nonsense. Humphrey never liked it. He was born in it and spent his childhood in it, but it never meant anything to him. Roger's the only one of the children who loves it. He's romantic, of course, and perhaps it gives him something it's never given us."

James took out his watch again.

"Well, if I'm to have time to look in on the aunts as I promised . ." he said.

II

MRS. HAYTON carefully checked over the contents of the tea-table to make sure that everything was there. It was quite an Occasion, having James and Julia to tea. James had said that he wasn't sure that he would be able to come, so they mustn't count on him, but James always said that . . . It was just one of his little ways. He was afraid of being tied down to anything. He always said, too, that he had a dinner engagement in town, but Mrs. Hayton had long ceased believing in the engagement. It was a sort of shield interposed between James and possible claims on his time and interest.

She had been into Nettleford this morning to buy some ginger-breads. James as a little boy had been passionately fond of ginger-breads. She used to send him tins of them to school and he used to reply:

"Dear Aunt Lucy, Thank you for the gingerbreds. I hope you are well . . . Love from James."

He had been a beautiful writer even then and, on the whole, a good speller. He had soon tumbled to the 'a' in gingerbread.

Dear James! He had taken such a lot of trouble, fixing up the business of this flat for them. It seemed dreadful in a way to be living in Julia's old home, but, after all, once it was turned into flats, someone had to live in it, and it was nicer for Julia to have the family here than strangers . . . she only hoped that Letitia would be happy. Poor Letitia! She had had such a tragic life, she deserved a little happiness. She began to hum, then, remembering that Letitia was resting, checked herself with an apologetic little cough.

Letitia was the younger of the two sisters by eleven years. She had always outshone Lucy in brains, charm and intelligence, and Lucy (who had adored her from babyhood) had been content that it should be so. Lucy herself was so plain and dumpy and quiet that it was a surprise to everyone (herself included) when she got married. It was not, of course, such a brilliant marriage as Letitia's, for Letitia had married Lionel Drummond, a popular writer, whose books brought him in a considerable income and who lived in Chelsea, poised expertly on the dividing line between the world of fashion and the world of

Bohemia. For the thirty or so years of their married lives (Letitia married when she was twenty and Lucy when she was over thirty) the sisters wrote to each other regularly but seldom met. Lucy would occasionally ask Letitia to stay with her, but Letitia was generally too busy, and Lucy realized that the life she led with George in the Midlands—a life that satisfied every need of her nature, for George, though somewhat unpolished, was kind and generous and loved her dearly—had little to offer her more brilliant sister.

Letitia's letters described a life that was to Lucy as unreal as a fairy tale—a life of first nights and dinner-parties and concerts, of foreign travel and meetings with writers whose names were to Lucy only so many letters on the backs of library books and who held for her such a legendary glamour that she was childishly thrilled to find that they ate meals and walked about the streets like other people. She even saw occasional photographs of Letitia in groups in the illustrated papers, standing by the side of her husband—a tall distinguished-looking man with a pointed beard, whom Lucy had not met since the wedding.

The war put an end to this life, and for a year or two Letitia's letters were short and infrequent, but it was a shock to Lucy to learn from an almost illegible letter (Letitia's writing was never easy to read) that Lionel had "gone off with another woman," that he had been "consistently brutal" to Letitia throughout their married life, and that Letitia had always been "desperately unhappy" with him, though she had been too loyal to say so. It happened that George was ill at the time, so Lucy could do little but send a five-page letter of condolence, and when, a fortnight later, George died Lucy was too much distracted to do anything but wonder how she was going to face life without him.

Further letters from Letitia followed—expressing perfunctory sympathy, but hinting darkly that Lucy was well rid of George, or indeed any husband, and discussing her plans. She was, of course, going to divorce Lionel . . . She meant to make him pay a handsome alimony. After the war she would probably go to live in the South of France . . .

Then came a letter that roused Lucy from her lethargy. Lionel had been knocked down by an army lorry and killed. There would be no alimony, or indeed any money at all, for Lionel had been "improvident" and lived up to if not beyond his income. He had died in debt. There might be royalties from his work, but his work had been essentially "ephemeral" (Lucy had to look up the word in the dictionary), and the sales would probably dwindle to nothing after his death. In any case they would hardly keep Letitia in shoes. She was penniless, wrote Letitia, underlining the word several times. The river was the only solution . . .

Lucy wired to her to come at once, and Letitia came, looking tragic and beautiful in new (and very smart) mourning. They stayed in Lucy's house for a time, but Letitia did not care for the Midlands.

Like Mr. Belloc, she found them sodden and unkind. And Lucy was not happy either. She missed George and she felt apologetic to Letitia for everything—her house, her servants and her friends—because she knew that they were not the sort of thing that Letitia was accustomed to. So they went to a boarding house at Bath and from there to a boarding house at Harrogate, and from there to a boarding house at Tunbridge Wells. Then James told them about Westover and they agreed to take one of the flats.

Lucy thought it would be nice to be near Julia and the children, and Letitia thought it would do as well as anywhere else for the present. So the sisters settled into Westover and resumed the relationship of their girlhood—for to Lucy, maternal and self-effacing, Letitia was still the lovely brilliant young girl of thirty years ago, a little wayward, a little difficult, perhaps, but to be loved and cherished all the more on that account.

The domestic situation presented certain difficulties, as a morning charwoman was all that could be procured in the neighbourhood, and Lucy realized that Letitia, who had from her youth been "delicate"—with that indeterminate and convenient delicacy that has no connection with any specific disease—wanted a good deal of waiting on and naturally could not be expected to wait on herself. So Lucy (who suffered from rheumatism and could herself do little active work) engaged a "companion"—a quiet capable woman called Miss Parsons, who so far had managed very well, though there were times when she obviously got a little on Letitia's nerves—delicate organs that had always been peculiarly accessible.

Julia and James found Lucy sitting on the settee knitting sea-boot stockings for the Merchant Navy. (She had knitted them throughout the war and found it difficult to stop.)

At sixty-four Lucy was plainer and more dumpy than ever, but the radiating good humour of her face amply compensated for her lack of beauty. No one ever saw Lucy "put out." If she was a little depressed sometimes, she kept it to herself . . .

"*Isn't* this nice!" she said, beaming from one to the other. "Sit down, both of you. This is Miss Parsons, James" (as Miss Parsons came in from the kitchen, carrying a plate of sandwiches). "She very kindly looks after us, and really I don't know what we'd do without her."

Julia sat down and looked about her.

"How pretty your curtains are, Aunt Lucy!" she said.

"Yes, Letitia chose them," said Lucy, torn between pride in Letitia's taste and horror at what they had cost.

James wandered about the room, inspecting the furniture and the view from the window.

"Very snug little place," he boomed. "Very snug indeed. Best side of the house, too. Smaller rooms than those at the front but more pleasant. Pretty view over the garden. You'll have to do something about that garden, Julia. Overgrown. Gives a bad impression. Thought you'd got a gardener . . ."

Lucy and Miss Parsons had been looking at him with expressions of growing dismay. Miss Parsons glanced at a door at the further end of the room, and Lucy laid her hand, gently deprecating, on his arm.

"James, dear," she said, "please don't talk quite so loud. You see, Letitia——"

She looked helplessly at Miss Parsons.

"Mrs. Drummond lies down in the afternoon," explained Miss Parsons, "and we always keep very quiet till we know she's awake. It upsets her to be awakened."

"She's not strong, you know," said Lucy.

"Well, well," boomed James, then, remembering her injunction, sank his voice to a hoarse rasping whisper. "Bit awkward if she goes on sleeping, isn't it?"

"We always wait tea for her," whispered Aunt Lucy. Her bright face clouded over as her instincts of hospitality fought with the consideration that she felt was due to Letitia, "I'll make tea the *minute* I hear her."

Miss Parsons had put her ear to the door.

"I think she's stirring," she whispered. "I'll go and see if I can do anything for her . . ."

She tapped on the door—a tiny tap like the tap of a bird's beak. A voice said faintly: "Come in."

Miss Parsons opened the door a fraction of an inch and vanished miraculously through the chink.

The cloud passed from Lucy's face.

"I'll make the tea in a moment," she said, "as soon as I think she's ready. Now tell me all about our new neighbours, Julia. It will be nice for Letitia to have a little company. I'm not much of a companion for her. I'm not intellectual, you know, and she has——" Lucy's voice sank to a note of hushed admiration, "a wonderful intellect."

James looked at his watch.

"Haven't much time to spare," he said. "Got a dinner engagement in town, and I want to see these people . . ."

"Oh, I'll make tea now, James," said Lucy. "I expect Letitia will be ready any moment. The kettle's on the boil."

She went into the kitchen and, while she was away, Letitia could be heard through her closed bedroom door saying: "*Really*, Miss Parsons!" in a voice expressive of patience strained to breaking point.

James still wandered about, absent-mindedly valuing the contents of the room. Wouldn't fetch much in a sale, but sound old-fashioned stuff . . .

Julia's eyes had a dreamy far-away look in them. This room had been the nursery when the children were little. There had been an old-fashioned barred gate at which they used to make toast and a high fire-guard round it, over which their damp things used to be put to dry when they came in from winter walks. She could almost smell that peculiar five o'clock smell of toast and damp tweed . . . On really wet afternoons they used to sit round the big table in the middle of the room painting or cutting out . . Colin's toy fort had been in that corner . . . The bookcase had been there, filled to overflowing with children's animals in various stages of dilapidation. Laura's shelf had been the only tidy one. Richard and Rachel used to spread their toy farm right over the floor so that you couldn't move without treading on a barn or a cow. . . .

The Hornby train had been Roger's hobby. He kept it in the old greenhouse in the garden. The lines were fixed round the stage and he made imitation scenery, with bits of sponge painted green and fixed on to pieces of wood for trees. Richard and Rachel would sometimes lend him cows from their farm to put in his fields.

She used to read to them here in the evenings, sitting on the shabby old horsehair armchair by the fire. They loved being read to—even Colin and Laura. When she was reading *Alice in Wonderland* to the little ones, Colin and Laura would often join them. Sometimes Humphrey would come in too . . . She saw herself sitting in the armchair with Richard and Rachel perched one on either arm of it, Roger cross-legged on the floor, and Colin and Laura in the chair opposite . . . and the door opening to admit Humphrey, pipe in mouth, his eyes smiling. Her mind sheered away from the memory, then she forced it to return, to relive the moment, to let Humphrey come in, sit on the edge of the table and sit there listening.

"Now I must really stop," she had said. "It's Rachel's bed-time."

"You can't stop there, woman," Humphrey had said. "Go on. '—change lobsters and retire in the same order'." He knew the book almost by heart. So she read to the end of the chapter and he carried Rachel pick-a-back into the night nursery, with Richard hanging on behind shouting:

" 'Will you walk a little faster?' said a whiting to a snail,
    There's a porpoise close behind us, and he's treading on my tail'."

When first she heard of Humphrey's death, she had not been able to bear her memories of him and had determinedly shut them out. Then she had thought that perhaps by shutting them out she was shutting Humphrey out, too, so she compelled herself to admit them. At first it had hurt horribly—like the coming to life of a frost-bitten limb—but gradually the pain was growing less and sometimes she almost recaptured that sense of peace and happiness that his living presence had always given her.

The door opened and Lucy came in with the teapot and hot-water jug.

"Now!" she said, settling down comfortably by the table. "Let's have some tea. Sugar for you, James, isn't it, and not for Julia?

You must have the scones while they're hot. And now tell me about the other tenants. Two brothers and their wives, isn't it?"

"Yes," said Julia vaguely. "The Fieldings. I haven't seen them yet."

"References excellent," said James. "Actually I've only met the elder brother. They've both been married since the war. I gather that the two wives haven't met yet . . . And the others are more or less local people, Mrs. and Miss Pollock. Came to Nettleford just before the war. Good-class house and bills paid regularly. Lease of house run out. That's why they're moving."

"I think I know them by sight," said Julia. "The daughter's a cripple, isn't she?"

"I believe so . . ."

Letitia entered, followed by Miss Parsons.

Letitia was a strikingly handsome woman, tall, slender, aristocratic-looking, with white hair always beautifully "set," a high bridged nose, a delicate complexion and deep blue eyes. Though she was fifty-three people still turned in the street to look at her. She dressed tastefully and at considerable expense and had on now a black after-noon dress, so faultlessly cut that it made Lucy's ready-made "for the not so slender" (as the advertisement put it) look outrageously baggy.

She stood for a moment in the doorway, as if to ensure an effective entrance, then swept forward to greet Julia and James.

"My dear, how nice!" she said, kissing Julia. "We're such close neighbours now and yet we see so little of each other."

"I'm so busy with the house and children," said Julia apologetically.

Letitia turned to James with a deepening and intensifying of her charm.

"Now, James, this *is* a treat. We really *do* feel honoured . . ."

James smiled a smile of sheepish ingenuous pleasure.

Letitia's wonderful with men, thought Lucy, watching her sister with simple pride. Ever since she was a girl, she's been wonderful with men. Lucy herself had always been afraid of men, paralysed by the consciousness of her plainness and lack of charm. She had accepted George chiefly because she felt so grateful to him for noticing her at all.

Letitia glanced at the tea-table and the faint line between her delicate brows deepened.

"Oh . . . you've made the tea."

There was a conscience-stricken silence.

"Only a few moments ago," said Lucy.

"I'll make you a fresh pot, Mrs. Drummond," said Miss Parsons, and went quickly from the room.

Letitia turned to the others with a deprecating smile.

"I'm not really fussy, but I can't drink stewed tea."

"It's only been made a few minutes, Aunt Letitia," murmured Julia, but Letitia ignored her, directing all the armour of her charm upon James again.

"Tell me about London, James," she said. "I'm an exile now, you know."

James' gaze rested appreciatively on his aunt. He had a weakness for a good-looking, well turned-out woman, provided there was no possibility of an "entanglement." James dreaded "entanglements."

Blossoming in the sunshine of her charm, he held forth about the changed conditions in London, gave his views on the political situation, and explained a recent legal case to her that she pretended not to understand, losing his usual brusqueness and the self-distrust that underlay it, even forgetting his non-existent dinner engagement.

"Have one of these gingerbreads, James dear," said Lucy.

"No, thank you."

"You used to like them, dear."

"Did I?" said James vaguely.

He had quite forgotten the little boy who used to nibble gingerbreads under the bedclothes in the dormitory and awake the next morning to the sharp discomfort of their crumbs. James was not interested in his own childhood or anyone else's. He considered childhood merely as a state of immaturity, and thought that the sooner it was over the better.

"More tea, Mrs. Drummond?" said Miss Parsons, who was pouring out.

The deep blue eyes sent her a quick unsmiling glance as Letitia answered:

"Yes, please, and with less milk in it. I thought you knew how I liked my tea."

Miss Parsons flushed slightly as she took the cup that Letitia handed her.

When they had finished tea, Lucy and Miss Parsons carried the tea-things into the kitchen, and Julia followed them in her vague indeterminate fashion. The kitchen had been Roger's bedroom. Roger had been bitterly angry when he heard that the house was to be turned into flats and had said that he would never set foot in it again. He couldn't bear to think of his bedroom's being Aunt Lucy's kitchen. . . .

We're three widows, she thought suddenly and inconsequently— I and Aunt Lucy and Aunt Letitia. It's funny that one can never really believe that other people have gone through the same things that one's gone through oneself. Nothing will make me believe that anyone else ever felt as I did when I heard that Humphrey had been killed, though I know really that millions of women must have done.

"There's no need for *three* to be doing the washing-up," said Miss Parsons.

She was quite different when Letitia was not there—friendly and cheerful and even sometimes dryly humorous.

"I want another of those sandwiches," said Lucy, taking one from the cakestand. "That's what I've come out for."

They all laughed and Julia said:

"I can still see the place in the wall where Roger shot at a fly with his air-gun. Humphrey was furious."

Inside the sitting-room Letitia was continuing her process of charming James.

"It's *such* a treat to me to see you, James dear. You're part of the larger world that I'm cut off from now. In Chelsea, of course, I used to know such a lot of interesting people. I miss it. This— is a great change for me."

James was charmed, but not quite beyond the bounds of common-sense.

"Lucky to have it to come to," he said.

Letitia gave him a tremulous smile.

"As if I didn't know that!" she said. "And Lucy and I get on so well. I have to limit my interests to hers, of course, and I feel it a bit of a strain sometimes. I miss the artistic interest that used to fill my life."

"Yes, yes, of course," boomed James sympathetically.

"Now, don't say it's good for me," she said, "because I know it is. It's good discipline for me to be cut off from all the interests that mean so much to me, and to be a poor relation."

"Oh, I say!" remonstrated James.

"Well, I am, you know," she smiled. "Lucy's very kind, and she doesn't mean to make me feel it, but—naturally she's used to having her own way. She's always led a comfortable, happy life, with everything just as she likes it, and it *does* tend to make people a little selfish."

"Something in that, I suppose," agreed James thoughtfully.

"Well, that's how I try to look at it," said Letitia with her brave smile. "I *try* to see all this," she waved her hand round the room, "as a lesson to be learnt. I'm too sensitive, too proud, too dependent on—well, beauty, and all this" —again she waved her hand around in a gesture that included Lucy's solid mahogany furniture and Turkey carpet and the heavy oil paintings on the wall—"jars on me. You know what my own house was like, James."

James remembered occasional dinners with Lionel and Letitia in the Chelsea house—Letitia moving gracefully among the Sheraton and Hepplewhite that had been sold to pay Lionel's debts.

"Yes, yes," he said. "It's hard on you, Aunt Letitia."

"Oh no," she disclaimed lightly, "don't make me think that. I don't want to. If I can bring a little happiness into Lucy's life—and I know I do—out of the wreck of my own happiness, that's all I want. When your own life's shipwrecked, that's all that remains, isn't it?—to bring happiness to others."

James, who was quite a simple man, despite his practical ability and legal acumen, was deeply touched.

Letitia gazed dreamily into the distance.

"One thing I'm thankful for, James, is that I never let people know how unhappy my married life was. You thought I was happy, didn't you? Everyone did. I was too proud to let people know how much I suffered."

"He seemed a good chap," said James tactlessly.

"He was a *brute*," said Letitia in a low tense voice, "but don't let's talk about him." Then, recovering her bright brave manner, she reached the point which she had been leading up to ever since she began the conversation. "I sometimes wonder whether I shall ever have a day in London again—dinner and a theatre and perhaps a night at a hotel. How I used to take it all for granted and what a treat it would be to me now!"

"Ah, you're thinking of the old days," said James. "Not what it was before the war—London, you know. Crowded restaurants. Rotten food. Not much better than the war-time stuff in my opinion."

Julia came out of the kitchen, followed by Lucy and Miss Parsons.

"Time we went," said James.

"I thought I heard a car," said Julia.

"Go and look out of the landing window, Miss Parsons," said Letitia. She flung orders curtly at Miss Parsons, scorning Lucy's "Would you mind?" and "Oh, Miss Parsons, could I trouble you to . . .?" She despised Miss Parsons because she had to work for her living.

She always despised women who had to work for their living. She could not have told why—perhaps because of the implication that they lacked the charm or looks that would have induced some man to do it for them.

Julia went across to the mirror and moved back a strand of hair that had fallen over her forehead.

"I don't look very tidy, do I?" she said, "but it doesn't matter. It's the house they've come to see, not me."

She turned away from the glass, and, as she did so, the strand of hair fell back over her forehead again.

"Yes, there's a car at the door," said Miss Parsons, returning.

"Come along, Julia," said James.

Going downstairs with her, he wondered whether to put in a word for Aunt Letitia. He didn't interfere in other people's affairs as a rule, but Letitia—so brave and beautiful in the wreck of her happiness —had roused the sleeping knight-errant in him.

"Keep an eye on Aunt Letitia, won't you, Julia?" was all he could think of saying.

"Yes, I've felt that someone ought to do that ever since I heard she was going to live with Aunt Lucy," said Julia cryptically.

Letitia stood by the window of her bedroom, gazing down onto the neglected garden, drumming her long white fingers on the back

of the chair. She was possessed by that feeling of reaction that
always succeeded the exertion of her charm and by a feeling of anger
against James. Stupid, pompous, prosy, self-centred *dolt!* How
little it would have cost him to ask her up to London for a few days,
take her out and pay her hotel bills. She couldn't have asked him
more plainly, or been more ungraciously refused . . . The anger
turned itself slowly, venomously, upon Lionel—Lionel, whom she had
all these years made the scapegoat for her mistakes, the outlet for her
"moods." He had eluded her to the last, baulking her of her revenge,
cheating her of the luxury that she had always looked to him to
provide. And she couldn't even make him suffer for it. His death
seemed a piece of deliberate malice.

She heard Lucy and Miss Parsons come back from the kitchen,
where they had been putting away the china and polishing up the
silver . . . then she heard low whispers in the sitting-room. The
sound increased her irritation till she could endure it no longer.

As she opened the door, she heard Miss Parsons say, "I think
six down must be 'shrewd'."

They were sitting together on the settee. Lucy was knitting her
sea-boot stocking again, and Miss Parsons was winding some wool
over her knee.

On the table in front of them was the morning paper open at the
crossword puzzle.

Lucy looked up and smiled.

"I thought you might be resting, dear," she said. Her heart was
still full of ingenuous pride in Letitia. "What an interesting talk
you had with James!"

Letitia said nothing.

"Would you like to sit here, dear?" went on Lucy in a conciliatory
tone. "I expect you're tired."

Letitia was, she knew, more sensitive and highly strung than
ordinary people. One had to be very careful not to irritate her.

"No, thank you."

"We're doing the crossword puzzle, dear."

"So I see." Letitia went to the back of the settee and looked
over their shoulders. "You've done quite a lot. When did you do
all that?"

Both Lucy and Miss Parsons looked guilty. Letitia's voice was
quite pleasant, but it accused them of a sort of conspiracy. And
actually it *was* a sort of conspiracy.

Letitia disliked crossword puzzles, but she also disliked to see
people around her engaged in anything that excluded her, so Lucy
and Miss Parsons had got into the habit of doing bits of crossword
puzzles in a furtive hurried manner whenever they were alone.

"Oh, just odd moments during the morning," said Lucy apologetically.

"You seem to have had a good many odd moments," said Letitia,
still in that pleasant voice.

That, of course, was aimed at Miss Parsons. Letitia was always accusing Miss Parsons indirectly of not earning her salary.

She glanced out of the window.

"James was quite right about the garden. It *is* neglected . . . Are you fond of gardening, Miss Parsons?"

"Not very, Mrs. Drummond."

Letitia laughed—a tinkling mirthless little laugh.

"No . . . it does involve hard work, of course."

Miss Parsons glanced up at her, then lowered her eyes again over the wool she was winding.

Lucy had put away the paper with the crossword puzzle. The atmosphere of wary uneasiness raised Letitia's spirits somewhat.

"Do sit down here and put your feet up, dear," said Lucy.

Miss Parsons gathered up her wool and moved to another chair.

"No, I have quite a lot to do," said Letitia. "I wonder if you'd do me a favour, darling?"

"Of course, Letitia," said Lucy eagerly.

"I want to rearrange a few things in my bedroom, and I don't feel equal to doing it alone, but if you'd kindly allow Miss Parsons to come and help me . . ."

There was a touch almost of timidity in the quietness of the voice, but it managed, none the less, to convey to Lucy the accusation of trying to keep Miss Parsons for her own selfish use, and to Miss Parsons the promise of a particularly harassing half-hour. After all, thought Letitia, if women worked for their living they should be made to work for it, not sit about on settees, winding wool and doing crossword puzzles. She had come upon some stockings with long ladders in them that she did not intend to wear again, but Miss Parsons might as well mend them. It would give her something to do.

Her depression gradually left her as she kept Miss Parsons running about the room, rearranging her things, moving her dressing-table from one side of the window to the other, for no particular reason except that it was a cumbersome piece of furniture, and Miss Parsons found difficulty in moving it. Perhaps, with her usual oversensitiveness, she had exaggerated James' imperviousness to her hints. He would think it over . . . She had prepared the way . . . James at present lived in rooms, but there was no reason at all why he should not take a nice house or flat in—Hampstead, say—with herself as housekeeper and, of course, a good staff of maids. He was quite well off. She saw herself presiding over James' dinnerparties, wearing the elegant toilettes that were so wasted here, charming his bachelor friends, again frequenting first nights and concerts, shopping in the exclusive houses she loved to patronise . . .

"Really, Miss Parsons," she said, "you don't seem to be getting on very fast. Why not take everything out before you try to move it?"

And Miss Parsons, by a supreme effort of will, forbore to remind her that that was what she herself had suggested doing at the beginning.

III

THE long grey car went slowly down the untidy avenue of Westover, turned out of the big iron gate, and, gathering speed on the empty country road, directed its course towards Nettleford.

Godfrey Fielding drove; his wife, Cynthia, sat next him; and Hubert, his brother, sprawled on the back seat.

"The furniture should fit in all right, I think, don't you?" said Godfrey. "Fortunately, they're big rooms. That stuff from Norways wouldn't go into anything small."

"I think we can make it look charming," said Cynthia. "The brother seems to be running the show, doesn't he? Mrs. Gideon hadn't much to say for herself. A vague little woman, but I liked her."

Godfrey Fielding was a large handsome man, with fair hair, grey eyes, regular features and a well-formed chin faintly cleft in the middle. He had a quiet, pleasant, assured manner, spoke very little, and perhaps gave the impression of being more intelligent than he really was.

When Cynthia first met him she had been on the point of becoming engaged to another man, but she had fallen so deeply in love with him that the other—a small dark slender man called Adrian Maple—had faded completely from her mind. She had set herself determinedly to win Godfrey, and she had succeeded. He was quite unaware of this, believing that it was he who had set to work to win her . . . but Cynthia knew that if she had not exerted herself, planned the campaign, manœuvred their every meeting, he would never have thought of her seriously as a wife. Beneath his air of being equal to any situation that might arise ran a vein of indolence. He was always inclined to follow the line of least resistance, to let things take their course . . . He found himself spending all his free time with her and reacted almost automatically to the situation, proposing just when and where she meant him to propose. They had been married in the first year of the war, and by now she felt she knew all there was to know about him. He was an overgrown public school boy of the best type, with the virtues and failings of that type—kindly, considerate, scrupulously honest and conscientious, making a fetish of physical fitness, so convinced of the rightness of his own point of view on any subject that he seldom troubled to dispute other people's, wholly uninterested in art and literature, but showing a slightly amused tolerance of those who were interested in them. His scale of values was rigid and undeviating. Men with the right backgrounds and standards were "decent chaps," the others did not exist for him, though he was uniformly courteous when contact with them was forced on him. He liked things to go smoothly on the surface and did not, unless he had to, look beneath . . .

Though the appearance of strength that had first attracted her had proved to be deceptive, Cynthia did not regret her bargain. She had got what she wanted—his physical perfection and his pleasant kindly companionship. It still thrilled her to enter a crowded restaurant with him and note the glances of interest they aroused—for her dark slender beauty was just the right foil for his blond masculinity. The sound of his slow, deep, well-modulated voice could still sometimes set her nerves a-tingle. And the schoolboy simplicity that underlay his man-of-the-world poise would sometimes catch at her heart as if she were his mother instead of his wife.

During the war Cynthia had helped to run a canteen, while Godfrey served overseas. He had made an excellent soldier and had won quick promotion, popular with his men and his brother officers, painstaking, efficient, fearless. He was perhaps lacking in initiative, but it so happened that initiative had never been demanded of him, and his short army career had been eminently successful. Demobilised, he returned to his niche in the Civil Service, and he and Cynthia took up their quarters in a London hotel, while they looked for a house.

Memories of his childhood turned his thoughts to the country.

"We must try to find a place within reach of town, where I can get up to work and back," he said. "Clear of the suburbs and near-suburbs, of course. If we could get something with some fishing and shooting . . . This doesn't sound bad."

And he would point out to her an advertisement in *Country Life* that would bring her delicate brows sharply together.

"But, *Godfrey*, we don't want ten acres."

"I daresay we could let some of the land."

"And £7,000!"

"It's not much for a place that size, you know."

"But we don't *want* a place that size. What should we do with it, anyway?"

"Oh . . ." he said vaguely, and by the far-away look in his eyes she knew that he was back in Norways, his old home. "One can always have people to stay for the shooting and that sort of thing."

"Godfrey, we *can't*. We can't afford to buy a place like that or to keep it up. I know you're thinking of Norways, but remember that it ruined your father. We've got to live within your income and we can't even *think* of a £7,000 house."

"All right," he said, smiling at her and yielding with a good grace, as he always did.

Godfrey's father had been a Norfolk squire who had shut his eyes to changing conditions and, by means of constant encroachment on his capital, continued obstinately to live the affluent life of his fathers. Fortunately he had died while his two sons were young and before his chaotic affairs had resulted in actual bankruptcy.

Godfrey had accepted his altered circumstances with characteristic good sportsmanship, but he had spent his boyhood as heir of Norways, in a house where the question of expense was never considered, against a background of old retainers, grooms, horses, lavish hospitality, and the habits of extravagance remained. It was Cynthia who had to balance the budget and restrain his inherent lordliness.

They had seen the advertisement of Westover in *The Times* and had got into touch with James at once: It seemed to solve the problem —for the time being at any rate. Impossible to visualise Godfrey in a suburban villa, and the cottage in country surroundings and within easy reach of London, which they had dreamed of, was still undiscovered.

"I don't like the house myself," little Mrs. Gideon had said naïvely, but Cynthia could see that Godfrey liked it.

Norways had stood in the same position, with a park and avenue in front, and the gardens behind. They belonged to the same period, too, though Norways had been built of warm red brick. She could tell by Godfrey's deliberately casual manner that it had touched the chord of his nostalgia for Norways . . .

Hubert had become involved in the business by the merest chance. He had been still at school at the time of his father's death, and had gone straight to an uncle in London, who had undertaken his training in accountancy. He had just completed his training and obtained a post when war broke out. For the first three years of the war he had been stationed in a small town in Ireland, and there he had married a girl whom Godfrey and Cynthia had not yet seen.

He had met Godfrey and Cynthia for dinner in town about a month ago and they had told him about Westover.

"I had to drag Godfrey away from the most *ridiculous* places," said Cynthia. "Places with ten or twenty bedrooms . . ."

"They were cheap at the price," smiled Godfrey, stroking his short fair moustache.

"But *what* prices and *what* places! Even this place is too big. The flat has three large bedrooms, which is more than we need. I suppose it's not really expensive, but it's more than I thought we'd have to pay for that accommodation."

"I've been looking about for a place, too," said Hubert vaguely. "It's no use having Trixie over here till I've got somewhere for her to come to, but it seems pretty hopeless."

And then Godfrey had said in his easy casual way:

"Why not join forces with us? Have one of the bedrooms. That'll leave the third for a dressing-room or spare. And the dining- and sitting-rooms are plenty big enough to hold the four of us."

Cynthia had looked at him in helpless dismay.

"I don't suppose they want to live on the top of us like that, Godfrey," she had said.

But the hint was wasted on Hubert. His rather morose face lit up with pleasure.

"I say! Do you really mean it? We'd love to . . ." He turned to Cynthia. "You'll like Trixie. She's awfully easy to get on with."

It was useless to say any more. The brothers were delighted with the arrangement.

"And with just the four of us, the sharing of expenses should be easy," said Godfrey. "I'm not much of a mathematician, but I can divide by two."

"It's simply a splendid idea," said Hubert eagerly. "If you're sure you don't mind. . . ."

Hubert was as unlike Godfrey as possible—thin, dark, with something tense and finely strung about him. He looked younger even than his years, and generally a little sulky and defiant as if he had a secret grudge against life. Like Godfrey, he was quiet and reserved, but whereas Godfrey's quietness held an easy poise and assurance, Hubert's was shy and awkward, and was alternated by bursts of vivacity from which he would lapse suddenly into a hotly self-conscious silence.

"Jolly to have old Hubert with us," Godfrey had said to Cynthia afterwards, "and a help to have the expenses halved. Don't ever call me extravagant again, old lady. I thought of it, you didn't."

She shrugged.

"You're taking a lot for granted, you know. There's Trixie to be reckoned with."

"Oh, she'll be all right," he said easily.

"I'd feel more certain about that if I'd met her."

"She's going to meet us when we go over the house."

But she had not come.

"She said it was a long journey just for that," explained Hubert. "She said that if I O.K.'d it she was sure it would be all right."

Both he and Godfrey were quite casual about it—didn't seem to think that her not having met Trixie mattered.

"I have an idea that she's not terribly domesticated," went on Hubert. "I mean, you make any arrangement you like about the house, and she'll fit in."

He seemed, in fact, to know very little about his wife . . . Cynthia suspected that it was one of those cases of which the war had supplied so many examples—a young man, far from his home and family, driven by loneliness into the arms of the nearest friendly young woman, often encouraged into them by the young woman's family in the hopes of gaining something from the alliance.

Hubert's army career had been undistinguished. He had hated the life consistently and had remained a private till the end of the war.

Hubert himself apparently felt no qualms. She was a "sweet little thing," she would "agree to anything they wanted." He showed them a snapshot of her taken before the war, so blurred that it conveyed little beyond a shady hat, a flowered print dress, and a pair of legs that were definitely out of focus. He had asked her to have a photograph taken but so far she hadn't had one . . .

"She says she can't be bothered," he said, smiling indulgently.

It was an odd situation, thought Cynthia, but such a common one in these days that the young people themselves saw nothing odd in it.

She made no further protest. The brothers had fixed the matter up between them, taking her consent for granted. She had checked her inclination to reproach Godfrey as soon as they were alone together after his carelessly issued invitation. It was all settled now and she had never been a nagging wife . . .

Moreover, she was tired of hotel life, deeply in love with her husband, longing to have him to herself . . . She saw the two of them in the spacious rooms of Westover . . . Hubert and Trixie just shadows in the background.

"What did you think of the place, Hubert?" Godfrey said over his shoulder.

Hubert leant his long lanky body forward, elbows on knees.

"Grand!" he said. "Just the place. I'll write to Trixie to-night."

"Right!" smiled Godfrey. "Well, let's pull up for a drink."

He stopped the car in front of a small country pub, and they went into the bar.

"The first on me," said Hubert, going to the counter.

He spoke nonchalantly, trying to hide his secret exultation. The deepest and most secret emotion of his life was his adoration of Godfrey. The difference in their ages had made it impossible for them to meet on an equal footing in childhood and, perhaps because life had never brought them into closer contact, Hubert's boyish hero-worship had persisted into maturity. Godfrey had always been kind-hearted, and the small boy, black-haired and black-eyed (a "little changeling" his nurse called him), given to sudden fits of rage and sudden hysterical bursts of weeping, had amused and touched him. When with the child, he showed him the tenderness he showed to all young weak things, protecting him from injustice, interesting himself in his pursuits, flinging presents at him with careless generosity . . . when away from him, he never gave him a thought. But to Hubert every hero he read of or heard of was Godfrey . . . So that the chance invitation to dinner and its sequel caused him keener delight than he ever remembered feeling before. Trixie, too, he was sure, would be delighted. He had told her about Godfrey and how wonderful he was . . .

Trixie . . . It was odd how little he remembered her. When he tried to think of her he saw only the cosy little kitchen, with its air of comfort and welcome, the blazing fire, the bacon and eggs on the table, the brown earthenware teapot on the hob, the jolly Cockney mother, her broad waist always spanned by apron-strings, the wry-faced humorous Irish father . . . the blessed, blessed, blessed release from camp life. He had been sent overseas a week after his marriage and had seen little of his wife since. But he knew that she was very young, rather spoilt and utterly inexperienced in housekeeping, and he had been feeling somewhat worried by the situation. Now it would be all right. Cynthia would help and guide her—Cynthia, who was Godfrey's wife and therefore perfect. He had the same feeling he used to have at Norways when Godfrey came home from school or college—a feeling of happiness and relief, as if all his troubles were over.

He was talking animatedly now, as they sat at the table, drinking pink gins, his dark eyes shining, a lock of his dark hair falling over his brow.

He looks tired and—hungry somehow, thought Cynthia, and, despite herself, pity for him stirred at her heart. He's expecting something from Westover and Godfrey and me that we can't give him. He's going to be terribly disappointed . . .

Godfrey watched him with an amused indulgent smile, as if he were still the little boy who had poured forth nursery confidences at Norways . . . a "queer young 'un" . . . a "nice kid."

"I'll see to the garden," Hubert was saying. "I'd like to do that. It's been horribly neglected . . . Who will there be besides ourselves? That old couple of aunts and their companion? *They* won't be much trouble. And who else?"

"The Pollocks, I think the name is," said Cynthia. "Mother and daughter—vaguely local and eminently respectable. We sound rather a dull crowd on the whole."

Hubert laughed.

"All the better. It's such a peaceful spot. A hectic crowd would spoil it. And, after all, it's near enough to London for us to go up there if we feel like making whoopee."

"Do you belong to a club, Hubert?" said Godfrey.

"No . . ."

"I'll put you up for mine if you like."

Hubert's face glowed with pleasure at the offer.

"That's awfully decent of you, Godfrey, but, as a matter of fact, I think I'd better not just at present. I expect it'll be a bit expensive settling down to housekeeping. There may not be anything over for clubs."

"Godfrey never thinks of that," said Cynthia, and the two men laughed.

"Cynthia," said Godfrey, "has a niggly little mind. She thinks in halfpennies and ounces. She can't do things on a large scale."

"Just as well for someone to think in halfpennies," said Cynthia. She looked at her watch. "Oughtn't we to be starting? How are you going back, Godfrey? Didn't you say that we came by a longer way than we need have done?"

"Yes . . . I believe the map's in the car."

"I'll get it," said Hubert, springing up. "Don't drink my gin . . ."

Cynthia looked after him with a smile that was half a frown.

"He's terribly excited about it all."

"Nice kid," said Godfrey easily. He looked round the room— the comfortably old-fashioned saloon of a country pub. "Decent little place. We must come out here and have a drink when the respectability of the other inmates gets on our nerves."

"Godfrey, I'm not happy about this," said Cynthia.

"About what, my dear?"

"About this—joining forces with Hubert and Trixie. *Must* I call her Trixie? It's a name that's always been my pet abomination. I suppose she's called Beatrice really. I shall call her Beatrice . . . We know nothing about her."

"Probably quite a decent sort . . ."

Cynthia shrugged.

"She may be or she may not. Anyway, even if she is, we shall find this living on top of each other a bit trying."

"Why should we? Hubert's a nice kid, and I've never seen as much of him as I should have liked. I think it an excellent arrangement. What's your objection to it?"

"I was reading William Godwin's *Life of Mary Wollstonecraft* the other day," she said slowly, "and when he describes how she lived with her sisters—and it was *not* a success—he says in his own inimitably pompous fashion, 'Co-habitation is a point of delicate experiment and is, in a majority of instances, pregnant with ill-humour and unhappiness'."

Godfrey laughed.

"Rubbish! It depends on whether people are easy to get on with or not. I am and you are and Hubert is, and I bet Trixie is."

She smiled.

"The truth is that you don't know me and you don't know Hubert, and none of us knows Trixie."

"Now you're talking nonsense!" he said. "Have another drink?"

"I think I will."

Hubert returned with the map. He was still bubbling over with excitement.

"We can fix up the tennis court. It's all overgrown at present . . . and I believe there's some quite inexpensive way of making a swimming pool."

"Cynthia's pretending that we shan't get on. Says we don't know each other. I told her it was damn nonsense."

Hubert drained his glass and smiled at her.

"Of course it is. You and Godfrey and I know each other pretty well. Actually, I've never seen very much of Trixie, though I'm married to her, but she's awfully sweet. You'll love her when you get to know her."

"Oh, we'll all shake down all right," said Godfrey, opening the map.

IV

MRS. GIDEON walked slowly homeward along the country lane. On one side was the wood and on the other a field, where the haymakers had been at work, and the air was sweet with the scent of newly-mown hay and the hundred other mingled scents of a midsummer evening. The lacy gossamer of cow-parsley still foamed in the hedges, and through the trees flamed the vivid purple of loosestrife from a clearing in the wood.

It was on an evening like this that Humphrey had proposed to her. They had been playing tennis. She was wearing a white linen dress with a red belt. He had turned to her suddenly and—no, she hadn't learnt to face quite all the memories without flinching . . .

Her mind sheered away from this one to consider the afternoon she had just spent at Westover. The Fieldings seemed nice people— pleasant and well-bred and with an air of what Jane Austen called "consequence." That sort of thing, James had given her to understand, was very important when letting a place. Especially with the first tenants. It set a standard . . . There were only the Pollocks to come now, and they should be moving in soon.

James had hurried off to catch his train as soon as the Fieldings had gone. She thought again that it was a good thing he had not been able to accept her invitation to dinner. He was so correct that a closer acquaintance with her *ménage* would probably horrify him. He would disapprove of the haphazard nature of her housekeeping and of the familiarity with which the children treated her. It was better that the interest he undoubtedly felt in them all should continue to be shown from a distance.

She smiled to herself as she remembered how Letitia had exerted herself to charm him this afternoon. Humphrey had always been amused by Letitia. He had seen through her the first time he met her, but he had enjoyed watching what he called her "airs and graces." He had liked her husband and admired the patience and forbearance he showed her, though, he said, they were wasted on Letitia. "A bit of wholesome brutality,"he had added,"is what the woman needs."

She glanced at her watch. She must hurry instead of dawdling along like this. Colin and Laura would be home by now and she ought to be seeing about dinner. In glancing at her watch she noticed the baggy uneven skirt of her knitted suit and it struck her for the first time that she ought to have put on something else. She had always been vague about clothes. She seemed to lack the flair that is inborn in most women. She never knew what to wear or when to wear it, and the older her clothes were the more she clung to them. Fortunately, Humphrey hadn't minded. Once she had said to him, "I'm sorry you've got such a dowdy wife, Humphrey," and he had replied, "I should hate a wife who was merely dowdy, but you, my dear, are so outrageous that there's a certain distinction about you."

The suit she had on now seemed all right to her, but she had had it a good many years and probably it had shocked James and outraged those nice people, the Fieldings. Oh, well, she didn't care. The worst part of it all, she knew, was her not caring . . . Often, when she was going anywhere, Laura left directions as to what she was to

put on, but to-day Laura must have forgotten . . . Still, it didn't
really matter what the Fieldings thought of her. Mrs. Gideon could
never understand that it mattered what anyone thought of her, but
the children seemed to think it did . . .

She had reached the house now, Greenways. Most people thought
it was a silly name, but she liked it. It was a cheerful modern compact
little house, built of red brick with green-painted door and window
frames. A narrow path led up to the front door, flanked by lavender
bushes and cottage lilies. It seemed to welcome her, as Westover
had never done. She had been brought up in a large country house
and married from there to Westover, but she had always preferred
small cosy houses.

The front door stood open, and so did the garden door at the end
of the hall, showing a glimpse of her herbaceous border, still gay with
helenium and Japanese anemones and phloxes . . . Mrs. Gideon
looked after the garden herself, with the aid of a jobbing gardener
who came once a week, and enjoyed "grubbing about," as the children
put it. She felt a deep maternal tenderness for her plants and it gave
her real satisfaction to hoe and water them and know that they were
comfortable—the same sort of feeling she had when she left her babies
bathed and fed and sleeping in their cots. In her other gardens there
had been gardeners who didn't expect her to do more than cut blooms
for the house—and often grudged her even those—and she loved this
little plot that belonged to her entirely. She liked doing the sort of
things that you can do in a small house and garden—hanging bits of
washing on the line, and talking to the next-door neighbour over the
fence.

"I'm afraid you've got a suburban soul," Colin had said and she
had replied, "I'm afraid I have."

She walked through the house to the garden, where Colin and
Laura were sitting in deck chairs at the end of the lawn under the
apple tree. There was a table between them with a bottle of beer
for Colin and a jug of orangeade for Laura.

"So you're both back," she said, smiling at them. "How
nice!"

Colin had got up from his chair, but Mrs Gideon sat down on the
grass beside them. She had an incurable habit of sitting on the floor
indoors and on the grass out of doors.

"Have you had terribly tiring days?" she went on solicitously.

"Terribly," said Colin. "I've interviewed a client who wants to
sue her next-door neighbour for enticing her cat away from her by
means of sardines and cream, and Laura has coped with a severe case
of infantile tantrums . . . Beer or orangeade?"

"Neither, thank you . . . Tell me about it, Laura darling." Mrs.
Gideon spoke persuasively and a little nervously, for the smile had
faded from Laura's face, and her eyes were fixed sternly on her mother's
costume. "Was Mrs. Court there?"

But it was useless.

"Blanche, *darling*," said Laura in a voice of horror, "you've not been to see those people in *that!*"

Mrs. Gideon's name was not Blanche. Her elder children had first named her the White Queen, and then shortened it to Blanche. Only Roger, who was very correct, disapproved of this and continued to address her as Mother.

"In what, dear?" said Mrs. Gideon innocently.

"That ghastly old knitted suit."

"What's wrong with it?"

"Wrong with it!" exploded Laura. "Everything's wrong with it. You've had it for at least eight years. It's appalling. You promised me to keep it for gardening."

"Well, I did do some gardening in it this morning, dear," said Mrs. Gideon, as if that exonerated her completely.

"I should think you did," groaned Laura. "It's got a green smudge down one side and fertiliser all up one sleeve, and a hole at the back."

Mrs. Gideon stood up and looked at the offending garment, conscientiously trying to see what was wrong with it.

"And it's *miles* too long, even for gardening," went on Laura. "It's a pre-war length. I told you not to wear it again till I'd shortened it for you."

"I hate short skirts," said Mrs. Gideon. "They show the rucks in your stockings."

"What's the *use* of all the trouble I take over you?" groaned Laura. "You've got that new coat and skirt, which is really beautifully tailored, and which for some unknown reason you never wear. And that two-piece that I made you get at Debenham's. And you must wear *that* to go and see these Fielding people."

"Well, you see," explained Mrs. Gideon, "I put it on when I got up this morning to do housework and gardening in, and I suppose it never occurred to me to change it. I feel comfortable in it. I've got to know it and it's got to know me. I always feel—*shy* with new clothes. And, after all, dear," searching for an excuse that would appeal to Laura, "if I don't wear them, they can't get shabby, can they?"

"You're incorrigible," said Laura. "Quite incorrigible, but it's my own fault. I ought to have put something out for you and left you definite instructions."

"I still don't see that it makes any difference what I wear," said Mrs. Gideon with gentle persistence.

And, strangely enough, thought Colin, she was right. He had often been surprised by the deference and respect with which his gentle dowdy little mother was treated wherever she went.

She met his eyes and they exchanged smiles—conspiratorial, affectionate smiles—the conspiracy directed against Laura, the affection including her. *Doesn't* she boss and *isn't* she a pet! their glances

said.   Colin and Laura had been friends and allies since childhood,
sharing the same friends and interests.

It struck Mrs. Gideon how like Humphrey Colin was growing.
He had always had Humphrey's features—the same blue eyes and
long mobile mouth, even the same slight bend in the nose, but now,
as his face lost the smooth mask of youth, it was falling into the
same lines of kindliness and good humour, with the same suggestion
of quiet strength behind it.   More and more they were all beginning
to turn to him for advice, instinctively to yield him his father's place.
"Ask Colin," she would say when the children wanted permission to
do something or were in any difficulty.   He assumed no authority
but took endless pains to help them.   He had inherited, too,
Humphrey's deep love of home and family.   With plenty of friends
and outside interests, his real life was here in this small crowded
house with her and the children.

Perhaps it's not fair on him, she thought.   We shift the responsibility for everything on to his shoulders.   And he's so young . . .

"What was Uncle James like?" said Laura.   "As ghastly as ever?"

"He was just the same," said Mrs. Gideon, who was so deeply
imbued with respect for her brother that, though she could not help
laughing at him with the children, she always felt guilty in doing so.
"He asked about you all.   He couldn't come to dinner . . ."

"Thank Heaven for that," said Colin.

"Fancy asking him!" said Laura.

"He's very kind," said Mrs. Gideon.   "I think he's really very
fond of you all, but you—scare him."

"Not so much as he scares us."

Mrs. Gideon laughed and looked round the garden, moving the
errant lock of hair from her eyes.

"Where are the others?"

"Roger's gone into the village and the Two are in the tree."

At the bottom of the garden there grew a holm-oak whose branches
forked conveniently not far from the ground, leaving a large empty
space.   Colin had made a rope ladder and nailed planks across the
place where the branch forked, forming a sort of platform.   This was
the scene of most of Richard's and Rachel's games.   It was a ship,
caravan, aeroplane, tank or anything they happened to need.   The
branches screened them from sight, and they had a tent that they
could fix up on the platform.

Rachel's voice was suddenly heard, upraised in the tantalising
laugh that always goaded Richard to fury.

"Now there'll be trouble," sighed Mrs. Gideon.

There was the sound of a scramble, and Rachel appeared, running
round the lawn, brandishing a cardboard cylinder.   Richard followed
her, his face a small tense mask of fury.

Rachel was a sturdy child of eight, with a round rosy face, a
small determined mouth and light brown curls tipped with gold.
Richard was eighteen months older—taller than Rachel, but slenderly

built, with a thin pale freckled face, vividly blue eyes and gingery hair. Both wore grey flannel shorts and yellow shirts.

Richard caught up Rachel just as she was passing Mrs. Gideon and hit out at her savagely. She turned on him, as furious as he, and hit back.

"Richard!" expostulated Mrs. Gideon.

"Go on," said Colin, leaning back in his chair and watching them. "That's right, Rachel. Give it him back. No kicking now! Go on, Richard . . . Don't funk . . . No hair pulling! . . ."

The fight gradually developed into a wrestling match, and at last Richard, red in the face with exertion and anger, got Rachel on to the ground and held her there.

"Say you're beat," he said fiercely between his teeth.

Lying there relaxed, she looked up at him, and suddenly began to giggle. The fury faded from his face and he began to giggle too. They sat on the grass side by side, laughing and breathless.

"Darling, you shouldn't hit a girl or anyone younger than yourself," said Mrs. Gideon.

"They're quite well matched," said Colin. "It was rather a pretty fight. I think Richard's black eye will be just a shade blacker than Rachel's. I'd give you two a few boxing lessons if we could get some gloves."

"Oh Colin!" said Rachel rapturously. "*Will* you?"

"But you shouldn't quarrel, you know, children," murmured Mrs. Gideon.

"I've forgotten what we were quarrelling about," said Rachel. "What was it?"

"You wouldn't give me the telescope," said Richard. "It was my turn to be Nelson and you wouldn't give me the telescope."

"Oh yes . . . I was tired of being an ordinary ship, anyway. . . . Let's have it an invasion barge."

"All right."

"And you won the fight," generously, "so you can be Monty."

They raced back to their tree, and Richard's childish high-pitched voice was heard calling out orders to an invisible army.

"Here's Roger," said Laura.

Roger joined them, standing a little apart, leaning against the apple tree and looking down at them. He was tall for his age, almost as tall as Colin—thin and dark and rather sardonic-looking. He bore a faint resemblance to Lord Byron, which he carefully cultivated.

"Well, darling," said Mrs. Gideon, smiling at him.

She was obscurely aware of the wall that separated Roger from the rest of his family and anxious to break it down. It made her a little nervous with him.

"Your Uncle James was asking after you, dear," she went on. "I promised to send him your report."

"You won't do that this time," said Roger with his Byronic smile, "because I've burnt it."

"Oh Roger, how naughty of you!"

"I haven't got much of a brain, but I don't want Uncle James pawing over the bit I've got . . . Did you go to Westover?"

"Yes," groaned Laura. "In that knitted suit. Can you beat it?"

"What's the place like now?" said Roger, trying to speak casually, "I suppose they've messed it up beyond recognition."

He was the only one of them to whom Westover meant anything, and he loved it with a deep romantic passion. To him it was not a shabby pretentious erection of stucco. It was a dream castle, a fairy palace, heart-stirringly beautiful behind its veil of trees. He had refused to go near it since he had heard it was to be turned into flats, but his thoughts brooded over it longingly as he lay awake at night. He despised the others for their acquiescence in their exile, for their easy acceptance of this, to him, hogger-mugger suburban existence. The element of picnicking in his mother's housekeeping that seemed to amuse, even delight Colin and Laura, outraged him. He cherished his grievances, believing himself to be of finer clay, of more inherent aristocracy than the rest. This imagined superiority helped him to combat a feeling of hurt loneliness. He was patently the "odd man out" in the little family. Colin and Laura at one end, Richard and Rachel at the other. He wandered unhappily, though with apparent self-sufficiency, in a sort of no man's land between. The fact that the other four lived at home while he went to boarding school emphasised his isolation. He kept his grievances to himself, subtly relishing them, maintaining good surface relations with the others, even imitating their casual friendly fashion of intercourse, but never relinquishing his secret sense of difference.

"Nothing could mess it up as much as the military did," said Laura.

"I don't mean that. That was inevitable. I meant this—turning it into flats." His lip curled scornfully.

"That, too, was, in the circumstances, inevitable," said Colin quietly.

Roger looked at him, and the deepest, most obscure of his grievances stirred at his heart. He resented bitterly, and for no reason that he could have explained, Colin's resemblance to their father. Dramatising every situation, idealising always the unattainable, he had built up a character of his father that would have surprised no one more than that gentleman himself, endowing him with every possible and impossible virtue. At this altar he worshipped and—as he liked to think—alone, for he alone, he felt, truly knew and mourned his father; and his father, and his father alone, could have understood and appreciated him. Sometimes he played with the idea that his father had not really been killed and would come home. He pictured the moment of his return and always it was just the two of them . . .

He resented the cheerfulness of the others, and his mother's cheerfulness in particular. Sometimes he wondered if she ever thought of his father at all. "I haven't forgotten," he assured the upright soldierly figure in the leather frame on his dressing-table. "I'll never forget . . ."

And that Colin, so ordinary, so unworthy to hold any part in this secret communion, should wear his father's likeness, was a sort of desecration in his eyes. Even his voice . . . "That, too, was, in the circumstances, inevitable." It might have been his father speaking.

For this reason he hardened himself against Colin, and secretly combated his influence in every way he could, refusing to yield to a trick of voice and features that was an insult to the memory it summoned.

Mrs. Gideon looked at her watch.

"Oh dear!" she said. "What about dinner?"

Laura smiled at her—the smile of tender amusement with a touch of mock severity that she always accorded her mother's vagueness.

"Blanche, darling, *what* a time to remember dinner! I got it all in train as soon as I came in."

"I know I don't deserve you, Laura," said Mrs. Gideon humbly.

"You don't, do you?" said Laura, "but actually I'd hate a mother who was too domesticated. It wouldn't give me scope. I enjoy pottering and there isn't room in any house for two potterers."

Laura loved trying out new recipes, altering the arrangement of the furniture, bottling and making jam . . .

"Our little home-maker!" teased Colin, and she reached out a hand to tweak his hair.

"Colin!" called Richard from the tree.

"Uh-huh," grunted Colin, turning his head in the direction of the sound.

"How many men are there in an invasion barge?"

Laura got up slowly.

"Well, I suppose it's time to set the table."

"I'll do that," said Mrs. Gideon eagerly. "It would make me feel less guilty."

"Let's do it together," said Laura, putting her arm through her mother's.

They went indoors. Roger stood, leaning against the tree, looking after them. Colin glanced up at him, sensing something of the secret turmoil of his spirit.

"Feel like doing a spot of work during the holidays, Roger?" he said.

"Not particularly, thanks," drawled Roger.

"They want someone to help with the Amateur Dramatic Society in the village. Jackson was producing for them and he's been taken ill. Heart trouble. He's had to give up everything."

Roger was silent for a few moments. Colin could not have hit on anything that would appeal to him more. The Amateur Dramatic Society had been started by his father, who had always taken a keen interest in it, frequently mentioning it in the letters he wrote from the front. He had asked how it was getting on in the last letter they had ever had from him . . .

"Do you think I could?" he said, forgetting to be superior and aloof.

"You've done it at school."

"They were only form plays."

"I'm sure you could manage it. Anyway, no one else has the foggiest idea of it, so if you don't take it on, the whole thing will fall through."

"What are they doing?"

"Galsworthy's *Loyalties*. Ambitious, of course, but these people always hitch their wagons to stars."

"I'd like to try, if you think I'd be any good."

"I think you'd be just the right person. Get into touch with Derek Frame. He's the secretary now. He was in a flat spin about it, and when I suggested you he jumped at the idea."

"Yes, I will."

He stood gazing into the distance, a look of eagerness on his sensitive young face, all its moroseness gone.

Colin threw him a glance of affectionate amusement. That should keep the young cub out of mischief, he thought.

Laura appeared in the open doorway, ringing the dinner gong.

V

"The train must be late," said Cynthia.

Godfrey looked up from his paper.

"I expect it is. They generally are on Saturdays. There's no hurry, is there?"

"N-no, but I want to get it over."

He smiled.

"You're not nervous, surely?"

The idea of Cynthia's being nervous amused him.

"Yes, I am," she admitted. "I'm more than nervous. I'm— frightened. Right from the beginning, I've had a feeling that it wasn't going to be a success."

"And right from the beginning I've had a feeling that it was . . . Even if it isn't, what does it matter? There's no harm done. We can just split forces again. There needn't be any unpleasantness."

She looked at him in silence for a few seconds, then said:

"You're incredible, Godfrey."

"In what way?"

"I believe that, however much unpleasantness there was, you just wouldn't see it. You'd just determinedly not see it."

His eyes were fixed on her quizzically.

"Isn't that the best way of dealing with unpleasantness?"

"It's your way."

"Come and sit down," he urged her affectionately. "You're getting all strung up, and it isn't like you. They may not be here for half-an-hour or more. You can't stand at the window watching all that time."

She came slowly back into the room. She was always *soignée* to the last detail, but he realized that to-day she had taken even more pains than usual over her appearance. The black dress she had on, with its cravat of soft lace, had only arrived last week from the London dressmaker. Like all her things, it was expensive and perfectly cut. She was not extravagant—she took great care of her clothes, brushing them and pressing them back into shape after each wearing—but everything about her had to be fresh and immaculate and the best of its kind. Her dark hair, dressed close to her head, shone like silk where the light caught it. A diamond sparkled in each small finely-shaped ear. As she came towards him he caught a whiff of her best perfume—the one she only used on special occasions.

"It's such a charming room. I wonder if it will seem overcrowded with four of us sitting about."

"Why on earth should it? There were more than four of the Gideons."

"You like the idea of living *en famille*, don't you?"

"Yes . . . Young Hubert's a nice kid."

"He's not a child now, you know . . ." She returned restlessly to the window. "I wish I had some idea what she was like."

"She's young Hubert's wife," said Godfrey, "that's enough for me. We shall pull together all right. Don't you worry."

She looked at him, partly in amusement, partly in exasperation.

"I envy you, Godfrey. Life's so simple for you."

"Well, life *is* simple," he said, "if only you let it be simple, if you don't twist and torture it . . . Look at me, just reading the newspaper—and honestly for the minute till you mentioned it I'd forgotten that we were waiting for Hubert and Trixie—and you pacing about like a caged lion."

She crossed the room, laying her hand on his hair in a fugitive caress as she passed him, and opened the further door, throwing a frowning critical glance around.

"I've made it as nice as I can, but a room never looks as welcoming in summer as in winter. A fire makes such a difference."

"Come and sit down, woman," said Godfrey.

There was a knock at the outer door and Cynthia went to open it. Letitia stood there, smiling uncertainly.

"I just wondered if I could help at all," she said. "I knew you were expecting your brother and sister-in-law. Could I make tea or anything? I'd love to."

"Oh . . . no, thanks," said Cynthia, "but it's awfully kind of you. Do come in."

"No, no," said Letitia. "I don't want to intrude in any way.
I only thought——"

"Do come in," said Cynthia with unusual urgency. The visitor
would be a sort of buffer state between her and Hubert's wife. The
presence of an outsider often helps to tide over awkward family
situations. "You must stay to tea . . . yes, you must."

"Well . . ." said Letitia, who had been drawn to the flat by
curiosity and fully intended to stay to tea, "If you're sure I shan't be
in the way and if I can help . . ."

"Of course you can help," said Cynthia, "and of course you won't
be in the way. There's nothing really to do . . . I've got everything
ready in the kitchen . . ."

They went into the little kitchen that had been improvised from
one of the original dressing-rooms. Sink, refrigerator, gas cooker,
enamel-topped kitchen table, gleamed spotlessly white. The walls
were painted cream, and curtains of blue American cloth hung at the
window. The kettle was on a low gas and there was a laden tea-tray
on the table.

"It's charming!" said Letitia, gazing round. "I envy you it. I'd
love to potter about ours, but—well, you know, Lucy's a bit touchy
about my—interfering in any way. Everything's hers, of course, and
she has a strong sense of possession. When one's a poor relation
one has to tread very carefully, but she's terribly kind and generous
to me."

Cynthia nodded understandingly, glad of anything to take her
thoughts off the meeting that loomed ahead.

She had seen very little of Letitia since coming to Westover, but
what she had seen, she had liked. Letitia had offered her help tactfully and unobtrusively on several occasions, and once or twice they
had met in the garden or hall and stayed for a moment or two to
talk.

From various things that Letitia had let slip, Cynthia understood
that she had had an unhappy married life, had been left penniless by
her husband and was now dependent on the charity of her fat dowdy
sister, who was, Cynthia had gathered, not very easy to live with.

Cynthia had felt sorry for her and inclined to establish friendly
relations. Both had lived in London, and they had a common language
of plays, books, restaurants . . . Neither was at home in this hybrid
apartment-house atmosphere. Laughingly they had confided in each
other that they were not country-lovers.

"It was all right just for August or for a day or a week-end,"
Cynthia said.

"And one got a little tired of it even then," said Letitia.

"But Godfrey loves it."

"So does Lucy."

"And, of course, these days one simply can't get a house in town—
not really in town. I'd rather have this than a suburb."

"Oh, so would I."

And to-day, Letitia, with her air of fashionable sophistication, seemed more than ever to belong to Cynthia's world, to be her ally against the alien forces that were about to invade it.

As she wandered about the kitchen now, admiring the fittings, discussing kitchens in general ("Why do men architects *never* put a light over the sink?") and the domestic situation in general, Cynthia found all her tension relaxing and had for the moment quite forgotten Hubert and Trixie, when Godfrey called:

"Here they are, Cynthia."

She sprang up, her heart beating unevenly, and went back to the sitting-room. As she reached it, the other door opened, and Hubert came in. His face wore a nervous eager smile.

"Here's Trixie," he said, standing aside.

The girl who entered had on a coat and skirt of not very good tweed, not very well tailored, and a tumbled blouse of artificial silk, strained tightly across loose breasts. Her hat was of the cheaper variety, making up in fussiness what it lacked in style. But she was beautiful —with deep violet-blue eyes in a heart-shaped face, cloudy dark hair and skin of transparent pallor. Cynthia's first feeling had been one of revulsion, but she conquered it quickly, and stepped forward to kiss the newcomer.

"My dear," she said, "we're all so glad to see you. You won't mind if I call you Beatrice, will you? I love the name, and I've never cared for Trixie."

"It's good enough for me," said Godfrey, kissing her in his turn. "It's splendid to have you here, Trixie. What sort of a journey did you have?"

"Not too bad," said the girl.

She had a deep musical voice with the suspicion of a brogue.

"Well, I'm sure you'd like a wash," said Cynthia briskly. "Come and I'll show you your room. Then we'll have tea."

She opened the bedroom door and stood aside. Trixie entered, looking round at the kidney-shaped dressing-table, with its chintz skirt, the peach-coloured curtains, the twin beds, with coverlets and padded headpieces of chintz, the bow-fronted mahogany chest, the Queen Anne writing-table, whose polished surface reflected the bowl of roses that Cynthia had put there this afternoon. She looked in silence—wary and on the defensive.

"I do hope you'll be happy here," said Cynthia.

She strove desperately to instil into her voice more friendliness than she felt, but was aware that she spoke distantly, patronisingly, as if she were showing a new housemaid to her room.

"You'll let me know if you want anything, won't you?" she went on. "Is there anything I can do for you now?"

Trixie slowly turned her thickly-lashed violet eyes to her sister-in-law. "No, thank you," she said.

She's—heavy, thought Cynthia. I've always hated the type. That heavy white skin and deep voice. Those slack breasts and broad hips . . . Why doesn't she wear decent corsets or at least have clothes that fit her? That skirt looks frightful behind. Not that it looks much better in front . . . If she's got a mind at all, it will be as slow and torpid as the rest of her . . . I knew it wouldn't be a success, but we'll have to go through with it now. I'll do my best. I honestly will do my best . . . She's so—ungracious. She hasn't said a word about the room and I took so much trouble over it . . . She determined perversely to drag some word of appreciation out of the newcomer.

"I hope you like the room?" she said.

"Yes, thank you," said Trixie, not taking her eyes from Cynthia's face.

Cynthia shrugged.

"Well, I'll leave you to have a wash. Come to the sitting-room when you're ready."

She returned to the kitchen, where Letitia was warming the teapot.

"She looks very young, doesn't she?" said Letitia.

It was a safe enough thing to say till one saw which way the wind was blowing.

"Yes . . . I believe she's only nineteen," said Cynthia.

Somehow the bond between them seemed strengthened by the innocuous interchange.

"We might as well make the tea now," said Cynthia. "The other two are ready and if she's a long time we can make a fresh pot."

"It's such a treat for me to have this peep into your home and see all your lovely things," said Letitia. "You have such perfect taste. It's silly, of course, to be dependent on—atmosphere, but somehow I always have been. Poor Lucy has no taste at all. To-day, as soon as I looked at your charming sitting-room, I felt a dozen weights drop from my spirit."

The flattery was shameless, but Cynthia welcomed it. She still felt a little piqued by Trixie's lack of appreciation.

"I've always been interested in what's called 'interior decoration'," said Cynthia. "The local builder was horrified when I wanted the panelling stippled. He didn't even know how to do it till I showed him."

"It looks charming. I noticed it as soon as I went in."

"It suits the room . . . Well, tea's ready and I hope she is."

Though they had barely mentioned Trixie since her arrival, they seemed tacitly to have formed a defensive alliance against her.

Cynthia carried in the tray and Letitia the cake-stand. Godfrey and Hubert stood talking together by the window. Over Hubert was an air of poignant defenceless happiness that caught Cynthia unawares and tugged at her heart. It was clear that, after almost forgetting what his wife was like, he had fallen passionately in love with her . . . And Godfrey was genial, expansive, delighted with this family gathering to which he had looked forward for so long.

Their conversation was trivial and superficial—enquiries about the journey, arrangements for meeting in town for lunch to-morrow—but no one could have seen them without being aware of the bond of affection between them. Strangely, it was still the bond of their childhood. Godfrey gave the invitation to lunch in kindly patronising fashion, with still that touch of amusement that had always marked his manner to Hubert; and Hubert, despite his absorption in Trixie, was delighted and gratified to be asked to lunch by the elder brother.

Almost as soon as Letitia and Cynthia had set the tea on the low table by the fireplace, Trixie entered. She had taken off her coat, and washed her face, but obviously had not done her hair again. She had not troubled with make-up, either, but the pallor of her skin was flawless in its transparency, emphasising the violet-blue of her eyes and the redness of the curving lips that owed nothing to lipstick.

Cynthia, looking at her, was aware of a sudden stab of jealousy. She's lovely, she thought. She's shapeless and slovenly and second-rate and sulky and—lovely. Lovely and gloriously young. Shame followed hot on the heels of her jealousy. I mustn't be like this. I must be kind to her. She's miles away from her home and family. I'm much older than she is. I'm responsible for her . . . She tried to whip up a feeling of tenderness for the girl and failed.

Godfrey and Hubert were fussing about her, moving an armchair for her, fetching a table for her tea-cup, handing plates and cake-stand. Really, thought Cynthia impatiently, Godfrey might leave that to Hubert. It doesn't need two of them . . .

Trixie looked up at them with a sudden smile. It was the first time Cynthia had seen her smile—a slow lazy smile, delicious and disarming.

"You two aren't a bit alike, are you?" she said.

"No, they used to call me Monkey Brand when I was a kid," said Hubert.

"Why did they stop?" she asked.

Hubert gave a shout of laughter.

It's intolerable the way they're all ignoring me, thought Cynthia. Aloud she said:

"Do try a piece of this currant cake, Beatrice. It's made from an old family recipe that dates from the days before baking powder was invented, when they used powdered ammonia instead. I've got it written out in my great-grandmother's handwriting."

There was a silence, and Cynthia continued in her suave slightly drawling voice:

"Her generation was, of course, completely domesticated. It's strange to think that the war's brought us round in a sort of circle to the same state, and that, after emancipating ourselves at great cost, we returned to kitchen and still-room and pantry, using their recipes and bottling and preserving, instead of leaving it all to the manufacturers as we used to."

"Yes," said Trixie. She took a piece of cake and said, "Thanks."

As she looked at Cynthia, the smile faded from her face and that wary, sulky, almost defiant expression took its place.

Cynthia felt hurt. I'm doing all I can to make her welcome, and she treats me like a schoolmistress.

"Do you know this part of the world at all?" Letitia said with perfunctory politeness.

"No, but," Trixie turned dancing eyes on Hubert, "Mr. Fielding's been describing it all the way down in the train, so that I felt I'd lived here all my life before I even got here."

Godfrey laughed at Hubert's expression of comical discomfiture.

"I didn't know I was boring you as much as that," said Hubert.

"Well, you might have found something else to talk about after all that time."

Despite Cynthia's efforts, they were divided again into two groups—Trixie and the two men by the window, Letitia and Cynthia at the tea-table.

When Cynthia and Letitia got up to clear away, Trixie made no move to help them. Godfrey and Hubert offered to help, but obviously without meaning their efforts to be taken seriously.

"Are you too tired to write to your mother, darling?" said Hubert. "I think you ought to—just to let her know that you've got here all right. The post goes at six."

She rose, smiling lazily at him, and went to sit down at the writing-table.

"I never can think of what to say to people in letters," she said.

"No, you can't," agreed Hubert. "You write the rottenest letters of anyone I know."

She took up the pen, wrote a word at the head of a sheet of plain note-paper, then held it over her shoulder to Hubert and Godfrey.

"Is that the way you spell it?"

Cynthia, passing from the tea-table to the door, glanced at the word Westover, written in a large childish unformed hand, enclosed in inverted commas.

"Yes," said Hubert. "Now get on with it. Shall I draw lines for you? Try and write half a page, at any rate. It's more than you ever wrote to me."

"Oh, you liar!" she chuckled.

"Your people live in Eire, don't they?" said Godfrey.

"That's right."

" 'That's right'," mocked Hubert. "Where did you pick that up? Are you a colleen or a Cockney?"

Cynthia stole a glance through the half-open door. Both men were smiling at Trixie as though she were an amusing child. Again that hurt feeling swept over her. She had been working all day to make a success of this home-coming, and it was a bitter disappointment. With the hurt was a curious feeling of loneliness. The affectionate admiration of the two men had been the background of her life for the past weeks, and she had valued and enjoyed it more than she had realized. Now suddenly it seemed to be diverted to the other woman, and so contemptible was the other woman in her eyes that their admiration was cheapened and debased, hardly any longer worth the having.

"I feel ashamed of letting you help like this," she said to Letitia. "We won't do the washing-up, of course."

Yet she felt reluctant to leave the warm shelter of the kitchen for the sitting-room, whose atmosphere of graciousness and serenity was now completely spoilt.

"Of course we'll do it," said Letitia. "There's not much. I like washing-up."

(Lucy and Miss Parsons would have been surprised to hear her say this.)

"Very well. If you're sure you don't mind . . ."

She had closed the kitchen door, but she could hear Trixie's warm lazy voice and the voices and laughter of the men.

Letitia's spirits rose as Cynthia's sank, though she veiled her cheerfulness under a manner of grave sympathy. The happiness and unity of these Fieldings had depressed her ever since they came to Westover, as other people's happiness and unity always depressed her . . . and the element of discord she had noted this afternoon had given her a sensation almost of exhilaration.

She glanced speculatively at Cynthia.

"You're going to have a very difficult time, my dear."

Cynthia was silent for a few moments. She would have liked to resent the remark as an impertinence, but the sympathy of Letitia's voice and expression was too much for her.

She was surprised by a sudden catch in her throat and turned away as she answered:

"Oh well . . . she's very young, but she's certainly less congenial than I'd hoped she'd be."

"I thought you were wonderful with her."

"She didn't respond much, did she?"

"Oh, you can see the type she is," said Letitia, growing bolder. "She's obviously no use for women . . . It's a good thing that your husband is so devoted to you. And yet I thought mine was . . . They're queer kittle-kattle, men."

The sound of Godfrey's laughter was heard again from the sitting-room.

A feeling of satisfaction warmed Letitia's heart. The little seed of doubt had been sown . . .

"Such pretty china!" she went on, brightly, as she put the last tea-cup in the glass cupboard, "but all your things are charming."

"It was my grandmother's," said Cynthia. "I've got almost the whole set, including a monumental slop basin."

"Oh yes, I know those Victorian slop basins. Aren't they fantastic! . . . Well, I really must go now. Lucy doesn't like my leaving her, and I've intruded on your family party quite long enough. I won't disturb the others. Say good-bye to them for me, won't you? It's so good of you to have let me come at all. And now I'll just slip quietly away . . . Good-bye, my dear. I hope so much to see a little more of you if you don't find an old woman like me too boring . . ."

"Do come again," said Cynthia warmly. "Come whenever you like."

And Letitia went back along the corridor with a little smile on her lips.

It died away, however, as she approached Lucy's flat. The wireless was on, and the strains of "Just a Song at Twilight" reached her even before she opened the door, augmented by the discordant voices of an unseen audience.

Lucy and Miss Parsons, sitting side by side on the settee knitting, the paper open at the crossword puzzle on the table before them, presented a picture of happiness and tranquillity that roused afresh all Letitia's resentment. Her lips were set in a tight line, as she went across to the wireless and switched it off.

"Do you mind?" she said politely. "You know how I hate that sort of rubbish."

"I'm sorry, dear," said Lucy humbly, "I didn't realize that you'd come back. What about tea? Miss Parsons and I have had ours, but the kettle's on and we can make you a pot in two minutes."

"I've had tea with the Fieldings, thank you," said Letitia.

"Has Mrs. Hubert arrived?" said Lucy, who took a passionate interest in her neighbours.

"Yes . . ." said Letitia.

She knew that Lucy was longing to know about Mrs. Hubert, so said nothing further except, "I'm a little tired. I think I'll go and rest before dinner."

She went into her bedroom and, closing the door, sat in the easy chair and took up a novel from the bedside table. In the sitting-room with Lucy and Miss Parsons, she was in the habit of reading formidably highbrow books—she found that they had a quelling effect on them—but when alone she generally read something lighter.

There was a long silence next door, broken at last by furtive little whispers. The tranquillity and contentment that had enclosed the other two and seemed deliberately to exclude her had vanished, so Letitia, for her part, became tranquil and content . . .

VI

GODFREY, Hubert and Trixie were still laughing and talking together when Cynthia returned to her chair and took up her needlework. She smiled at them, determined not to spoil the atmosphere of easy friendliness. But it seemed to have been broken by her very entrance.

The two men sprang to their feet, and the smile faded from Trixie's face, giving place to that guarded sulky look.

"Mrs. Drummond gone?" said Godfrey.

"Yes. She asked me to say good-bye to you for her. She didn't want to disturb you."

"Good-looking old lady," said Hubert.

"Bit high-hat, isn't she?" said Trixie.

"Oh, she's quite a decent soul," said Godfrey.

"Who else lives here?" said Trixie.

"Only ourselves and Mrs. Drummond and her sister and sister's companion at present. Some more people are supposed to be coming soon—the Pollocks. I'm not sure what the family consists of—mother and daughter, I believe."

"I'd better tell you about our domestic arrangements, Beatrice," said Cynthia. (I'm trying to be nice, she said to herself despairingly, but I seem to make them all uncomfortable whenever I speak. Or am I imagining it? She's only been here three hours and the whole situation's got on my nerves already. But I mustn't start making a mountain out of a molehill. I must just be natural and friendly . . .) "We've only so far been able to get a woman to do the rough work in the morning and another woman to come in at night to cook the dinner, so we must divide the work between us, as far as possible. I suggest that we get the breakfast in turns, and that we each do our own rooms, except, of course, on the day when the woman does them. There'll be just the two of us for lunch, so I'll see to that, if you like, and we can perhaps get the tea in turn. There's no need to make any definite arrangement about that. I'm hoping, of course, that we shall have a little more domestic help as time goes on, but till then we must just manage between us."

"O.K.," said Trixie without much interest.

"I'm a great standby," said Godfrey. "My washing-up has to be seen to be believed."

"I bet it has," grinned Trixie.

"And I," said Hubert proudly, "can make hash."

"I bet you can, too," giggled Trixie; "of anything you try your hand at."

Cynthia rose and folded up her needlework.

"Well," she said pleasantly, "I'll go and have a wash before dinner."

"Come along, darling," said Hubert, holding out his hand to Trixie and pulling her out of the chair.

Laughing and half-reluctant, she allowed him to draw her into the bedroom.

"Well, what the heck am I supposed to do?" she said when the door had closed on them. "I washed just before tea. Does she expect me to wash again?"

"You want to change into a dress or something, don't you?" he said, smiling at her.

"No, you bet your life I don't. Still, anything to oblige."

She knelt by her trunk, which had not yet been unpacked, and began to throw its contents on to the floor around her. Hubert sat on the bed and lit a cigarette.

"What does she want me to put on? This?" She held up an elaborate backless pink dance frock.

"Heavens, no! Just a dress, that's all. I mean, she's got that black dress on, so she won't change, but, when she's been wearing a skirt and jumper, she changes into a dress for dinner. A sort of—afternoon dress, I suppose it is."

"It would be. You're all mad. Afternoon dress for night. Evening dress for breakfast, I suppose. What do *you* do? Change into silk knee-breeches or pyjamas or what?"

"No, you little idiot! I've got a suit on, so I don't change, but, if Godfrey and I have been messing about in flannels, we change into suits for dinner."

"Oh well, we live and learn. Seems a blasted waste of time to me. Will this do?" She held up a dress of patterned silk.

"That's just right," he said approvingly.

"Good! It'll be the first thing that has been, and I bet *she'll* sneer at it."

"She's a dear, Trixie. You mustn't get her wrong."

"Oh, I'm not getting her wrong. She hates me. I saw it in her face the minute I came into the room. She covered it up quick, but not quite quick enough . . ."

Sitting on the floor, she drew a silk stocking on to one bare leg, then looked up at him, pursing her lips and arching her eyebrows. "Ay'd bettah tell you abaht ah domestic arraingements, Be-ah-trice." Her mimicry of Cynthia's voice and manner was so comical that Hubert laughed despite himself. "Do trai a piece of this caike, Bee-ah-trice. It's maide from pah-dah-ded ammoniah."

He slipped a hand over her mouth and she lay back on the floor giggling, then sat up and shook off his hand. "Bee-ah-trice, blast her! If Trixie was good enough for my people, it's good enough for her. Well, if her ladyship's going to try and come it over me, she's got a surprise coming to her. I've got the devil's own temper, you know . . . Did you know?"

"No."

"You don't know anything about me. I can scratch and bite and scream the house down."

"All right, you little vixen! Well, hurry up. I'm tired of holding this dress."

There was still a smile on his thin nervous face, but he was looking at her uncertainly. Her gaminesque impudence and fresh childish beauty delighted him, but there was a sense of foreboding at his heart. Perhaps, after all, things weren't going to go as smoothly as he'd thought they would. Despite his love for Trixie, perhaps because of it, he felt uncertain of his ground, afraid of alienating her by clumsiness or lack of understanding.

He guessed that her flippancy hid a secret nervousness, but he did not know her well enough to be able to reassure her. Her manner, gay and affectionate though it was, held him at arm's length.

She was just ready when the dinner-bell rang.

"Come on," she said. "If I'm late she'll start looking down her high and mighty nose at me again."

"Now listen, Trixie," he said, taking her by the shoulders, "Cynthia's a dear. She doesn't quite know what to make of you. She's a bit nervous though you may not guess it. You've *got* to get on with Cynthia, d'you hear?"

She looked up at him, her violet-blue eyes soft with laughter.

"Why the hell should I call her Cynthia? If she won't call me by my name, why should I call her by hers? . . I won't. I'll call her Victori-ah. It suits her, too. Bee-ah-trice and Victori-ah! What a couple!"

"Don't you dare, Trixie."

Still laughing, she raised rosy pouting lips to him and he kissed her, fiercely, hungrily.

"It's good to have you here, Trix," he said. He gave a little nervous laugh. "D'you know, I'd almost forgotten what you were like."

"I'd quite forgotten what you were like. It all happened so quick, didn't it? . . . I didn't want to come, you know. Mum and Dad had an awful job to make me."

"Why?"

"It didn't seem real. You didn't seem real . . . I was happy at home. I didn't want to leave them . . I felt I must've been crazy to go and get married and that they'd no right to hold me to it. I cried my eyes out . . ."

He kissed her again more tenderly.

"It's all right now, isn't it?"

"I dunno yet . . . It may be or it mayn't . . . Come on. We'll get into trouble."

He looked round the room. She had not unpacked yet, and the carpet was still littered with the things she had flung out of her trunk. Her skirt lay on the floor where she had stepped out of it. Her blouse and stockings were thrown anyhow on to the bed. Her shoes were on a chair.

"Hadn't we better just tidy it up?" he said.

"Oh come on," she said. "We'll do it to-night. Don't *you* start turning into a Victori-ah."

"Well?" said Godfrey, when Hubert and Trixie had gone to bed. Cynthia looked up at him with a faint smile and said nothing.

He perched on the arm of her chair and slipped an arm round her, drawing her to him.

"You look tired," he said. "You've worked too hard getting things ready. You must rest to-morrow."

She was still silent, and both were aware of the constraint in the atmosphere.

"You don't like her, do you?" he said at last.

"Do you?"

"I asked you first, but—well, yes, I do. She's just a child. There's something very attractive about her."

"To a man, no doubt. She's lovely and brimming over with sex-appeal, but I couldn't get on terms with her at all. She seems to have no means of communication but that cheap back-chat that all girls of her class use, I suppose, to attract men."

"Don't be catty, Cynthia."

She stiffened and withdrew from his embrace. He went over to the fireplace and put a light to his pipe. Then he said quietly:

"You know, I don't think it wise of you to call her Beatrice."

She set her lips obstinately.

"I'm going to stick to it, now I've started. I've always loathed the name Trixie, though I must admit that it suits her."

He sent her a quizzical glance over his pipe.

"I know what's in your mind, you hard-boiled little snob! She talks about Hubert as Mr. Fielding and she puts Westover in inverted commas and she says 'That's right' and she holds her knife as if it were a pen and eats her sweet with a spoon instead of a fork and does a hundred other little things, I daresay, that were supposed to 'class' people in the old days. My dear, they're words in a dead language. They don't mean anything any more."

She smiled faintly.

"They mean enough for you to have noticed them."

"Well, we were brought up to speak the language and we do it instinctively, and notice when other people don't, but we've got to realize that it doesn't mean anything and, really, never did. Hubert doesn't even notice it."

"Oh Hubert! He's so much in love that he doesn't know whether he's standing on his head or his heels."

"And that's all that matters to me."

"Yes, I don't matter, do I?" she said in a voice suddenly tremulous with anger. "She's been as insolent to me as she could be all evening, but you don't mind that. I'm expected to sit by and watch the two of you behave like a couple of moonstruck suburban youths—and enjoy it." She stopped suddenly, aghast at her outburst. "I'm sorry, Godfrey. I don't know what came over me. I don't generally make scenes, do I?"

"You're tired, my dear. Let's go to bed and forget it."

She looked up at him.

"Don't let her come between us, will you, Godfrey? All evening I felt so—cut off from you. You can talk her language and I can't."

"What on earth do you mean by that? The girl's Hubert's wife, and I was trying to make her feel at home, which was more·than you seemed to want to do."

"Godfrey, we *mustn't* quarrel about her."

He smiled down at her.

"You're doing all the quarrelling that's being done. Listen, darling. This is only a temporary arrangement. We'd all rather have houses of our own, but we can't get them. It's just a question of making the best of things for the present. There'll be difficulties, of course, but we must just——" he paused.

"Ignore them?" she supplied, rather dryly.

"Well, why not?" He drew her to her feet and kissed her, holding her closely. "It's all right now, isn't it?"

She smiled tremulously.

"Yes . . ."

But she knew it wasn't.

VII

MRS. POLLOCK flitted from room to room, straightening a cushion here, altering an ornament there. She was a vivid little woman, with dark hair, bright eyes and a trim neat figure, and she moved with the quick grace of a dragon-fly. Her mother had been a French woman, and Mrs. Pollock herself had spent her childhood and girlhood in France. From her mother she had inherited her instinct for style and from her English father (a scholar and dilettante) she had acquired a cultivated and critical taste for the arts . . . Next to her daughter, the chief interests of her life were music, literature and dress.

She had come to Westover last week, and was still feeling exhilarated by the "move." Workmen and charwomen had drooped and wearied, but Mrs. Pollock, upheld by her inexhaustible store of energy, had never flagged. She had outworked them all, though her slightest action had to be accompanied by streams of excited French-English and abundant gesticulation. And now everything was finally in place, and the result satisfied even Mrs. Pollock.

The dining-room held her eighteenth-century French furniture and engravings. The sitting-room, which she called the salon, was gay with Sèvres china, gilt wall mirrors, and painted cabinets. The soft colours of the Chinese carpet harmonised with the eau-de-nil walls and the gold brocade curtains. The third little room she called the boudoir, and in that she had frankly compromised with "English bourgeois taste." It was, she knew, Ann-Marie's favourite room. There were deep leather armchairs, a solid bureau, a gate-legged table and a comfortable old-fashioned sofa. Books lined the walls . . . Mrs. Pollock bought books with almost feverish enthusiasm, sending weekly orders to London for any book that caught her fancy in the pages of the literary reviews. She had a fierce contempt for the "cairculating library."

She moved a bowl of flowers from one table to another, moved a mirror on the wall that was hanging a fraction of an inch out of the straight, picked up an almost invisible piece of fluff from the carpet and dropped it into the wastepaper basket, then held out her arm with a quick darting movement, characteristic of her, to consult her watch. It was time for Ann-Marie to come back from work . . .

There was no reason at all why Ann-Marie should go to work. Mrs. Pollock's marriage had been a marriage of convenience, and her husband had fulfilled his part of the bargain by dying six years after the marriage and leaving her handsomely provided for. Mrs. Pollock's sense of the dramatic, with which she was liberally endowed, had prompted her to give an impressive representation of an inconsolable widow, but actually she had felt little grief. Like Mrs. Norris, she consoled herself for the death of her husband by considering that she could do very well without him . . . and proceeded to devote herself to Ann-Marie. Since the child's birth she had concentrated on her all the passion of her nature. Ann-Marie, trotting by Maman's side in the most exquisite of little French frocks, the daintiest of little French bonnets, was one of the prettiest pictures you could imagine. "Like a little doll," people said . . . And indeed the small grave face, china-blue eyes, and silky ringlets made the comparison not inapt.

In spite of the almost innumerable safeguards by which she was surrounded, however, Ann-Marie succumbed to infantile paralysis only a year after her father's death, and lay fever-tossed and pain-racked on the little white curtained bed beneath the white satin eiderdown. Mrs. Pollock was so distracted that for a time she had to take to her own bed, much to the relief of everyone concerned. There, propped up by pillows, the tears streaming down her face, she informed the Almighty with Gallic vehemence that if He took her Little Flower she would follow . . .

Ann-Marie recovered—to trail a useless foot and hobble slowly and painfully about the house. Had she been allowed to go to school and play with other children, her lameness might have made little difference to her, but Mrs. Pollock considered the idea "barbarous . . . inhuman."

"Other children they would make her suffer so. They are cruel, those other children. All the time she would feel the difference. It would poison her spirit . . ."

So Ann-Marie continued to be a familiar sight in the neighbourhood, still dressed in her most exquisite of French frocks, the daintiest of French bonnets, but wheeled everywhere now in a little invalid chair made, to Mrs. Pollock's order, in the shape of a swan.

As time went on, the question of Ann-Marie's education arose. Even a governess Mrs. Pollock considered to be out of the question.

"She is so sensitive, my Little Flower, and they are hard, these governesses. They do not love. They do not understand. I only understand because I only love."

So Mrs. Pollock proceeded to educate her Little Flower with the enthusiasm and intensity she brought to bear on anything she undertook.

Ann-Marie enjoyed the lessons, particularly the history lessons, for in them Mrs. Pollock would give dramatic renderings of any scene that appealed to her own imagination, often moving both herself and Little Flower to tears. As Mary Queen of Scots, she showed a deplorable lack of self-control before the block in Fotheringay Castle, but, as Charles I, she demanded the five members with flashing eye and curling lip. Elizabeth and Cromwell were blood-soaked villains to be mentioned, if mentioned at all, in the same breath as Nero or Charles Peace. Thus Ann-Marie acquired a certain historical background if little historical perspective.

When Ann-Marie was fourteen, Mrs. Pollock decided that she must travel. Debarred from the normal pleasures of youth, from dances, games and companionship in general (for Ann-Marie was allowed no friends. Friends, Mrs. Pollock considered, would emphasise her "difference") she must find pleasure in the scenery and culture of Europe. So Mrs. Pollock and Ann-Marie and a brand new invalid chair (no longer, of course, in the shape of a swan) went to Holland, Belgium, France, Germany, Italy . . . Ann-Marie was wheeled round churches, museums, picture galleries, was carried by smiling Neapolitans through the ruins of Pompeii, was driven round the chateaux of the Loire, over the Alps, sailed on the Italian lakes, went in steamers on the Rhine and the Rhone, attended the musical festival at Strasburg, the Passion Play at Oberammergau . . .

Wherever she went she received lessons in the language of the country from the best teachers obtainable, and Mrs. Pollock joined the lessons, giving them a life and colour they might otherwise have lacked, for the humblest pronoun, the most inoffensive preposition, could take on a personality of its own and rouse the deepest emotions in Mrs. Pollock's breast.

In 1939 Mrs. Pollock and Ann-Marie had returned to England from a visit to Egypt, which had included a voyage down the Nile, the inevitable visit to Luxor and the Pyramids, and a sudden conviction on the part of Mrs. Pollock that she was the reincarnation of a priestess at the shrine of Isis.

In spite of all this, Ann-Marie looked more pale and peaky than ever, and Mrs. Pollock decided on a course of country air and complete relaxation. A London house agent sent her the address of a house near Nettleford, which seemed to fulfil all their requirements, and Ann-Marie and Mrs. Pollock had just moved into it when war broke out. And then, for the first time in her life, Ann-Marie showed signs of self-will. She wanted to "do something for the war."

"The war!" said Mrs. Pollock, waving her hands in a gesture of contempt. "It is foolish, the war. Like all wars, it serves no purpose. Civilized people ignore wars."

Ann-Marie's lips took on an unaccustomed line of firmness.

"I can't feel like that about it, Maman," she said.

Mrs. Pollock was nonplussed by this strangely independent attitude on the part of her Little Flower, uncertain whether to be cut to the quick or merely amused.

"*Chérie*," she said at last, "you know that I would give the heart out of my bosom to make you one of those heftee young women who stride about so ungainly in khakee and air-blue, but my darleeng must remember that she is not like other girls."

"I don't mean—that, but there must be something I could do. Men are being called up. I could take a man's place."

"Darleeng!" said Mrs. Pollock with a rippling laugh of pure amusement. "A man's place? *You?*"

A faint flush overspread the pallor of Ann-Marie's face.

"There is—sedentary work. I could do that."

"Darleeng, Maman knows her Little Flower . . . Her Little Flower is too fragile . . ."

"I'm not," said Ann-Marie stubbornly. "I could sit at a desk and write letters or add figures. I could learn to type."

"Type!" screamed Mrs. Pollock in horror. "Are you mad, *chérie?*"

But Ann-Marie continued to show an obstinacy and determination that she had never shown before.

"My little one," pleaded Mrs. Pollock hysterically, "you must not, I pray you, put yourself in the place of a girl who works for her living. You have too much physical and moral delicacy for such a life. You have been gently nurtured, guarded, shielded . . ."

But Ann-Marie was not listening. She was studying the Situations Vacant columns of the daily paper.

"Here's an advertisement for 'shirt hands'," she said. "I suppose it's sewing and I could sit down to it. Of course, it doesn't release a man but it would release a girl for one of the Women's Services."

Mrs. Pollock paled and choked and—set to work. Mr. Chapman, her solicitor in Nettleford, had told her, when last she saw him, that his secretary had left to join the A.T.S. and that he had not been able to find another. All the educated girls in the neighbourhood, he said, seemed to be doing war work.

Mrs. Pollock entered into a little conspiracy with him. He was to engage Ann-Marie temporarily, till she was cured of this folly. A week, Mrs. Pollock considered optimistically, should be enough. Fortunately, Mr. Chapman passed the house on his way to Nettleford and could both pick up Ann-Marie in his car and drop her on his way home, thus sparing her all unnecessary exertion. It would be doing her, said Mrs. Pollock with an eloquent gesture, a real kindness. She would be eternally grateful. Ann-Marie was so delicate, so fragile that she would soon realize how impossible such work was for her. Mr. Chapman was a little surprised by the request, but she was a good client, so he agreed.

From Mrs. Pollock's point of view, however, the conspiracy proved a failure. Ann-Marie continued to work as Mr. Chapman's secretary, had continued now for five years. She was quick and dependable, and Mr. Chapman had no intention of parting with her if he could help it.

When the war ended it was a shock to Mrs. Pollock to discover that Ann-Marie wished to continue her work (Mr. Chapman's former secretary seemed to have joined in the conspiracy by marrying a sergeant in the Signals), but, after a suitable display of horror and distress, she consented. During the years of the war, she had gradually accustomed herself to the arrangement. Though it took Ann-Marie from her during the day, it enabled her to use the day as a preparation, of gradually increasing crescendo, for her return. The elaborate dinners that she planned each night (dainty dinners with subtle flavourings, for Ann-Marie had a poor appetite and must be tempted) often necessitated a journey into Nettleford in the morning and the opening of proceedings at the gas cooker by 3 o'clock in the afternoon. So that, when Ann-Marie returned at about five o'clock, the stage was set and Mrs. Pollock ready to play her part in the scene of reunion—a scene that often reached surprising heights of drama.

The situation had its redeeming features. Mr. Chapman was eminently respectable, and Ann-Marie worked by herself in a little room that opened off his office and so was spared those contacts with the crude outside world from which Mrs. Pollock had always tried to shield her.

There was the sound of wheels on the gravel and, looking out of the window, Mrs. Pollock saw Ann-Marie being helped from the car by Mr. Chapman.

She darted to the door.

"*Darleeng!*" she cried, flinging herself upon the small slight figure.

Mr. Chapman raised his hat, returned to the car and drove off.

Mrs. Pollock slipped an arm round Ann-Marie and helped her along the passage to the boudoir.

There Ann-Marie lay on the sofa, propped up by cushions, looking pale and fragile, while Mrs. Pollock stripped off her shoes and stockings, and, holding the slender feet tenderly in her lap, began to massage expertly, chattering the while about her day's doings, telling whom she had met, what they had said, what she had said, giving amusing little descriptions and imitations, frequently stopping the massage to enable her to make those swift darting gesticulations without which any form of intercourse was impossible for her. Ann-Marie's clear laugh rang out time after time . . .

"And now, *chérie*, if you feel rested . . ."

Then the routine of the evening began—the steaming scented bath, the dressing of Ann-Marie in one of those elaborate picture frocks in which Mrs. Pollock loved to see her, the brushing and arranging of the silky golden hair. Every evening Ann-Marie was dressed as if for a party, just to sit at the candle-lit table for a tête-à-tête dinner with her mother.

Mrs. Pollock sang to herself as she fastened the last gleaming curl in place. She was so happy, tending her Little Flower . . .

Back on the sofa in the boudoir, Ann-Marie sipped her glass of sherry, while Mrs. Pollock put on the gramophone a record of Ravel's "Ma Mère l'Oye."

"This is a surprise for you, *chérie*," she said. "I brought it from London last week, and," she smiled roguishly, "I have another surprise for you. After dinner you shall know. And dinner itself is yet another surprise, for I have managed to obtain—Ah, but I will not tell you. It would spoil the surprise."

"You are so good, Maman," said Ann-Marie.

"You think you will be happy in this Westover, my little one?"

"Yes, Maman."

"And now," with a dramatic flourish of both hands, "we must leesen."

Lips parted, eyes bright, sitting upright in her chair, tense with emotion, Mrs. Pollock drank in the strains of "Ma Mère l'Oye," her hands moving with the music.

Ann-Marie lay on the sofa, the full flounced dress of midnight blue taffeta spread out around her, the golden head propped up by cushions, sipping her sherry and fighting a treacherous feeling of boredom. The feeling had visited her more and more frequently lately, bringing with it a bitter sense of shame. That she should be *bored*, surrounded by Maman's love on every side, her life filled with interests, pleasures, treats carefully prepared by Maman. It was incredible . . . All day she longed for her return to the gay happy little world in which she and Maman lived apart, in which they were all in all to each other, and yet lately it had been spoilt by this nagging little feeling of boredom. Ann-Marie felt shocked and bewildered. . . . It was wicked, ungrateful—horrible . . .

The strains of the record died away . . .

"How it stimulates and inspires!" said Mrs. Pollock. "One feels, does one not, my child? as if one had drunk of nectar and ambrosia. . . . And now we must turn to food for the body, *chérie*. Maman will not be a moment, my darleeng. Dinner will soon be ready."

"Mr. Hassock came into the office to-day, Maman," said Ann-Marie abruptly.

Mrs. Pollock stood motionless—very motionless for her—on her way to the door.

"Yes?" she said.

"He wants to take me to the new play at St. James' next Saturday."

Mrs. Pollock's immobility vanished. Her eyes flashed, her hands fluttered, her whole body quivered.

"Oh, my darleeng, it would be too much for you."

"He'd take me all the way in the car," said Ann-Marie with a touch—just a touch—of sulkiness in her voice. "I went with him before, you know."

"And it was too much for you. My Little Flower was drooping with fatigue. You were too exhausted, you remember, my precious, to go to the office even on the Monday . . . Think of it, _chérie_ . . . Remember . . ."

Ann-Marie was silent, thinking of it, remembering . . .

Mr. Hassock was a client of Mr. Chapman's who had conceived an admiration for Ann-Marie and had asked Mr. Chapman to introduce him to her. He was a personal friend of Mr. Chapman's, a bachelor of considerable wealth and unblemished reputation, and Mrs. Pollock could have no possible objection to the acquaintance. Ann-Marie had been tremulously excited when he suggested taking her to London to a theatre. It seemed to offer a miraculous entry into the normal world that had till now been closed to her. To go to the theatre with a man like other girls . . . Mrs. Pollock had done all she could to discourage the idea, but Ann-Marie had been calmly, quietly insistent. Beneath her çalm and quiet she felt, strangely, that she was fighting for her existence. Mrs. Pollock gave way and stood, a tragic figure, on the front doorstep, waving good-bye with desperate courage till the car was out of sight.

But as the day wore on the brightness faded from the prospect for Ann-Marie. Mr. Hassock, despite his good looks and perfect manners, was dull; was pompous and self-important and humourless and—devastatingly dull. His conversation consisted of a flow of platitudes, his comments on the play were banal and even, Ann-Marie considered, idiotic. She missed Maman's sparkling wit and gaiety, her quick keen judgments, her rapier-like criticisms. Maman looked at things from unexpected angles. She made you laugh, she made you think. Throughout the afternoon to which she had looked forward for so long, Ann-Marie was bored and tired and homesick. She was not, of course, quite as tired as Maman made out, though at the time she had believed she was. Maman's cries of horror at her appearance persuaded her that she had reached the last stages of collapse. It was lovely to return to the warm familiar atmosphere of Maman's love and protection—like coming in from the cold and rain to a glowing fire. She relaxed in it, lying in bed all Sunday and Monday in a state of listlessness that, under Maman's guidance, she interpreted as exhaustion. Well, that's the end of that, she had thought, as she sat propped up by pillows, gratefully drinking a bouillon made by Maman's skilled hands. But it wasn't quite the end. For something deep down in Ann-Marie—something that she tried her hardest to conquer, because she felt that it was wicked—still chafed at the enclosed world in which she lived, still longed for escape . . . And still Mr. Hassock, respectfully, suavely admiring, seemed to provide the only means of escape. She had felt something of the old flutter of excitement this afternoon when he had suggested another visit to the theatre.

"I'll ask Maman," she had said.

"Tell her I'll take care of you," said Mr. Hassock, smiling down at her. "She can trust me to do that."

"I'd like to see the play, Maman," said Ann-Marie, a little plaintively.

"Of course, my darleeng," said Mrs. Pollock. "I myself had been thinking that we must see that play, but next Saturday is the concert at Albert Hall. We will go to that. I will order the car to-morrow. I was looking at the paper this morning, and I said to myself, 'There are many things in London that Ann-Marie and I must see.' There is to be an exhibition of Modern French Art. We must certainly go to that, *chérie*. Yes, we must arrange some expeditions. And Maman can look after her Little Flower as no one else can, note when she is tired, take care that she does not exhaust herself . . . And now you shall have the second surprise, my little one. It is the book of poems of which I read you the review in the newspaper last Sunday. I sent for it for you . . . Here it is."

Smiling fondly, Mrs. Pollock took a small book from the drawer of her bureau and handed it to Ann-Marie.

"Oh, *thank* you, Maman," said Ann-Marie, but there was something a little forced in her enthusiasm.

"And now," said Mrs. Pollock brightly, "Maman will go and see to her *pièce de résistance* that is still in the oven."

Her voice could be heard in the kitchen, as she moved to and fro, upraised in gay little snatches of song.

Ann-Marie lay on the sofa, turning over the pages of the book but without looking at any of them. She was wondering whether it was worth while to fight for this visit to the theatre with Mr. Hassock. If only she liked him better . . . If only she had enjoyed the day she spent with him before . . . That day, she had to admit, had been a failure, but it had been an escape, too (she could not have told from what) and it was the only escape that had so far offered itself. Perhaps she had expected too much . . . She didn't quite know what she had expected—certainly not anything that would lead to love and marriage. Maman had shown her plainly (though without putting it into actual words) that love and marriage were not for her, that with her the things of the mind must take their place, and that the things of the mind were more satisfying and lasting.

She closed the book and lay gazing into space. I'm wicked, she thought despairingly, I'm discontented and ungrateful and *wicked*. For the things of the mind bore me . . .

"And now, *chérie*," said Mrs. Pollock, appearing suddenly in the doorway and flinging out her arms, "dinner ees sairved."

Dinner was over. Ann-Marie was lying on the settee in the salon, and Mrs. Pollock was reading aloud from the new book of poems, when Letitia knocked softly at the door.

Mrs. Pollock answered the knock.

"I hope I'm not disturbing you," said Letitia, smiling round as she entered. "How cosy you look! It's quite a picture."

"Be seated, Madame," said Mrs. Pollock with frigid politeness. She did not want visitors. She had always managed so far to discourage them wherever she had lived. They tired Ann-Marie, they brought cold blasts of alien influence into the warm happy world that she and Ann-Marie inhabited together.

"I don't want to disturb you," said Letitia, "but I'm giving a little party on Friday week—just a small cocktail party, so that we can all get to know each other, and I *do* so hope that you can both come. Our flat is just above this."

"Eet ees very kind of you," said Mrs. Pollock who, when on her dignity, always became aggressively French in accent and manner, "but my daughtair ees not strong and such functions overtire her."

"Oh, but, Maman . . ." said Ann-Marie eagerly, raising herself on her elbow, "I—It wouldn't tire me. Just upstairs. It's not like— going out somewhere."

Letitia smiled charmingly at Mrs. Pollock.

"It will be a very quiet party. Just ourselves and the Fieldings, who have the other upstairs flat, and the Gideons, who used to live here. Almost a family party. It wouldn't be complete without you. We're all so anxious to know you."

Mrs. Pollock hesitated. It sounded harmless enough. Nothing there to overtire her Little Flower. And—it might make her forget this outrageous man who wanted to drag her up to London again. Mrs. Pollock was not really jealous of Mr. Hassock. She was shrewd enough to realize that he bored and irritated Ann-Marie, but—he unsettled her, too. If Little Flower wanted to go to this very dull party, she should go. It would distract her mind from other things.

"I thank you," she said graciously to Letitia. "We accept your kind invitation weeth much pleasure."

There was dismissal in her tone, but Letitia did not go. She stayed for an hour or so longer.

When she went, she left Mrs. Pollock with an excellent opinion of both Letitia and herself, but a very poor opinion of the other occupants of the flats.

VIII

MRS. GIDEON sat in the garden darning socks. With three boys the process of sock darning seemed an endless one, and she could never, as she expressed it, "catch up."

Through the open window of the kitchen, where Trixie, Richard and Rachel were making toffee, came the sound of laughter and scuffling.

"You mustn't eat it till it's set."

"It won't ever set."

"Oo, it's lovely."

"You've got a blob of it on your nose."

"Look! It pulls out like elastic."

"You're *ruining* it."

"Let's eat it now. It's *lovely* as it is."

"Hi! You're taking too much."

Trixie had been over to Greenways a good deal lately. When with Richard and Rachel, she seemed to become a child herself, entering into all their games as though there were no difference in age between them. Mrs. Gideon was fond of her and liked having her there, but she felt worried by the situation, and sometimes wondered what would come of it. She's such a baby, she thought. It seems absurd to expect her to behave like a grown-up person. But she's a married woman, responsible for other people's happiness. She's going to hurt them or be hurt by them—terribly.

Richard came racing out with the pan of toffee, pursued by the other two, who were laughing too much to catch him. He dodged round the apple tree and ran back into the kitchen.

Mrs. Gideon put away her sock and went indoors. The three were scuffling on the kitchen floor.

"What a mess everything's in! Get up and put it straight. And do you call this toffee?"

"It's lovely, Mummy. It just hasn't set, that's all, but it's lovely! Try some."

"No, thank you . . . It's tea-time. Put the kettle on, Rachel, and tidy yourselves up, for goodness' sake. *Look* at you! You're covered with toffee."

They crowded laughing round the mirror on the kitchen wall, then ran to the tap over the sink to wash, pushing each other about and splashing each other.

Trixie came back to the kitchen, took off her apron and threw it on to a chair.

"Put that away, you untidy little monkey!" said Mrs. Gideon. "You know where it came from."

Trixie grinned, folded it up and put it into a drawer.

"Trixie's staying to tea, isn't she?" demanded the children.

"Oh yes, *please*," pleaded Trixie.

"What about Mrs. Fielding?" said Mrs. Gideon. "Will she be expecting you?"

"Oh, *her*," said Trixie with a grimace. "No, it doesn't matter for tea. She just gets her own. If I'm there, she gets mine too." She pursed her lips and assumed a drawling, high-pitched voice. "Weel you hev another cup of tea, Bee-ah-trice?"

"Now, Trixie, none of that, you naughty girl!" said Mrs. Gideon severely. "She doesn't talk like that at all and you know quite well she doesn't. In any case, I won't have you making fun of her here, and I've told you that before."

Trixie rubbed her head against Mrs. Gideon's shoulder, like a pony nuzzling.

"I'm sorry."

"You be a good girl," said Mrs. Gideon, patting her cheek. "Take the tea-things out into the garden while I make the sandwiches."

"Let's not have chairs," said Richard. "Let's have a picnic."

"All right. But wash your face again. You've still got toffee on it."

"It's not toffee. It's his old freckles," jeered Rachel.

Richard threw the kitchen towel at her and plunged his face under the tap, soaking his hair and the top part of his blouse.

"Hello, Toffee-face!" teased Rachel when he emerged.

He leapt in pursuit of her, knocking over a chair, and they disappeared into the garden.

Mrs. Gideon murmured "Children, children!" in mechanical expostulation, as she got out the bread and butter and tomatoes from the larder.

"Carry the tea-things out, Trixie, there's a good girl. Put the tablecloth on the grass . . . And make those two monkeys behave themselves."

The cloth was spread under the apple tree and they all sat on the grass around it.

"Let's have a real picnic and ask people to it," said Rachel, her mouth full of tomato sandwich.

"In the wood," said Richard.

"*Can* we, Mummy?"

"I don't see why not," said Mrs. Gideon. "We'll ask Colin to-night."

"You'll come, won't you, Trixie?"

"Of course I will."

The two chattered away excitedly, making arrangements for the picnic, and Trixie fell silent. She was so happy in this atmosphere of carefree family affection. It made her different, more her real self, not sulky, as she was with Cynthia, or silly and flirtatious, as she was with Hubert and Godfrey. (It was funny to call yourself flirtatious with your own husband, but it was the only word she could think of.) She could talk to Mrs. Gideon about Mum and Dad. She'd rather die than mention them to Cynthia—or even to Hubert and Godfrey. . . . They wouldn't understand . . .

They carried the tea in, and Mrs. Gideon returned to her deck chair and darning-basket. Rachel and Richard went to play on the tree-platform, calling to Trixie to join them, but she continued to sit on the grass by Mrs. Gideon's chair.

"I like being here," she said suddenly. "I wish I didn't have to go back."

"Don't be silly," said Mrs. Gideon.

"It's not silly. I love you all here . . . It's fun playing with Richard and Rachel. I've got two little cousins at home about their age and I used to go and spend every Saturday with them and play with them . . . They live in the town. They'd love it here."

"You must have them to stay with you."

"Not with her looking down her nose at them!"

"Now, Trixie!"

Trixie leant her head against Mrs. Gideon's knee.

"Sorry . . . You know, the last Sunday I was at home Mum and Dad and I went into the country. Are you tired of me talking about Mum and Dad?"

"No, darling. Go on."

The saga of Mum and Dad was resumed. "Mum and Dad" . . . "Me and Mum" . . . "Me and Dad." Most people would have been bored, but Mrs. Gideon was deeply interested . . . She felt that she knew the little house as well as if she had lived in it, the seldom used parlour, the cosy kitchen-living-room, the bustling kindly "Mum," the humorous adoring "Dad."

"They spoilt you, you know," she said.

"Who?"

"Mum and Dad. Mum specially."

"I know," said Trixie. "Mum said she knew they had done. She said I was a little Irish slut and it was her fault, because she'd always waited on me and tidied up after me, and never made me tidy up for myself. She said she'd kept me a baby too long, but I'd got to start my own life now I was married. She said I mustn't go back to them, however homesick I was."

"Are you homesick?"

Trixie nodded.

"Sometimes. But she said I'd wanted to marry him and I must stand by it. She said I was old enough to know my own mind."

Mrs. Gideon looked down at her anxiously.

"You're happy, dear, aren't you?"

"Oh, yes," said Trixie vaguely. She clapped her hand to her mouth suddenly. "*Gosh!*"

"What is it?"

"I never did our room before I came out. I'm always forgetting."

"Oh, Trixie!"

"I'll do it when I get back Perhaps she won't have gone in . . ."

"You'd better go now and do it."

"I suppose I had. Oh dear! And it's the evening of Mrs. Drummond's party. You're coming, aren't you?"

Mrs. Gideon smiled.

"Yes. All of us. Aunt Lucy insisted that Rachel and Richard must come too."

"Oh, good!"

Laura and Colin came into the garden through the house.

They generally met after work and came home together.

"Hello, darlings," said Mrs. Gideon. "Have you had tea?"

"No," said Laura, "I'll go and make it. Don't you dare get up, Blanche."

Rachel and Richard swarmed down the tree.

"Colin, can we have a picnic and ask people? Mummy says we can if you say so."

"All right," said Colin, "if you'll help and not leave all the work to other people."

"Oh, Colin, we *wouldn't* do that."

He grimaced at them.

"Wouldn't you? You would if I know you, you lazy little brats. Go and get some deck chairs out. We can't all sit on the grass. Hello, Trixie."

Like the others, he had come almost to accept Trixie as a member of the family. She seemed to be in and out of the house most of the time.

She smiled up at him rather shyly.

The Two came back across the lawn, dragging deck chairs. Colin sat down and they hung over his shoulder, standing on a rung of his chair.

"We've been making toffee, Colin. Will you have some?"

"No, thanks."

"Colin, can we all ask four persons each to the picnic?"

"As many as you like, if you'll stop breathing down my neck."

"I'm not breathing down it now, am I, Colin? D'you think you'd have time to mend our tank to-night? We don't know what's wrong with it, but it won't tank any longer."

"I'll see. Now for Heaven's sake stop smothering me. I can't see to breathe with the two of you on top of me like this . . . Go and get the table for Laura."

"See to breathe," echoed Rachel in delight.

Laura had come out with a tray of tea. She looked unsmilingly at Trixie as she set it down.

"Let's all have another tea," said Mrs. Gideon. "I made heaps of sandwiches, and I hate watching other people eat."

"So do I," said Rachel. "Come on, Trixie."

Trixie and the Two sat on the grass round the tablecloth, the others on deck chairs round the table.

Roger came in at the garden gate. Watching them over the hedge as he approached, he had thought how complete they looked without him, and had wondered if they'd miss him at all if he died suddenly.

The performance of *Loyalties* was to be given at the end of the holidays, and he had been rehearsing in the Village Hall all afternoon.

. . . On the way home he had subjected himself to his favourite form of torture, which was to force himself in imagination to perform the act of heroism by which his father had won the D.S.O. a few months before he was killed. Colonel Gideon had captured a machine-gun nest single-handed in the face of enemy fire. Roger tried to do the same, but always he turned and ran back when he was halfway there. He could never force himself to face the rain of bullets that his father had faced without flinching. And in some way, by not being able to do so, he felt that he was betraying his father.

He was passing the group in the garden with a muttered greeting when Mrs. Gideon said:

"Come and have a cup of tea, Roger."

He hesitated, then sat down a little way from the rest, as if to emphasise his isolation. Laura handed him his tea, and the others went on talking about the picnic, Laura's work, the party to-night. He thought, none of them takes the slightest interest in me. I've been slaving at the rehearsal all afternoon, and they don't even ask about it . . .

"Rehearsal go off all right, Roger?" said Colin.

"Yes, thanks," said Roger shortly, resenting Colin's interest as fiercely as a moment ago he had resented his lack of it. Patronising beast, he said to himself and, liking the sound of it, repeated, Patronising beast.

"You children must get ready now if you're going to Aunt Lucy's," said Mrs. Gideon. "I've put your things out. Run along. . . . And—Trixie, child, are you still here? Run off at once. And do your room the *second* you get in."

"It'll take me hours," said Trixie with her slow smile. "I always leave it in a frightful mess."

"Well, don't leave it in a mess again. It's not easy to be tidy if you're naturally untidy, I know, but just keep on trying. I have to. I'm just as bad as you, and I keep on trying."

"You're not like that," said Laura with a sudden sharpness in her voice. "You don't know what to wear or how to wear it, but you're not—slovenly."

Mrs. Gideon looked at her in surprise and she flushed. She didn't know why she disliked this girl so much. She had disliked her from the moment she first saw her—in the post office with her husband the day after her arrival.

Mrs. Gideon walked to the gate with Trixie.

"You'll be a good girl when you get home, won't you, Trixie?"

"Yes."

"Promise?"

"Yes."

Mrs. Gideon took the heart-shaped face in her hands and kissed it.

"Now off you go!"

When she returned to the garden, Laura had gone indoors and Colin and Roger were alone. Colin was taking the children's tank to pieces. Roger was apparently absorbed in his copy of *Loyalties*.

"You'd better go and change, too, Roger," said Mrs. Gideon. "You can't go to Aunt Letitia's party in those old flannels."

"I'm not going to Aunt Letitia's party," said Roger, his eye still on his book.

"Oh, Roger!"

"I've already told you that I'm never going to set foot in the place again."

Mrs. Gideon looked at him unhappily. He'd stay at home by himself, feeling lonely and miserable and believing that no one wanted him.

"Roger, darling, I'd like you to come with us."

Roger went on reading his book without speaking.

Colin looked up from the dismembered tank.

"Get a move on, Roger," he said impatiently. "You heard what Mother said."

Roger gave him a long slow look. He'd have a show-down with Colin one of these days—let him see that he wasn't a kid to be ordered about. But he'd choose his own time and place, and it wouldn't be here or now. Besides, right down at the bottom of his heart he rather wanted to go to the party . . .

He slipped his book into his pocket and went indoors.

Cynthia was at the window when Trixie came up the drive. She had run most of the way from Greenways and was hot and breathless, her hair falling untidily about her face. Cynthia turned away from the window, her lips a tight line.

All the happiness of her life with Godfrey seemed to have been spoilt by the arrival of Hubert's wife. The little seed of discord dropped by Letitia had failed to flower. Cynthia knew that Godfrey's inherent decency and real affection for Hubert would prevent his ever falling in love with her, but he *was* fond of her and in a way that Cynthia found particularly galling. When she saw him laughing at her sallies, or her funny little ways, there was a protective tenderness behind his amusement that brought a pang to her heart. That's how he would have been with his daughter, she thought. He'd like to have children. There's something in him that needs children. And I don't want them . . .

She was older than Godfrey. She could never forget that it was she who had engineered their marriage. It gave an element of precariousness to his love for her. Secretly she was always afraid of losing him. She needed, she considered, all the weapons of her charm and beauty to hold him . . . The idea of pregnancy revolted her. To lose the taut slender elegance she preserved with such care, to become shapeless and sagging, to have to stop going about with him, to be a drag, a responsibility . . . She had seen women who were bearing children go horribly to pieces. And—she managed all their business affairs. She couldn't afford to lose her hold on the reins even for a few months. When he had suggested having children, she had put him off. "Let's wait till we're a bit more settled," she had said. She had intended to continue putting him off. He would not have persisted. He would soon have resigned himself. But now this girl had made her see what she was cheating him of, and she could not bear to think that she was cheating him of anything.

That, of course, was not the girl's fault. She could not in justice have disliked her for that alone. She disliked her because she was slovenly, lazy and common. Everything about her offended Cynthia's fastidiousness. She had ignored Cynthia's suggestion that they should get the breakfast ready in turns. She lay in bed in the morning till ten or eleven, or, if she did get up, slopped about the flat in a dressing-gown, her face unwashed, her hair undone. She wore grubby blouses, creased dresses, grease-spotted skirts. It never seemed to occur to her that she could remedy these defects. She shirked her share of the housework. She left a trail of her things about wherever she went. The look of shining immaculate freshness that the flat had worn before her arrival seemed to have vanished . . . There were times when Cynthia's conscience suggested to her that she might have helped matters by a little tactful advice and guidance, but she disliked the girl too much to try. Her dislike had been gathering force with the weeks, and this afternoon it had come to a head. She had looked into Trixie's and Hubert's bedroom about three o'clock to find the bed unmade, the slops unemptied, the floor strewn with Trixie's clothes, the furniture undusted, the carpet unswept, the windows tight closed, the atmosphere unbearably fusty. She had stood there motionless looking about her, so angry that for a few moments she saw the room through a kind of mist . . . Then she set to work, making the beds, emptying the slops, dusting, cleaning, polishing. When she had finished, the place was as fresh and sweet as Cynthia's own bed-room. She had meant to speak to Trixie about it as soon as she came in, but she realized gradually that she could not trust herself to do so. At the very thought of the girl, her heart quickened and a curious feeling of breathlessness came over her.

Trixie burst noisily into the room. Cynthia, reading a book by the window, did not speak but the look she turned on her sent a wave of icy coldness through Trixie's body. She had met little dislike, or even criticism, in her short life before . . . She crossed the sitting-room into her bedroom, closed the door and gazed around her. So she'd done it. Done it and then looked on her as if she was a bit of filth. The beast, the *beast!* She sat down on the bed, trembling, and a slow sultry anger gathered at her heart.

Godfrey and Hubert came in together. Hubert seemed tired and dispirited. The happiness he had looked forward to seemed still to elude him. He disliked his work and had always disliked it, but he had been given no choice in the matter and realized that he had been fortunate to have a job to come back to after the war. He had disliked the Army even more . . . That would have worried him little if his home life had been what he had hoped it would be. But Trixie was evasive . . . As a wife she was amenable enough, but he never seemed to get any nearer her. She imposed a wall of flippancy between them. Sometimes he felt that, when his passion for her died, it would leave no common ground on which they could meet.

Cynthia raised her eyes from her book. There was a tight closed look on her face.

"May I have a word with you, Hubert?" she said.

He followed her into the little kitchen.

"Hubert, do you mind speaking to Beatrice about keeping your bedroom more tidy? I went in there at three o'clock this afternoon, and it hadn't been touched. It was in a disgusting mess." She noticed how tired and worried he looked, and, despite herself, compunction stirred at her heart. "I hate bothering you like this, but——"

"That's all right, Cynthia. I'll speak to her. I'm—terribly sorry."

He went into the bedroom. Trixie still sat on the bed. She turned hot angry eyes on to him. He stood for a moment screwing up his courage. Best to get it over quickly.

"Trixie," he blurted out, "Cynthia's asked me to speak to you about the bedroom."

The anger that Trixie had been holding in check broke its dam . . . It was like a flood, sweeping her and everything else along with it.

"Leave me alone!" she shouted. "Get out! I won't have you all nagging at me. I'm sick of it. I hate her. I hate you, too. I hate you all."

She collapsed suddenly on the bed, sobbing wildly.

He went to her and put a hand on her shoulder in a bewildered uncertain way.

"Trixie . . ."

She raised her tear-stained face.

"Get out!" she screamed hysterically. "Get out!"

He hesitated, then went away, closing the door behind him.

Godfrey was pouring out a glass of sherry.

"Have a drink, old chap," he said, looking with sympathy and compassion at Hubert's white strained face. "We might as well fortify ourselves for the party."

Hubert took his glass with a shaking hand.

"I don't expect there'll be anything fit to drink there," Godfrey went on smoothly. "There never is at a woman's party."

He could hear the sound of muffled sobs from the bedroom, but such scenes were best ignored. They blew over if one took no notice.

"Sherry, Cynthia?"

"No, thank you."

She sat tense, her eyes on her book, her face still wearing that tight closed look . . .

IX

THE sitting-room was gay with bowls of roses and tall jars of delphiniums and lilies.

Letitia had been busy herself—and had kept Lucy and Miss Parsons busy—all day. Her temper had worn thin, and her voice taken a sharp edge long before the preparations were complete. Lucy and Miss Parsons didn't seem to have the least idea how such things should be done. Luc̵ ̵ad even suggested sweet biscuits . . . The glasses had had to be h̵ ̵, and Letitia would have liked to hire a waiter as well, but hired wa..ers seemed to be unknown in Nettleford. She had invited the Fieldings, the Gideons, the Pollocks, James (she was surprised and gratified when James accepted the invitation) and several local people whom she had come to know.

The guests were beginning to arrive, and already the room was full of the cheerful hum of conversation. Letitia moved about with a fixed sweet smile. Several things had contributed to put her out. For one thing, people persisted in treating Lucy as if she were the hostess. It was, of course, Lucy's flat, and Lucy had paid for the drinks, but Letitia had made it quite clear to everyone, when she invited them, that it was her party. Lucy looked as dowdy as ever in an old-fashioned dress of patterned silk (and what a pattern!) but people clustered round and talked to her, and Letitia found it galling. She had thought that Lucy's very presence would spoil the party, and had even suggested with an air of solicitude that perhaps she would find it too tiring and might prefer to stay in her bedroom, but Lucy, though touched by Letitia's unusual consideration, had said quite firmly that it wouldn't tire her at all and that she enjoyed parties.

Another thing that had annoyed Letitia was that Lucy had asked Julia to bring Rachel and Richard. Letitia had wanted her party to be a replica of the smart parties she used to give in Chelsea, and one did not ask children to such parties. And here they were, drinking orangeade out of tumblers, wolfing cheese straws, and getting over-excited. They were with James now—both talking to him at the same time, as they always did, chattering away, telling him about their boxing lessons, their rabbits, and inviting him to their picnic.

As he listened to them, James' face lost its usual firm pursed look, becoming softened, almost human . . .

Roger came up with a plate of cheese straws. James took one, and his eyes followed Roger, as he moved away, with a look of interest.

Roger was a good-looking boy . . . . All Julia's children were good-looking and attractive. Even Julia herself looked charming to-day, having obviously been dressed by Laura for the occasion, wearing the new two-piece and a becoming hat, her greying hair smooth and tidy. This, obscurely, Letitia felt to be the crowning insult, for she liked to think of Julia as dowdy and negligible. To Letitia her own superiority was as the breath of life, and it had to be fed perpetually by the inferiority of the people around her.

It wasn't right, she reflected, that Julia's family should monopolise and exploit James like this. James was Julia's brother, of course, but he'd done as much for her as any brother could be expected to do for a sister. Poor James! Someone ought to protect him from them.

Roger approached her with his plate of cheese straws. She took one and detained him, exerting all her charm, asking about the play, flattering him subtly. He had been rather shy of her—she was so smart and handsome and belonged to the magic world of London writers and artists, which he looked on with awe and wonder—but he responded instinctively, losing his schoolboy awkwardness, telling her about the play, describing the difficulties and humours of the production. None of his own family, he thought a little resentfully, had shown as much interest in it as Aunt Letitia.

She was looking at him with laughing eyes.

"And have you brought your report for your Uncle James to see like a good little boy?" she said.

Her smile seemed to unite them in a conspiracy of friendly mockery, directed against Uncle James.

He grinned.

"No. I've burnt it."

"It was a *very* good one, I suppose," she teased.

"No, it was rotten," he smiled, though actually it had been quite good.

"Oh, you ought to have given Uncle James an opportunity to say, 'Did better than this when I was at school, my boy'."

There was delicious mockery of James' pompous manner in her voice.

" 'Happiest time of your life, my boy'," said Roger, continuing the mockery. " 'Make the most of it. Make the most of it'."

She laughed gaily.

"You naughty boy! And we're both neglecting our duty. You should be taking these cheese straws round and I should be looking after my guests . . . Here are two more."

There was a momentary sensation as Mrs. Pollock and Ann-Marie entered—Ann-Marie ridiculously overdressed in an ankle-length, full-gathered dress of grey chiffon, with a flame-coloured sash, leaning on her mother's arm and walking with a stick.

Mrs. Pollock greeted Letitia, then gave herself up to attendance on Ann-Marie, selecting the most comfortable armchair for her and sending Colin, who had moved the chair forward, back to their own room for a footstool.

"You know the Vicar, don't you, Mrs. Pollock?" said Letitia.

With something of the expression of a member of the old French aristocracy facing a mob of *sans culottes*, Mrs. Pollock turned to greet the Vicar and his sister.

The Vicar was a short tubby Pickwickian little man, with a round rosy face, a shock of iron-grey hair and a nervous habit of filling up any pauses in the conversation by little cooing noises while he tried to think of something to say. He had a boundless love for his fellow-creatures, but was almost painfully inarticulate. His sister was even shorter than he was and as thin as he was tubby. She had a tiny face, always tensely set, piercing brown eyes and an abrupt authoritative manner. She always looked swamped by her clothes, as she bought garments of stock size and had neither the time nor the patience to get them altered to fit her. Her coats trailed down to her tiny ankles, the shoulders reached her pin-like elbows. Despite all this, she had a devastating dignity and was known significantly as "Miss Vicar." Her brother was seldom seen without her, and she lived in constant dread of his getting married. The two had a certain local fame as the fastest Litany team in the diocese. It was said that together (for no other parishioners ever attended the service, which took place at eleven o'clock on Wednesday and Friday, except occasionally to time them with a certain proprietary pride) they could get through it in just over two minutes. The Vicar could say three petitions without drawing breath, and his sister neatly slipped in the responses—as one word—while he was saying the last word of one clause and the first of the next. His sermons were undistinguished, consisting chiefly of his little cooing noise, but the congregation was used to it and did not mind.

Colin had fetched Ann-Marie a drink and sat down on the empty chair by her side. He looked at the pale pointed face in its frame of silky golden hair above the grey chiffon dress and thought, She looks like a starving child . . .

"I know you by sight, of course," he said. "I've seen you in Chapman's car. He's the rival firm and we don't come across him much. You're his secretary, aren't you?"

Ann-Marie met so few strangers that she was painfully shy with them and had formed the habit of covering up her shyness by an assumption of Maman's manner—broken English, gesticulations and all.

"Yes, and you, too, I know by sight. You work for Mr. Greig, yes? And you lived here before the war and now live in the house called Greenways. You are a large familee."

"Quite correct," said Colin.

Mrs. Pollock, abandoning her frozen pose, which she could never retain for very long, began to scold the Vicar for the ugliness of his stained-glass windows and the incompetence of his choir and organist.

"There is no religion without beauty. To me beauty *ees* religion. Those colours, they freeze the very blood in my veins—those reds and purples, like a hit in the face. Who could pray with a hit in the face? And your organist, he has no soul, no mind, no heart. He play his organ as if it were a sausage machine. An organ should stir the emotions, move the depths of the feelings and he play eet as a sausage machine. If I should attend your church, Vicar, I should become a devil-worshipper."

The Vicar cooed apologetically, and his sister began to make slighting and provocative remarks about the Roman Catholic Church to which she quite mistakenly imagined Mrs. Pollock to belong.

Mrs. Gideon was feeling a little worried because Trixie wasn't there. She had asked Mrs. Fielding about her and Mrs. Fielding had replied shortly that she had a headache. There was an air of constraint over the Fieldings. She hoped there had not been any trouble. But it was time to take the Two home now.

"Say good-bye to Aunt Letitia and Aunt Lucy, and thank them for the party," she said to them.

"Good-bye, Aunt Letitia," said Rachel. "Thank you for the party. When this was the nursery there was a picture of Jesus in His cradle over the mantelpiece."

"Don't be silly, Rachel," said Richard severely. "It was a manger."

"I *meant* a manger," said Rachel.

Mrs. Gideon glanced round the room. Colin was talking to Ann-Marie, Laura to Hubert Fielding and Roger to Derek Frame, the Secretary of the Dramatic Society.

She went into the passage, wondering whether to slip along to Trixie's room . . . and finally decided not to. It savoured of "interference"—a fault to which she was specially prone. Besides, it was after the children's bedtime.

"We've been to a cocktail party," said Richard proudly. "I bet no one else in my form has. We've had cocktails."

"We only had orangeade," Rachel reminded him.

"If it was a cocktail party, they were cocktails. I shall call them cocktails, anyway . . . Mummy, may we just go and see if the old swing's still there? The one Daddy put up for us in the stable for wet days."

"If you're quick. I'll walk on and you must catch me up before I've got to the gate."

"Yes, we will, we promise."

They ran off and she walked through the neglected garden to the green gate in the wall.

Letitia watched her from the upstairs window then turned sharply at the sound of Lucy's voice. Lucy, who should have remained quietly in the background, deeply and humbly impressed, was laughing and talking to the people round her.

"I never cross my bridges till I come to them," said someone.

"I often wonder how people who do that do it," said Lucy. "I mean, cross bridges before they come to them . . . It sounds so difficult."

And everyone laughed as if she had said something amusing.

Letitia joined the group.

"Have you everything you want, darling?" she said solicitously to Lucy.

"Yes, thank you," said Lucy. "Aren't these little sardine things that Miss Parsons made delicious?"

"Would you believe it?" smiled Letitia to the others. "Lucy actually wanted to provide sweet cakes and sugar biscuits."

She had a vague idea of "showing up" Lucy's ignorance by the revelation, but Lucy only beamed round like a happy child.

"Well," she said, "this is the first cocktail party I've ever been to in my life."

James suddenly found himself standing next Miss Parsons. Mellowed by four gins and the festive atmosphere, he began to tell her about himself—how hard he had worked to achieve his position, how by the exercise of exemplary industry he had become the head partner in the firm he represented . . . He held forth on the legal system of England, contrasting it with the legal systems of other countries. He quoted almost word for word a letter he had written to *The Spectator* on some obscure legal point that their leader writer had seemed to misunderstand.

And something in Miss Parsons rebelled. Everyone she had spoken to this evening had talked to her about themselves. All the people she ever met talked to her about themselves. She was sick of listening to the story of other people's lives. And she suddenly determined to tell James the story of her own life whether he wanted to hear it or not . . . The worm in her had turned at last, driven to desperation by James' pompous monologue. She told him of her childhood in the country vicarage where her father (a modern language specialist) had taught her French, German, Spanish and Italian. She even told him, fixing a stern eye on him and daring him not to listen, about her pony and dog and rabbit—the dog who had a passion for gooseberries and went about most of the summer with a bleeding nose, because he couldn't resist thrusting it into the gooseberry bushes. ("I used to spend my pocket money on vaseline, but it never seemed to make it any better"); the rabbit who always came lolloping into the drawing-room through the open French windows for his saucer of milk on summer afternoons at tea-time; the broad-backed pony on which she played at highwayman, wearing a black mask with a black skirt of her mother's over her shoulders as a cape. She didn't even stop there. She went on to tell him how, when she was eighteen, she obtained a good post with a commercial firm, translating their foreign correspondence. They sent her abroad. "It was very interesting," she said, "while it lasted."

Then she stopped, giving him his chance of escape. She had, as it were, worked the poison out of her system. She had forced someone to listen to her for at least five minutes. She had told them the story of her life instead of listening to the story of theirs. Refreshed and recompensed, she was ready to listen again . . .

James had listened restlessly at first. She was essentially the sort of person one talked to, not the sort of person who talked. She had no right, he felt resentfully, to reverse their obvious rôles. Then, despite himself, he became interested.

"What happened?" he said. "Why didn't it last?"

"I was sent for because my mother was ill and the doctor said she couldn't live more than a year, so I stayed . . . She lived for twenty years, but every year they said she couldn't live much longer, so I stayed . . . She couldn't bear anyone but me to look after her. She became senile towards the end, but even so, she always fretted when I wasn't there. She died last year . . ."

James tried to imagine those years, but he hadn't much imagination, so he gave up the attempt.

"Why didn't you go back to the work you'd been doing before?" he asked.

She shrugged.

"I'd—been away too long. I'd—forgotten things. I'd become like people who've served a prison sentence. I suppose you know about them. They lose their initiative."

"They get it back, you know."

She shrugged.

"Perhaps . . . I just took the first job that offered itself and it was this."

James coughed his dry harsh cough.

"Well, it must be quite a pleasant job. I mean, my Aunt Letitia must be a delightful person to work for."

"Delightful," said Miss Parsons rather dryly.

"Miss Parsons!" called Letitia.

"I must go," said Miss Parsons to James. "Thank you for playing the wedding guest to my Ancient Mariner."

"Not at all," said James, with his frosty smile.

He watched her cross the room to Letitia, making mental calculations about her age. She must be forty. He'd thought her older, but that was probably the way she did her hair and the way she dressed.

She had a round fresh-coloured face and pleasant brown eyes. Her dark hair was only slightly flecked with grey . . .

Suddenly he saw her as a child, rubbing vaseline on her dog's nose, playing highwayman in the black mask, kneeling on the drawing-room floor to give the rabbit his saucer of milk at tea-time.

Then he thought of the wastage of the long years, during which her youth had slipped away from her. She must always have been kind and cheerful, or her mother would not have clung to her presence as she did . . .

Letitia came up to him, laying her hand affectionately on his arm.

"James, dear, I've been longing for a little talk with you . . ."

Hubert sat on the settee with Laura, wondering what was happening to him. As soon as he and Laura began to talk, all his depression and weariness had vanished, and a strange sense of peace had stolen over him. He hardly knew what they had talked about. It was enough just to listen to her low gentle voice . . . like a spring of water washing away the dust and grime of his soul. There was something—cleansing in just being with her . . .

Laura's eyes were wandering round the room. Poor Colin still seemed to be marooned with that terribly affected French girl. She ought to rescue him, but she didn't want to yet.

"You used to live here, didn't you?" said Hubert.

"Yes . . ."

"It must be hateful for you to see it all cut up into flats like that." She smiled.

"Everyone thinks so, but we don't feel like that at all. Except Roger. The rest of us love the silly little house we're in now. Roger's got a renaissance soul and we haven't. We've got modern villa souls. Poor Roger! He thinks it's terrible of us not to mind. Besides, it was ghastly to run, you know, from a woman's point of view. Stone floors and long passages and the dining-room miles away from the kitchen, and frightfully inadequate heating and a boiler that ate tons of coke a day . . . Uncle James has been very clever about modernising it, hasn't he? And we're lucky not to have to go right away, because I love the country round here, don't you?"

"I haven't seen much of it. I just go to work and come back . . ."

"Oh, but it's lovely—once you get off the main road, of course. All main roads are the same and pretty hideous. But there are some glorious walks through the woods. The children want to have a picnic soon. Will you come to it?"

"I'd like to."

She looked at his thin face, its youth marred by lines of weariness and depression.

"I expect it's rather hateful going up to London every day."

He found himself telling her all about himself—about his work, and how irksome and uninteresting he found it, about his boyhood at Norways, about Godfrey . . . He did not mention Trixie, but her friendliness and understanding seemed to envelop him so completely that there was no need to tell her anything in words. She understood because she was in some way part of himself. He thought of the girl he had left sobbing on the bed. She was a stranger . . . even her face seemed blurred and indistinct when he tried to recall it. But he knew every line of this delicate flower-like face, had, it seemed, known it all his life . . . Foreboding seized him, as he realized what was happening, but beneath the foreboding was still this radiant all-illuminating happiness.

Cynthia and Godfrey passed him.

"We're going now, Hubert," said Cynthia.

"No hurry, old chap," said Godfrey, giving him a glance of sympathy as he thought of the scene to which the poor kid must inevitably return.

The curtain of depression closed down again on Hubert's spirit as he read the thought in Godfrey's mind.

"I'll be along in a minute," he said.

"James, darling," Letitia was saying, "I sometimes feel so worried about your living in those poky little London rooms. They are poky, aren't they?"

James felt touched by her solicitude.

"Oh no, they're really quite comfortable, you know. Quite comfortable. But, as a matter of fact, I shall have to leave them. The lease has run out, and they're going to be turned into offices."

Letitia toned down the instinctive reaction of pleasure to one of condolence.

"Oh, I *am* sorry, dear. How worrying for you! And what are you going to do?"

"Find others, I suppose."

"Oh no, James . . . I simply hate to think of you at the mercy of these grasping London landladies. Honestly, it worries me terribly sometimes."

James' grim little face had softened. Beneath his brusque manner was a secret hunger for affection that had never been even partially satisfied.

"They're not bad, Aunt Letitia. Not bad at all."

"James, I'd love to think of you in a little flat . . . Somewhere cheerful. A service flat. You'd be independent of any landlady's vagaries then. Chelsea or somewhere like that. Not too near your depressing old offices, of course."

His mouth relaxed into its faint reluctant smile.

"Well, well, I don't know . . . Since I've been coming over here to look after Julia's business, I've sometimes been tempted to come a little farther into the country."

"Not *too* far, James dear," said Letitia.

"No, no, not too far, but I hope to take Colin into the firm eventually and ease off work a little myself . . . Pleasant in the country, you know."

"In the summer," agreed Letitia, "but not in the winter, James. A service flat in London or a little place *just* outside. You'll need a housekeeper, of course, but no need to look too far ahead, just yet, is there? We'll both keep an eye open for a suitable place. That's the first step . . ."

"Well, I don't know," said James, with a sudden panic-stricken idea that he was being rushed. "Very comfortable really, as I am."

"Oh yes," said Letitia lightly. "No need to make any definite plans, but I shall know no peace of mind, dear, till I'm sure you're being properly looked after."

She was feeling very pleased with herself. The interview had gone off exactly as she had meant it to. She had sown the seed . . . It would probably need a little coaxing and watering, but it would grow.

His eyes had wandered to the garden where Roger was walking across the lawn. That would give her the next opening she wanted.

"Isn't he getting tall!" she said.

"Yes," said James. There was a shy pride in his voice. "Nice boy. Nice manners."

Letitia smiled—a motherly indulgent smile.

"Yes, but *wasn't* it naughty of him to burn his report because he was ashamed of your seeing it!"

"Eh, what?" said James, startled.

"Didn't you know, James? Perhaps I oughtn't to have mentioned it. Children are such monkeys, aren't they? It was such a bad report, and he was so frightened of your seeing it that he burnt it."

James was conscious of a heavy weight of disappointment at his heart. He had derived a deep sense of gratification from the thought that he was giving Roger the chance of a good education. It had never even occurred to him that Roger was not making the most of his chances.

"It must have been pretty bad," he said slowly, without his usual abruptness.

"I believe it was," said Letitia. "Well, he told me himself it was. But one mustn't be hard on him, James. Boys will be boys. They're just thoughtless. They don't mean to be ungrateful and disrespectful. When Roger makes fun of you, imitating you and that sort of thing—I know that he does it out of pure thoughtlessness. I don't like it, of course, and I always reprove him, but one mustn't take it too seriously."

A dark flush crept over James' face. He was acutely sensitive to ridicule. So Roger made fun of him . . . imitated him . . . He cleared his throat and glanced at his watch.

"Well, I must be off," he said. "Got a dinner engagement in town."

As he went out of the room he met Roger in the doorway and passed him with a curt nod.

"Yes, I have been Mr. Chapman's secretary ever since the beginning of the war," Ann-Marie was saying. "I do not know how I manage the work, but somehow I do." She gave a gay brave little laugh.

"Why shouldn't you manage it?" said Colin. "I imagine it's quite an easy job."

She looked at him reproachfully.

"Oh, I don't mean the work. I mean . . . well, my lameness."

"You're not as lame as all that, surely?" said Colin.

She was aware of a sense of outrage. Her lameness had been her chief claim to distinctiveness since she was a child. It gave her any importance, any personality she had. To have it belittled like this was insufferable.

"A whole group of muscles from my hip to my toe is paralysed," she said coldly.

"Yes, but you've got one sound leg and can use the other as a sort of stick, can't you? I shouldn't think it was difficult for you to get about. I'm no doctor, of course."

"Obviously."

Her heart was beating fast with anger. The compassion and admiration that were her due were, for the first time in her memory, being withheld. It had been intolerable of him even to make her mention her lameness. It was, as a rule, tactfully ignored, recognized only by the general atmosphere of muted sympathy.

"Why, when I go up to London, to a theatre or concert, we have a car right from this door to the door of the theatre or concert hall."

"Do you often go?"

"Quite often. Last Saturday we went to hear a recital of Bartok's sonatina."

"Don't think I've ever heard of him," said Colin.

The amusement in his eyes was a sort of challenge. She wanted to impress him, to change the amusement to admiration and respect.

"He is one of the moderns," she said, sitting upright in her chair, using her mother's voice and gesticulations. "There is, of course, little of the old-fashioned soporific harmony in his work. But such music represents life. It reproduces emotion in sound. It excites and stimulates . . ."

"That sounds grand," said Colin, the amusement in his eyes deepening, "but what did you really think of it?"

"I have just told you," she said with dignity.

"No, you haven't. You've told me what you've heard other people saying about it. What did you think of it yourself?"

She was silent for some time, then said quite simply:

"I thought it rather noisy."

He laughed, and she flushed with annoyance.

"That wasn't meant to be funny," she said stiffly.

"Perhaps not, but it was. Do you never laugh?"

"Of course I do. Maman is witty. She imitates people. She can always make me laugh."

"I see . . . but you ought to learn to laugh at yourself as well as at other people, you know. Actually it's much more important to be able to laugh at oneself than to be able to laugh at other people."

"There is nothing in my own case for laughter," said Ann-Marie reproachfully.

"That's all the more reason why you should laugh at it."

"I do not understand you," she said helplessly. "Perhaps I am stupid. I go out so little and meet so few people."

"Why?"

"What do you mean?"

"Why do you go out so little and meet so few people?"

"It tires me. I am not strong."

"On the contrary you must be as strong as a horse to stand the life you lead. You have no exercise or fresh air. You go everywhere in closed cars, and you hardly ever even sit up in a chair. You're living the life of an elderly invalid and you're neither elderly nor an invalid. It's a miracle you've survived it so long."

She looked at him, her face stony with anger.

"If I were—like other women—I would get up now and leave you."

"I'm sorry," he said. "I know I've been outrageously rude, but I've been longing to say all this to you ever since I first saw you. Now I've said it, would you like me to go?"

"No," she said. "Please stay . . . It is not quite as you think. Sometimes we go into the country."

"In a closed car?"

"Naturally. There is no other means."

"Now, listen. We're having a picnic—a week on Saturday, I think. My young brother and sister started the idea, and we're asking everyone we know. It's to be in Barton Wood. Will you come?"

"I wish I could," she said wistfully.

"But you can."

"Can I get there by car?"

"You can go to the gate in Barton Lane by car and then walk through the wood to the clearing where we're going to have it."

"Walk!" she echoed in horror. "I could not walk so far."

"You could try."

"It's impossible. Maman would never agree."

"She would if you wanted it enough."

"Perhaps if we brought the invalid chair . . ."

"I'm not inviting an invalid chair to a picnic."

"Will you be there?"

"Of course."

"I mean—at the gate where the car stops. Will you meet me there?"

"Yes."

"I'll try . . . Yes, I should like to try . . ."

Mrs. Pollock darted up to them.

"Now, my darleeng, we must go. You look exhausted, feverish. Thank you, Mr. Gideon . . . if you weel open the door. I have made your adieux, *chérie*. I have explained that you were too tired to make them yourself."

When Ann-Marie was halfway down the passage she turned . . . Colin was standing at the door watching her. There was still amusement—but something else as well—in his eyes.

"Straight to bed, my little one," said Mrs. Pollock when they reached their flat. "You must be wearied to death. Eet was stupid, stupid. Such an evening shall not be inflicted upon us again."

"I think I ought to go out more and meet people, Maman," said Ann-Marie slowly. "Not going out makes me—not natural. I feel —I hear as I talk—that I'm not natural."

"My *darleeng!*" said Mrs. Pollock with a gay little peal of laughter. "That is absurd . . . The young man, Mr. Gideon, deed you like him?"

"No," said Ann-Marie decisively. "He had no manners and no sympathy."

"Ah, like all the Eenglish," said Mrs. Pollock, becoming more French than ever in her relief at hearing that Ann-Marie had not liked the good-looking young man who had been talking to her all the evening. "Now a bath and bed, my darleeng, and I will bring you up something to eat on a tray."

She took Ann-Marie to her bedroom and began tenderly to strip off the grey chiffon dress, the sheer silk stockings and satin shoes . . . Ann-Marie looked at the small but elaborate French gilt bed, with its hangings of rose-coloured ninon, its eiderdown of rose-coloured crêpe de chine . . . and suddenly felt ashamed of it. It was silly and childish and theatrical.

"I can get into the bath by myself, Maman."

"Darleeng, you cannot. You have never done it by yourself. I have always assisted you."

"But I can. There must be a way. It's only that I've never tried. If I—Look, that's it!"

Ann-Marie, perched on the edge of the bath, had lifted her useless leg over with her hand, swung over the other and, holding on to the edges of the bath with both hands, lowered her slender white body slowly and carefully into the scented water.

"There!" she said, smiling triumphantly.

Mrs. Pollock screamed.

"Darleeng! You must never do that again."

"I'm always going to do it," said Ann-Marie calmly. "After all, I'm not quite helpless. I have one sound leg . . ."

"But, my Little Flower——"

"Maman," said Ann-Marie, squeezing an enormous bath sponge against her thin breasts, "I wish you wouldn't call me Little Flower. It makes me sound like St. Thérèse of Lisieux and I'm not ... ."

X

THE picnic party was assembled in the wood and Mrs. Gideon and Laura were spreading the cloth and unpacking the baskets. The spot chosen for the picnic was a circular clearing, surrounded by silver birches, where the children had picnicked every summer since they could remember. Each of them claimed one particular spot as his or hers. The fallen tree-trunk was Rachel's and Richard's; the cut-down trunk that made a little stool, Roger's; the armchair formed by the roots of a tall oak tree, Laura's; the first branch of the oak, as broad as a sofa, had been Colin's.

The children (Richard and Rachel had invited three friends each) had fetched water from the stream and made a fire at the side of the clearing. Their faces and clothes were streaked with smoke and mud, but they were radiantly happy and the kettle was almost boiling.

"And you can't send us upstairs to wash," said Rachel, hopping about on one leg, "because there isn't any upstairs and there aren't any taps."

"Let's go and wash in the stream," shouted Richard.

"No, you don't," said Mrs. Gideon, who was arranging ginger biscuits on a plate. "I know what *that* means . . . There's plenty of hot water in the kettle, so come along and I'll clean up the worst bits of you as best I can."

"Shall I put the iced cake in the middle?" said Laura.

"Yes, darling," said Mrs. Gideon, "and the two sandwich cakes on either side."

She was feeling a little guilty towards Laura. She had been to early Service that morning (it was St. Bartholomew's Day and she liked St. Bartholomew) in the skirt of one costume and the coat of another. She had not realized it till she was on the way home and she had changed as soon as she got in, but she suspected that Laura had seen her from her bedroom window. There had been a twinkle in Laura's eyes at breakfast, though she had said nothing. Now she said innocently:

"Yes . . . I know you like things to match," and Mrs. Gideon said:

"So you *did* see," and they both laughed.

"Of course I saw," said Laura, "but I can't scold you. You look so sweet."

"I know I look all *right*," said Mrs. Gideon complacently. "I thought hard about everything I put on. I wasn't going to get into trouble twice in one day."

"You are a pet," laughed Laura.

Miss Parsons had arrived early and was putting little cartons of jelly and blancmange on the tablecloth. Her cotton dress and shady hat made her look younger than usual and she was singing to herself as she arranged the tea-things. Mrs. Gideon had invited Letitia and Lucy, too, but Lucy said that with her rheumatism her picnic days were over, and Letitia said bluntly that she had always detested them. Lucy had insisted that Miss Parsons should come, and, though Letitia, who considered that Miss Parsons' outings should be confined to her official "afternoon off," had found a dozen jobs to keep her at the last minute, Lucy had been unexpectedly firm, so Miss Parsons had changed into her new dress (it was maroon with white spots and suited her) and her summer hat (last year's but with a new maroon ribbon) and set off for the wood.

Letitia was now in the process of taking it out of Lucy by altering all the plans they had made for their holiday. She had already done it several times, and, when anything annoyed her, she did it again. Lucy had booked rooms in Torquay and then had to cancel them because Letitia, though it had been she who had suggested Torquay in the first place, had decided suddenly that it didn't suit her. Next, Lucy had booked rooms in a hotel at Bath, and had to cancel those because Letitia, having been given cold meat for lunch, which she always considered an insult, decided that she didn't want to stay in a hotel. There had followed apartments in Leamington Spa, a hotel in Cromer, and apartments in Weymouth. This afternoon Letitia had suddenly decided on a hotel in Bournemouth and, at the moment when Miss Parsons put out the last carton of jelly, Lucy was sitting down to cancel the rooms in Weymouth and engage rooms in Bournemouth.

"We'd better hire a car and chauffeur, too, while we're there," said Letitia carelessly.

Lucy would have liked to object to this on the score of expense, but, whenever she did so, Letitia had a migraine or accused her of grudging her her keep, or both, so Lucy had learnt never to mention expense unless she were driven to it.

Of the Fieldings only Hubert and Trixie had accepted the invitation, as Cynthia had arranged to meet Godfrey in town and spend the afternoon with him.

Trixie looked pale and sulky. Beneath her sulkiness was no longer the old childish petulance but real unhappiness . . .

The row about her bedroom had blown over. She had gone to bed, and, when Hubert came in after the party, had pretended to be asleep. Normal relations had been resumed the next morning, and things were, on the surface, smooth enough. She kept her bedroom tidy, but everything that she could possibly do to annoy or irritate Cynthia she did. Her hatred of Cynthia was like a cloud surrounding her on all sides, shutting out light and air. It was Cynthia, she was convinced, who had changed Hubert. She couldn't have told how Hubert had changed, but he had changed. He was as kind and attentive as ever, but there was a difference in him. It was as if only part of him were there. At first she had held him at arm's length to stop him coming too near her, but now she knew that she could let down her guard and he wouldn't even notice. She felt bewildered and unhappy and lonely. She lay awake in the night, hating Cynthia.

She had avoided the Gideons of late, ashamed of the hatred that filled her, yet determined to cherish it, shrinking from Mrs. Gideon's gentle searching eyes.

Mrs. Gideon came forward to greet her and drew her over to the fire where she was making the tea.

"What's the matter, darling?" she said.

"Nothing," said Trixie sullenly.

"Have you had a row with Mrs. Fielding?"

"No."

It was strange to think that they hadn't had a row, that they had always been polite to each other.

"Then have one, dear," urged Mrs. Gideon, "and get it over."

Trixie gave a crooked little smile.

"It'll be more than a row when it comes," she said. "If I'd got any arsenic I'd put it in her blasted China tea to-morrow."

"Now, Trixie," said Mrs. Gideon, shaking her head, "don't talk like that. You know you don't mean it. Here are the paper napkins. Go and put them out, there's a good girl."

The kindness of her voice sent a ray of comfort over Trixie, but it faded as she turned away.

Mrs. Gideon watched her with a worried frown. She was such a child—a pretty, wilful, unhappy child.

Colin was coming along the path with Ann-Marie. To Ann-Marie's surprise Maman had agreed to her attending the picnic. It happened that Mr. Hassock had rung up suggesting an expedition to town on the same day, and that a prior engagement gave a welcome excuse. Moreover, Mrs. Pollock believed that the car could take Ann-Marie right to the scene of the picnic and that Ann-Marie disliked young Mr. Gideon—neither of which was true.

Colin helped her out of the car, handed her her stick and walked beside her down the path. She thought he might have helped her more than he did . . .

"When I walk, even with my stick," she said, "it's my good leg that hurts . . . I get a sharp pain right down it. And if I stoop for more than a few seconds it hurts horribly."

"Really," he said, without interest.

She set her lips. He was horrid. She didn't know why she'd thought she liked him . . . She wished she hadn't come. If she hadn't come she would have been lying on the settee at home with Maman looking after her—reading to her or putting on records for her or talking to her—on the watch for the least sign of weariness. Only Maman understood.

She felt suddenly homesick for the love and warmth and sympathy of the little world that she and Maman shared. She would never try to go out of it again. She had learnt her lesson. She had felt

just the same when she went out with Mr. Hassock . . . She didn't
know why she'd tried again. It only made her miserable.

"Here we are!" said Colin cheerfully, as they reached the clearing.

"Oh, my dear," said Mrs. Gideon, "how splendid of you!   Come
and sit down here, then you can lean against this tree."

That compensated a little for Colin's lack of sympathy, but only
a little.

"Haven't you got crutches?" said Richard, raising a hot and smoke-
blackened face from the fire. "We hoped you'd come on crutches,
then we could have races on them."

"We're awfully good at crutches," said Rachel.   "The boy next
door had them once and we used to borrow them every day."

"So much so that the boy had to learn to walk without them,"
said Laura.   "The doctor was amazed at his progress."

"Haven't you even got one of those iron things?" said Rachel,
inspecting Ann-Marie's thin flail-like leg.   "I once knew a girl that
had one——"

"That's enough from you two," said Colin.   "Go and carry those
plates for your mother."

"Everything's ready, so do sit down," said Mrs. Gideon.   "I
think there are enough rugs and cushions and things . . ."

Mrs. Gideon had asked the Vicar to come, because she knew that
he liked picnics, and the Vicar, having ascertained that his sister was
to preside at a Women's Institute meeting that afternoon, had accepted
the invitation. He was very fond of his sister but liked occasionally
to go out by himself. His sister had, however, discovered his plan
in good time, and had handed over her duties to the Vice-President
in order to accompany him. She was now showing signs of trying
to turn the picnic into a parish treat, but was being gently though
firmly held in check by Mrs. Gideon.

The Vicar was sitting on Roger's tree-stump stirring his tea and
making happy little cooing noises. He loved being surrounded by
young people, especially when no one expected him to say anything
to them.

Roger had brought Derek Frame with him. Derek was a tall
fair good-looking young man who had been a pilot in the Air Force
during the war and was now working in his father's business.

"It's an odd thing," he said, looking round, "but, you know, all
this peace-time stuff still seems unreal to me. Only the war seems
real."

"It's the opposite with me," said Hubert. "Even while the war
was on, it didn't seem real. It seems like a dream now. I'm not
keen on my job, but I was jolly glad to get back to it."

"I always wanted to go into the old man's business," said Derek,
"but, now I'm in it, it's all as flat as a pancake. This working *against*
people gets me down . . . trying to 'do' the next man instead of
giving him a helping hand as one did in the war. The old man says
you must have competition, and the essence of competition is to

knock the next man out, and Heaven knows the old man's straight enough. It isn't that there's any funny business about it. It's that—well, when for five years you've been working *with* people—all pulling together—it sort of gets you down to have to start working *against* everyone, trying to queer their pitch. All decent chaps, too . . . Gosh!" he ended, "I sometimes think I'd give the rest of my life to have one day of the Battle of Britain back."

"It's difficult—this transition period," said Mrs. Gideon. "We've got to try to save what was good in the war attitude to help with the peace."

"So many vices become virtues," said Laura, "and the sooner they go back to being recognized as vices, the better. Mean people came into their own in the war. The sort of people who, even when they needn't, love to save bits of string and the insides of envelopes and mix marge with the butter and put bricks in the fireplace. They could indulge their vice to their heart's content in war-time, and wear haloes at the same time."

The Vicar cooed delightedly, but his sister said sternly, "Waste is waste whether in peace or war."

"Then there were the messy people," went on Laura, ignoring her, "the people who enjoy eating out of saucepans and doing without table-napkins and pigging it generally. That suddenly became a virtue, too."

"It's still a necessity," said Mrs. Gideon mildly, "because we still can't get maids—not here, at any rate."

"My mother says that the real heroines of the war were the house-wives," said Derek, "who went on dusting and scrubbing and waiting in fish queues and cooking up odds and ends of rations day after day. She says it would have been much easier to be a commando."

"One certainly got a little tired of it," smiled Miss Parsons.

"One still gets tired of it," said Mrs. Gideon. "I was dusting the bookshelves the other day, and I opened Berkeley's *Principles of Human Knowledge*, and, when I realized that dust didn't exist, and furniture didn't exist and dusters didn't exist, I thought why waste time over them, and I took a deck chair into the garden."

"But the deck chair didn't exist, neither did the garden, so how could you?" put in Richard.

Roger was thinking about his father and imagining him coming slowly down the little path between the trees to the clearing. He might easily have lost his memory . . . He had heard that a lot of men who had been reported killed came home after the last war—and quite a long time after. They'd lost their memories. No one knew that they were coming till they suddenly appeared . . . Suppose his father came home this afternoon. He'd go to Westover and find where they were and he'd come down that path. He fixed his eyes on the bend of the path, a queer feeling of excitement at his heart.

"Have one of these patties," said Colin to Ann-Marie. "My mother makes beautiful pastry."

"No, thank you," said Ann-Marie. "I've got a terribly small appetite. I hardly eat anything."

"That's nothing to be proud of," said Colin.

"I didn't say I was proud of it," said Ann-Marie in a small voice.

Why had he asked her to come, she wondered, if he only wanted to snub her? . . and again she longed for the haven of Maman's devotion and the familiar shelter of the beloved little boudoir.

But she *was* hungry. It must be eating in the open air. She stretched out a hand and took a patty.

The Two were already clamouring to start on what was for them the business of the day.

"May we go down to the stream and race boats, Mummy? . . . Come with us, Trixie . . ."

Trixie went with them slowly, glancing back at Hubert, who was sitting next to Laura.

"I have a feeling that something nice is going to happen to me," said Richard, leaping along the path.

"*What's* going to happen to you?" challenged Rachel.

"I don't know. Perhaps it'll be finding a robin's nest. I hope it'll be finding a robin's nest . . ."

He bent down and picked up a piece of a branch that had been blown from one of the trees. It was in the shape of a miniature walking-stick, with a little crook at one end.

"Oh *Richard!*" said Rachel in delight. "Isn't it lovely? A little walking-stick."

Richard considered it, frowning thoughtfully.

"You can have it," he said at last. "If anything nice happens to me, I want it to be finding a robin's nest."

"Oh, *thank* you," said Rachel, and ran down the path, twirling the little stick.

"Let's walk to the end of the wood," said Colin to Ann-Marie. "It's not far."

"I'm afraid it's too far for me," said Ann-Marie.

"Well, let's go as far as you can manage, anyway."

"All right . . ."

They walked along in silence. She felt shy and ill-at-ease. She didn't know what to say to him. She never knew what to say to people. She had thought before at the Drummonds' party that the remedy was to go out more. Now she knew that it wasn't. The remedy was not to go out at all. She was only happy and at her ease with Maman . . . darling Maman, who would never have let her go dragging along a rough woodland path like this, without any help but her stick. For the hundredth time she wished she hadn't come . . .

"Perhaps I ought to be going home now," she said. "Maman will be expecting me."

"Nonsense!" said Colin. "It's far too early to be going home. We're nearly at the end of the wood."

She looked at him helplessly, on the point of tears.

"Like to give up?" he said.

"No . . ."

They reached the end of the wood. A stile led to a field path.

"Let's take a rest," he said.

She sat down on the lowest step of the stile and he stood beside her. There was a silence, and, feeling that something was demanded of her, Ann-Marie assumed her company manner.

"Have you read the new book of poems by Palmyron?" she said.

He lit his pipe and looked down at her with a smile in his eyes. "No."

"It is wonderful. Maman was reading it to me last night. Of course," she shrugged her shoulders, and threw out her hands in one of Mrs. Pollock's gestures, "it is in what may be called the 'European tradition.' Many of the poems are—obscure; but that is only because the poet's thoughts are more complex and his feelings more intricate than those of the average reader. It is to a certain extent Imagist poetry. It calls for concentration. It——" she paused.

"Stimulates?" suggested Colin.

"Yes . . ." She looked at him accusingly. "You are laughing at me."

"I'm sorry, but—Why don't you be yourself?"

"What do you mean? I was being myself."

"No, you weren't. You were being someone else."

"Who?"

"I don't know. Your mother, I suppose. You know," slowly, "I don't believe that you're highbrow at all really. I think that really you're just a simple lowbrow like myself. You just repeat what you hear like a parrot."

She said nothing, gazing in front of her, as if she had not heard.

"There's a lovely view from the top of that field," he went on. "You can see the whole valley. Shall we go?"

She measured the distance with her eyes.

"It's a long way."

"Not very."

"You'd have to lift me over the stile."

"I will if you like, but you could manage it by yourself. Suppose you try and I'll help you if you need it."

She frowned at it thoughtfully, remembering the bath.

"I think I can manage."

She made a quick movement, lifted her useless leg over with her hand, and was soon on the other side.

"Good for you! Now come along."

She walked slowly up the path with the help of the stick, and sank down on the grass at the top of the hill. Her cheeks were flushed with the exercise, her eyes bright. She looked down at the valley beneath her, the woods and fields, the little farmhouses, standing toy-like in the distance among their trees, the river shining in the distance—and caught her breath.

"Oh, it's *lovely!*" she said. She turned and looked at him. "You know what you said a minute ago—that I wasn't really highbrow?"

"Yes."

"Well, I never thought of it before, but I don't believe I am."

He gave a shout of laughter, and a smile broke slowly over her face.

"We're getting somewhere, aren't we?" he said. "What's that queer name your mother calls you?"

"Ann-Marie? It isn't queer. It's my name."

"I couldn't call you that. I'm too insular. What do other people who call you by your Christian name call you?"

She considered.

"No one else calls me by my Christian name."

"I'm going to call you Ann, then. My name's Colin."

"Colin . . . It's a nice name . . ." She lay back on the grass and let the sun drench her. "Oh, it's lovely, lovely, lovely. I am glad I came."

"Come here again with me next Saturday. Just the two of us. Blanche shall pack us a picnic tea."

"Oh, I'd love to." Her radiance faded, and a shadow passed over her face. She sat up. "I don't know whether I can."

"Why not?"

"There's Maman."

"Wouldn't she let you?"

"She wouldn't—like it. Usually, she likes me to spend Saturdays with her. To-day she had some things to do at home and—there were reasons why she didn't mind my coming, but usually she looks forward all week to my Saturday afternoons. She might be—hurt."

"Bring her, too, if it's the only way."

She smiled, the delicious spontaneous smile that he had seen for the first time only a few moments ago.

"I can't imagine her here, can you?"

"Not exactly . . . Well, do your best, won't you?"

"Yes . . . Anyway," she lay back again and turned her face up to the sun, "let's not think of anything but here and now. It's—heavenly, isn't it?"

Mrs. Gideon, Miss Parsons and Miss Vicar were washing the tea-things in the stream, hindered by the children, who were paddling and racing bits of twig down the miniature waterfall.

"Trixie, darling, go and fetch the other tea-towel, will you?" said Mrs. Gideon. "This is soaked. It's in the wicker basket."

Trixie went back to the clearing.

The Vicar still sat on his perch, smoking a pipe and cooing to himself. Roger and Derek Frame were outstretched on the grass, discussing the next play.

"I don't see why we shouldn't try one of the Restoration comedies," said Roger.

"We couldn't," said Derek. "They'd shock the natives too much."

"One of the pre-Shakespearian things, then. *Friar Bacon and Friar Bungay* or something like that. Anything to get out of the rut of ex-West End successes."

At first Trixie didn't see Hubert and Laura. Then she saw them walking along the path. They had been to the other end of the wood and were coming back. They were talking earnestly, and Hubert's eyes were fixed on Laura's face.

Trixie returned to the stream.

"What's the matter, Trixie?" said Mrs. Gideon.

"Where's the tea-towel?" said Miss Parsons.

"The tea-towel?" said Trixie. "Oh, I've forgotten it."

"I'll get it," said Rachel, and ran back, twirling her little stick.

Colin was helping Ann-Marie into the car.

"Thank you so much," she said shyly. "I've had a lovely day."

"You've been a real sport," he said. "See you next Saturday?"

"I hope so."

When he reached the clearing again, most of the guests had gone and the last of the picnic things were being packed into the baskets.

Richard, over-tired and over-excited, his face streaked with perspiration and dirt, was in the process of working himself up into one of his "states." He was demanding his "walking-stick" from Rachel.

"I found it," he said.

"You *gave* it me," she said indignantly.

"I only gave it you because I thought I was going to find a robin's nest. I haven't found a robin's nest, so it's mine."

"It isn't."

"It is. I found it."

"You're a thief if you take it . . . You *gave* it me."

"I've explained about that. It's *mine*. *You're* a thief. I *hate* you . . ."

She dodged behind a tree. He ran after her, sobbing with rage.

"Children, children!" expostulated Mrs. Gideon.

Colin came up to them, pipe in mouth.

"Hi, you!" he said to Richard. "Go and tell Richard I want him."

Richard gulped and stared at him, open-mouthed.

"I *am* Richard," he said.

"Nonsense!" said Colin shortly. "Richard's ten years old. He's not a cry-baby."

Richard still stared at him, and a slow smile dawned on his grubby tear-stained face.

"Is he like me?" he said.

Colin considered him thoughtfully.

"He isn't unlike you, now you mention it. He's cleaner than you as a rule, and he doesn't go about with his stockings round his ankles."

Rachel, who was hopping about with delight, seized Richard's hand.

"Come on. Let's go and find him," she said, and dragged him, still a little bewildered, down to the stream. There she realized that she was carrying the little stick. "Here! You can have it," she said, handing it to him.

"I don't want it."

"Well, let's break it up and divide the pieces and race them down the stream."

A few minutes later they returned to the clearing. Rachel had washed Richard's face with her handkerchief, sleeked back his hair and pulled up his stockings.

He went to Colin, his golden freckled face solemn, his blue eyes dancing.

"That boy said you wanted me, Colin."

"Yes, I do. You can carry the knapsack and this basket. Who was the little beast, anyway?"

"No idea," grinned Richard. "Pretty lousy specimen, wasn't he?"

"I'll say he was. Blubbering and shouting . . . Where's Roger?"

"He's gone home with Derek Frame."

"Then we're the sole survivors. Quick march, Richard! I'll take that, Laura . . ." He looked at her. "You're very quiet."

"What do you want me to do?" said Laura. "Dance and sing?"

"Oh, let's all," said Rachel, and went dancing down the path singing, "What shall we do with the drunken sailor?"

When they reached the lane, Trixie and Hubert were there.

"Good Lord! Have you got all that to carry?" said Hubert.

"We brought it," said Richard.

"And it's much lighter now," said Rachel. "There are five of us, you know."

"Six with Roger," said Richard, proudly. "We're a large family."

"And all strong and healthy," said Rachel, "except that Roger had a boil on his neck last holidays."

"Stop *chattering*, children," said Mrs. Gideon. "Run along home."

"I'll come with you and give a hand," said Hubert, taking the basket from Mrs. Gideon. He turned to Trixie. "I won't be a minute, Trixie. I'll just help with this stuff as far as Greenways."

"Come, too, dear," said Mrs. Gideon.

"No, thanks," said Trixie, and, turning on her heel, walked on towards Westover.

XI

TRIXIE lay relaxed in the steaming lavender-scented water of her bath
. . . She was bewildered and unhappy . . . and she kept telling
herself that she need not be either. She had run down to the stream
with the children as soon as the picnic tea was over, and there was
no reason at all why Hubert should not have gone for a walk with
Laura. Naturally he would not want to race boats or paddle in the
stream with the children. The two of them had looked very serious,
but Hubert generally did look serious. And it was natural, too, that
he should have wanted to help the Gideons carry the things home . . .
But there was this strange feeling of loneliness and isolation that had
been oppressing her more and more lately . . . She couldn't understand it. She had been brought up in an atmosphere of uncritical
affection—"Mum's girl," "Dad's pet"—treated as a baby, spoilt and
indulged. Though she had been homesick when first she came to
Westover, she had not missed that atmosphere. Hubert's devotion
had taken its place. She had accepted his devotion carelessly as her
right, without valuing it, but she realized now how lost and desolate
she would be without it in this new and alien world.

Again she told herself that she could never be without it. Hubert
adored her . . . And Godfrey was fond of her, too. There had
always been something of Dad's amused tenderness in Godfrey's
affection. It had helped to make her feel at home.

It was only Cynthia . . . The familiar wave of hatred swept over
her. If it hadn't been for Cynthia everything would have been all
right. Cynthia looked on her as dirt, and tried to make everyone
else look on her as dirt. Even people outside the family noticed.
Mrs. Drummond, for instance . . . She had been rather kind to
Trixie lately, had stopped her in the corridor yesterday to talk to her
and had said with a little conspiratorial smile: "I suppose her ladyship's got you where she wants you by now." That had roused
afresh all Trixie's resentment against Cynthia, though she didn't like
Mrs. Drummond. Mrs. Drummond belonged too much to Cynthia's
world for Trixie to like her.

She heard Hubert come in and go to the bedroom, but she stayed
there soaking in the bath . . . Her thoughts turned to Mum and
Dad, and she saw them quite plainly in the warm friendly kitchen,
Dad in his shirt-sleeves sitting by the fire reading the newspaper,
Mum in her big apron bustling about getting the supper . . . Perhaps
they were talking about her. A lump rose in her throat, a desperate
longing swept over her. She imagined herself walking in at the door
. . . They would jump up to welcome her. She would be pressed
against Mum's broad bosom. Dad would take her by the shoulders
and look at her, his face beaming with joy and pride. But Mum had

told her she mustn't go back. And, rather to her surprise, she realized that she didn't want to. In any case, one couldn't go back. It was like a journey. The first part of the way might be easy and sunlit, and the next hard and dark, but, though one loved to think of the sunlit part, one couldn't turn back. One had to go on . . . Mum and Dad. Her heart brimmed over with love for them, so that for the moment there was no room even for her hatred of Cynthia . . .

A clock struck eight and she got out of the bath, pulled out the plug and carefully washed the porcelain. She would never forget the time she had found Cynthia in the bathroom, her face turned aside with an expression of fastidious disgust, washing away the "tide mark" of Trixie's bath. She had hated her for it, but ever since then she had been careful to wash the bath herself before she left it.

She went into the bedroom and looked around her uncertainly. Hubert had been in and changed. It was nearly dinner-time . . . She was tired and her head ached. She would just have dinner and then go straight to bed. She pulled on her pyjamas and thrust her feet into bedroom slippers. She took down her dressing-gown, then flung it on her bed and kicked off her slippers. The night was sultry and she felt stifled.

Cynthia tapped on her door.

"Dinner's ready, Beatrice," she said.

Cynthia had enjoyed her day in town with Godfrey and had hated coming back to Westover. They had had lunch at the Carlton, and Cynthia had been pleasantly aware that in the crowd of smart well-turned-out women, she more than held her own. There had followed stalls at the matinée of a clever sophisticated play, then tea at Godfrey's club. She felt that she had spent a "civilized" afternoon and dreaded the return to a home whose atmosphere was now completely spoilt for her. But, at least, she determined, she must counter Trixie's influence by every means in her power . . .

When she came home she changed into a dress of wine-coloured taffeta that she had seldom worn, put on her diamond earrings and a touch of her best perfume. Then she went to the dining-room and got out the best lace table-mats, taking off the quilted chintz ones they generally used. The lace mats looked lovely on the polished mahogany table with the bowl of roses in the centre. It was a gracious well-proportioned room—a fitting background for the Sheraton side-board and Chippendale chairs. When winter came they would dine by candlelight . . . Eighteenth-century furniture always looked at its best in candlelight . . . Her spirits rose as she looked round the room, glancing at her own charming reflection in the Queen Anne mirror on the wall. She felt like a general leading a successful counter attack. She had been giving in too easily. She must fight.

She went to the kitchen where the "woman" was preparing the dinner.

"We'll have the best dinner service, Mrs. Grimes," she said. "I like to use it occasionally."

The two brothers were drinking whisky in the sitting-room.
Godfrey had brought back a bottle of his favourite brand from London.
He was genial and expansive; Hubert was quiet; but as soon as she
entered she was aware, as always, of the bond of affection between
them. It soothed and comforted her. Those two, at any rate,
enjoyed living together. Nothing had as yet happened to impair
their relations.

"Whisky, Cynthia?" said Godfrey, as she entered.

"Thanks." She sat down with them. "What was the picnic like,
Hubert?"

"It was—very nice," said Hubert absently.

Something's worrying him, she thought. I wonder what it is . . .
"Who was there?"

"Oh . . . Mrs. Gideon and Colin and the children and Miss
Pollock and a few locals."

"Wasn't the daughter there—Laura?"

"Yes . . . yes, she was there."

"I believe old Hubert's got a touch of liver," said Godfrey. "It's
always the result of a picnic. Sitting on the damp grass and eating
cold pastry."

Hubert smiled.

"I didn't eat cold pastry and the grass wasn't damp."

"My nurse used to say that grass is always damp," said Cynthia.

"In the old days people sang glees at picnics," said Godfrey. "I
think all the zest must have gone out of them now that people don't
sing glees, though I suppose you can always get chased by a bull, or
sit on an ants' nest."

"This afternoon's was quite uneventful," said Hubert.

"Didn't you even play rounders?" said Cynthia.

"No."

"Then I don't call it a picnic. Actually, the picnic is an ana-
chronism. It belongs to the days of the pony-trap, the straw boater
and the concertina. And the Vicar should have been there."

"He was," said Hubert. "I forgot to mention him, but he was
there."

"Did he say grace?"

"No."

"Then it doesn't count."

They all laughed and she was aware again of the harmony that
seemed to fill the atmosphere when the three of them were together
without Trixie.

She glanced at her watch.

"I think dinner will be ready. I'll tell Beatrice."

They had just taken their seats when Trixie entered the dining-
room, barefoot, in her pyjamas, and slumped down at the table,
sprawling in her seat.

Cynthia looked at her with tightened lips. The pyjamas, of artificial silk, were tumbled, creased and (Trixie had worn them for a

week) grubby. Her hair was tousled after her bath, her nails imperfectly cleaned . . . A disgust that was almost nausea swept over Cynthia.

"I'll bring your dinner to your bedroom, Beatrice," she said shortly.

"Thanks. I'll have it here," said Trixie.

Cynthia rose to her feet. She was so blinded by anger that she could hardly see the tousled slovenly figure in front of her.

"I refuse to sit down at table with you in that state," she said. "I don't know where you learnt your manners, or what sort of a pigstye you were brought up in, but——"

Trixie had sprung up so violently that her chair fell to the floor behind her. Her eyes were blazing.

"You leave my people alone!" she shouted. "You——"

She choked and ran from the room, slamming the door, so that the glasses on the table rattled . . .

Hubert, the muscles of his face taut, hesitated a moment then followed her.

Cynthia sat down, her breast rising and falling rapidly, her eyes fixed on her plate, her lips still tight.

Godfrey reached out for the decanter and filled his wineglass.

"Never mind, old lady," he said easily. "Don't worry. It'll blow over . . ."

"Do you want it to blow over?"

"Well, of course . . . Anyway, let's forget it."

He talked pleasantly and casually about the afternoon they had spent in town and she answered shortly in monosyllables. She looked round the lovely room—at the Sheraton and Chippendale, the lace mats on the gleaming mahogany. It was all spoilt.

She poured out Godfrey's coffee in the sitting-room and then went to her bedroom. Godfrey sat drinking his coffee and trying to read the evening paper. Women's squabbles . . . Men mustn't take them too seriously, but they were a damn nuisance. They disturbed the even tenor of life that was to Godfrey so enormously important. Still—if you ignored them, they blew over in time . . .

He could hear the sound of voices in Trixie's bedroom. Trixie's shrill and hysterial—Hubert's low and pleading. Then Hubert came out. The furrows showed deeply in his thin cheeks.

"Godfrey," he said, "Trixie wants me to tell you that she won't speak to either of you again till Cynthia's apologised."

He spoke in a jerky monotonous voice as if he were repeating a lesson.

Godfrey put down his newspaper and stared at him with a slow hardening of his face.

"That's preposterous," he said.

"I can't help it. That's what she says. She thinks that Cynthia's insulted her people."

"I'll tell Cynthia what you say," said Godfrey shortly, and took up his paper to end the interview.

Hubert turned and went from the room.   For the first time in his life Godfrey had looked at him with coldness and hostility.   Till this minute he could not even have imagined those grey eyes without the old light of affection . . . but now he had seen them.   The foundations of his world seemed to be slipping away.

He went out of the front door and turned instinctively in the direction of Greenways.

Cynthia came back into the sitting-room and Godfrey repeated what Hubert had said.

She sat down and took up her needlework without comment.

"I told him it was preposterous," said Godfrey.

She threw him a quick glance, then lowered her eyes to her work again.

"I should have thought you'd have found more than that to say about it.   If any apologies are to be made, it should be the other way round."

"Quite."

The evening was an uncomfortable one.   It seemed to drag interminably.   Hubert did not return, and Trixie did not come out of her bedroom.   Godfrey tried to read a book.   Occasionally he glanced at Cynthia and, though her head was bent over her tapestry work, he could see that her lips were still tightly set . . . They were in for a pretty unpleasant time, he thought ruefully.   Trixie would show the immovable obstinacy of the spoilt child.   All day, as a rule, Godfrey looked forward to returning to the pleasant atmosphere of his home at night (for, despite what he called "occasional breezes," it had continued to be pleasant).   It would be pretty grim to have to come back each night to this.

Cynthia was folding up her work.

"I think I'll go to bed," she said.

Godfrey put down his book.

"Look here, Cynthia, aren't we taking all this a bit too seriously?"

"What do you mean?"

"Well, she's only a child and she's hopelessly ignorant.   We all know that.   But those people can be as mulish as hell.   If she's taken up this attitude it's going to mean a lot of unpleasantness."

"I still don't know what you mean."

"After all, it's only a few words.   It won't kill you, and then we can all forget it and settle down comfortably together again."

She looked at him in silence for a few minutes.   She had gone very white.

"Let's get this clear, Godfrey.   Are you asking me—*me*—to apologise to that little guttersnipe?"

His eyes shifted away from hers.

"I'm not asking you to do anything.   I'm merely pointing out that, if you do, it will save a lot of unpleasantness for all of us.   And it would be—generous, because we all know that you weren't in the wrong."

"I see." She put her work away in her work-basket. Her face was flint-like. "Very well." She opened the door of Trixie's bedroom and went in.

Trixie was lying on the bed, her face hidden on the pillows. She lifted a swollen tear-sodden face.

"Beatrice," said Cynthia, "I'm sorry if you consider that I have insulted your parents in any way." The words fell from her lips like knives. Then she went out and closed the door.

"Cynthia . . ." said Godfrey.

She gave him a look of bitter contempt and went to her bedroom without speaking.

XII

JAMES and Letitia were having lunch at the Berkeley. Letitia had heard of a suitable flat to let in Chelsea and had asked James to meet her and look over it. It was she who had suggested lunch at the Berkeley. In such matters James was a little lacking in initiative. He needed what she called a "lead." . . . He was nervous, too, about moving into a flat, apt to take fright at the smallest difficulty and bolt for cover to some non-existent rooms that he pretended to have found in Bloomsbury.

Letitia wore a black suit with an orchid in her buttonhole, and was entertaining James in her best fashion. The orchid had cost a considerable sum at a florist's in Piccadilly, but Letitia believed in expensive little touches like that and found it irksome that she could now indulge in so few of them.

As James' housekeeper she would, of course, expect a substantial salary. James must have plenty of money and he hardly spent any on himself. It was ridiculous that he should pay two hundred pounds a year for Roger's education. One could do quite a lot with two hundred pounds a year. Julia must be devoid of all pride to place herself under such an obligation . . . Poor old James! He had a curmudgeonly manner, but he was always anxious to do the right thing. He had even included Lucy and Miss Parsons in his invitation to lunch—when finally she had managed to squeeze it out of him. She had replied at once, accepting the invitation for herself, but refusing it for the other two, and had not mentioned it to them till she had posted the letter.

"James wondered if you two would care to have lunch with him," she said lightly, "but I told him that I was certain you wouldn't want to. You'd find it much too tiring, Lucy, with your rheumatism, and I'm sure Miss Parsons has other things to do."

Lucy had looked a little disappointed, but Miss Parsons' face had worn its usual inscrutable expression. James, though well-meaning, needed a little social training. One did not ask people's companions to lunch at the Berkeley. She was enjoying her lunch—sole, chicken and a delicious pineapple soufflé—and was hoping that it would be the first of many.

James, on his side, was experiencing the natural gratification of the male at appearing in public with a good-looking, well-dressed woman. Aunt Letitia must be getting on, of course, but she was still strikingly handsome. He had realized, as soon as he saw her, that she had been right in heading off his first tentative luncheon invitation from the City chop-house he had suggested and steering it towards the Berkeley. City chop-houses were definitely not her background. It suddenly occurred to him that Miss Parsons would have fitted quite well into either background. She would have sat there—quiet, pleasant, at her ease . . . Aunt Letitia's charm was a bit overpowering —it kept one on one's toes all the time so that one couldn't relax— but he could not help feeling flattered at being its target.

"I was sorry Aunt Lucy and Miss Parsons couldn't come," he said tactlessly.

Aunt Letitia made a little grimace, then laughed.

"I wasn't," she said. "When three women live together, James, they like to get away from each other occasionally."

"I suppose so," said James.

"One is a bit swamped by the family at Westover, you know. Lucy to the right, as it were, Julia to the left. They don't exactly volley and thunder—except Richard and Rachel—but one can never get away from them."

"Julia seems to manage very well at Greenways," said James. "I was a bit anxious about it at first. Never very businesslike, you know, Julia."

"But you do so much for her, James. Why, you pay all Roger's school fees, don't you?"

"Yes," said James, glad of an opportunity of airing his favourite grievance. "Two hundred a year, with extras and things. Deuce of a lot, when you come to think of it. I sometimes wonder whether it's worth it."

Letitia stored up the words for repeating to Roger with, if necessary, a few additions.

"I'm afraid I don't even wonder, James dear," she said. "I'm not a socialist, of course, but I do think that the public school system has had its day. And—another thing. In a place like that Roger's bound to mix with boys a good deal better off than himself. I suppose that's what makes him so dissatisfied with his own home."

"Is he dissatisfied with his own home?"

Letitia shrugged.

"You've only to watch him . . ."

"His father and Colin went there, you know. I was at Winchester myself, of course."

"Oh, it was all right in your day, but we're living in quite a different world now, and we must take a realistic view of things. The public schools are no answer to the post-war problems. I believe that the secondary schools are the answer. I simply can't think why everyone doesn't send their children to them. I always say to my friends, 'You pay money through the rates to provide excellent schools in the neighbourhood. Why ever don't you send your own children to them?' I'm afraid snobbery's at the bottom of it. And, of course, with a boy like Roger, who's difficult and not too steady to start with——"

A look of panic came into James' face. Essentially steady himself, he had a horror of anyone who wasn't.

"Isn't Roger steady?" he said.

Letitia smiled.

"I'm not going to crab Julia's children to you," she said. "Things haven't been easy for Julia, and it's not surprising that her children have got out of hand. I'm terribly fond of them, of course."

James was silent, wondering whether he had been precipitate in undertaking Roger's education; whether he was, after all, doing what was best for the boy himself. The pride he used to feel in his position had vanished of late.

"Where have you and Aunt Lucy decided to spend your holiday?" he said at last.

Letitia, who had been looking round the room, turned to him with a little smile. She had just seen Mrs. Fielding at another table, having lunch with a dark young man, whose expression and attitude showed every sign of devotion. He was leaning forward with his arms on the table, gazing into her face . . . Things were not going well with the Fieldings. Something had happened lately—she didn't know what—to make them worse than they had been before. Before, there had just been friction between the two women, but now the men were involved as well . . . All four were on bad terms with each other. Letitia had tried to lead Mrs. Fielding on to confide in her, but Mrs. Fielding seemed to have withdrawn behind her defences. She was distant and uncommunicative. The confidence that had seemed to exist between them on the day of Mrs. Hubert's arrival had vanished. As things got worse, Mrs. Fielding got more distant and more uncommunicative. And, of course, Mrs. Hubert was hopeless. Still—their unhappiness was obvious, and Letitia derived from it the gratification she always derived from other people's unhappiness . . . as if some part of the grudge she owed to Fate were being paid off.

"Nothing's really settled yet," she said, toning down her smile to express weariness and patience. "Things are—difficult for me, you know, James. Lucy holds the purse-strings."

James nodded sympathetically, understanding, as she meant him to understand, that Lucy was a little mean and more than a little unreasonable.

"Will Miss Parsons take her holiday at the same time?" he said.

"I know nothing of Miss Parsons' plans," said Letitia with a touch of irritation in her voice.

The flat was small, compact and cheerful, overlooking the Embankment. James was as timid as a startled deer over the matter, shyly interested one minute and the next darting back, panic-stricken, to the shelter of his mythical rooms in Bloomsbury.

"Of course," he kept saying, "there are these rooms in Bloomsbury . . ."

"But such a gloomy neighbourhood, James dear," said Letitia. "A man in your position should live in a good neighbourhood. You've worked hard and you've been successful and now you deserve comfort and pleasant surroundings. I always think that it's one's duty to live up to one's means and position."

"I suppose it would be more—expensive than rooms."

She shrugged.

"Very little, and, after all, the two hundred a year you spend on Roger's education would be far better spent giving yourself a few extra comforts than spoiling the boy for the life he will have to face."

"No, no," said James quickly, "No, no, no."

Letitia saw that she had gone too far and hastily retraced her steps.

"I didn't really mean it, James dear," she laughed. But she had planted her seed and perhaps it would grow . . .

He was gazing about the sunny little room, still with that comical expression of mingled pleasure and dismay.

"I suppose . . . Now, what would the place need in the way of staff?"

"You'd need a housekeeper, of course . . . and a maid. Perhaps a woman to do the rough work."

"That would come expensive."

She smiled at him.

"You're not a poor man, you know, James."

His wintry smile peeped out in response then vanished.

"Well, no . . . And you think that a—er—housekeeper would find the place quite easy to run?—with a maid and charwoman, of course."

"Quite, James."

"The kitchen's all right, isn't it?" he said. "Convenient and all that?"

"Oh yes. It's a kitchen any woman would love to work in."

"That's good."

"You know, James," she said slowly and thoughtfully. "I've sometimes thought of taking up a job . . ."

He was looking round the room again with a dreamy expression that made him seem quite unlike himself.

"Yes?" he said absently, then, shaking off his dreaminess and becoming himself again, "What were you saying, Aunt Letitia?"

"I said I'd sometimes thought of taking a job," said Letitia a little sharply.

"A job?"

"Well, it's not easy, living with Lucy. I'd rather be independent."

"Of course. What sort of a job?"

"I'm used to running a house, you know. You remember, don't you, James? our delightful home in the old days and the dinner-parties we used to give there. I think a post as housekeeper in a good district to a—widower or bachelor . . ." She waited expectantly.

"Yes, excellent idea," he said, but still in an abstracted fashion, as if he hadn't really heard what she said.

She sighed. These cautious people were very difficult to manage. Still, she felt fairly hopeful on the whole. James always hated to commit himself definitely, but he was certainly interested in the idea.

"Now, James, what about it?" she said, trying to force a decision. But James took fright again.

"There are a lot of things to be considered," he said, "a lot of things . . ."

"It will get snapped up by someone else if you wait too long."

"I'll take my chance of that," he said. "After all, there are always those rooms . . ." He looked at his watch. "Well, I suppose you want to be getting back to Westover."

"Oh, there's no great hurry," said Letitia, who thought that the least James could do after all her trouble was to give her tea and take her to a play or film. He seemed curiously lacking in the little courtesies of life. He would need a good deal of training, but Letitia felt herself equal to the task.

"As a matter of fact," said James, "I have to see Julia on some business, so I might as well run over to Pakenham with you . . . We shall just catch the 3.15."

"Very well," said Letitia, rather coldly.

They found Lucy comfortably entrenched behind her tea-tray, reading a Wild West story. Lucy had a childish passion for Wild West stories, but she never read them when Letitia was there, because Letitia could be very sarcastic about them. She slipped the book under a cushion as Letitia and James entered. It had a rather garish jacket depicting a beautiful girl in evening dress intervening in a fight between two cow-punchers in the primitive surroundings of a very Wild West bar.

"This is nice!" she said, beaming a welcome at them. "I didn't expect you for tea . . . I won't be a second making another pot. Mary's gone over to Greenways."

"Mary?" said James.

"Lucy has begun to call Miss Parsons by her Christian name," said Letitia, with an eloquent little curl of her lip.

"Oh . . . is Mary her Christian name?" said James.

"It appears so," said Letitia, as if the subject were too far beneath her notice for her to hold any definite views on it.

"Well," James looked at his watch again, "I don't think I'll stay for tea, thanks, Aunt Lucy. I'll get along to see Julia. I have to see her on some business."

"Did you have a successful day, dear?" said Lucy timidly, when James had gone.

Letitia didn't know whether she'd had a successful day or not. She'd put in a good deal of spade-work, and found it very tiring.

"Yes, thank you," she said shortly, "but it was all a bit of a rush, and I've got a migraine coming on . . . Oh, and Lucy——"

"Yes, dear?"

"I don't think Bournemouth would suit me, after all. It's very relaxing. I think perhaps somewhere in Scotland . . ."

James was halfway to Greenways when he met Miss Parsons coming back. She wore the maroon-spotted dress, and her shady hat threw a becoming shade over her pleasant brown eyes and sun-flushed cheeks. She looked very nice. Rather like a robin, thought James, which was the highest poetical flight his mind was capable of . . .

She was passing him with a quick nod, but he stopped her.

"Good afternoon, Miss Parsons. You've been to Greenways, I hear."

"Yes, I always spend my free afternoon there. Mrs. Gideon's very kind to me."

He turned to walk back with her.

"I was sorry you couldn't lunch with us," he said, his shyness increasing the natural pomposity of his manner.

She threw him an enigmatic glance.

"I was sorry, too," she said.

He walked beside her in silence for a few minutes, then said abruptly:

"Do you care for Chelsea?"

She looked at him in surprise.

"I've never thought about it," she said.

"It's considered not an unpleasant neighbourhood," he said. "There is the river."

"So I've always understood," said Miss Parsons.

Again they walked on in silence for some minutes. Again it was James who broke the silence. He gave a sudden rusty chuckle.

"That dog of yours who used to eat gooseberries off the bushes . . ."

She smiled.

"Fancy your remembering that!"

"I've often thought about it," said James, adding simply, "I don't know why."

"He was called Cerberus," said Miss Parsons, "and he was always trying to get into church. I remember once, at an Early Service, my father had forgotten to shut the vestry door, and Cerberus was up in the chancel before anyone could stop him, with his paws on the altar, trying to lick my father's face. Fortunately, it was at the end of the service."

James gave another rusty chuckle, then became serious.

"I was sorry to think of the way your career was cut short," he said.

"It's strange that you should mention that," said Miss Parsons, sinking her voice to a confidential note, "because I had a letter from a friend of my father's this morning. He's only just heard of my mother's death. He has a business in Milan—he went back to open it again as soon as the war ended—and he asks me to join him as his secretary, to deal with his foreign correspondence . . . He particularly wants an older woman, he says, as he always finds them more reliable. He offers a good salary."

"So you're going?" said James.

"I haven't made up my mind. I've written to ask for time to consider it. At first I had a horrible suspicion that he was doing it out of pity because he'd heard that I'd had to take a post as companion, and then I thought that he would hardly risk his firm's reputation just out of pity for a woman he hadn't seen for years. If I'd got the letter a few months ago I'd have refused the offer at once, but my self-confidence is gradually returning. I know now that I can pick up the threads again if I try. I've always kept up my reading in French and German and Italian even when I couldn't leave my mother . . . I've begun to realize lately that just pottering about a house isn't enough to occupy me."

"I suppose not," said James a little despondently.

"And yet at first I was frightened even of that. It proves that I'm getting my courage back."

"Milan," said James thoughtfully. "It's a long way from your friends."

"I haven't any friends," said Miss Parsons.

James opened his mouth to speak, then closed it again.

"You see," went on Miss Parsons, "my mother's illness isolated me for so many years. I lost the friends I'd had as a girl, and I had no opportunities of making new ones."

James nodded understandingly.

"My aunts will miss you," he said.

"I haven't told them about it yet. I may decide not to go, in which case I'd rather they didn't know anything about it. You won't tell them, will you?"

"No," said James.

"I don't know why I told you," said Miss Parsons. "I suppose it was because you happened to mention it."

When they reached Lucy's sitting-room, they found her at work on the sea-boot stocking.

The Wild West story was still under the cushion. Letitia was sitting very upright on the other side of the fireplace, reading Bates'

Naturalist on the Amazon. She wasn't interested in either naturalists or the Amazon, but it was as good a means as any for making Lucy feel inferior. She knew all about the Wild West story (half of its cover was quite visible beneath the cushion), and she knew that Lucy wouldn't dare to take it out as long as she continued to sit there reading Bates' *Naturalist on the Amazon* . . .

She raised her eyebrows slightly as James entered with Miss Parsons.

"I've just dropped in to say good-bye," said James. "Got a dinner engagement in town. Mustn't miss the train. Thank you for all your help, Aunt Letitia."

"Did you finish your business with Julia, dear?" said Lucy.

"Oh that!" said James with dignity. "It was not a matter of any great moment."

XIII

COLIN and Ann-Marie were walking along the field path towards Greenways. Ann-Marie walked without a stick, dragging her foot but covering the ground with a rapidity that would have seemed impossible a few weeks ago. She swung along happily, bareheaded, holding her face up to the sun. Her air of transparent fragility was deserting her. Her cheeks were sunburnt, her eyes bright. Colin, pipe in mouth, hands in pockets, accommodated his usually long loose stride to her uneven steps. She knew that she was different, that the whole world was different . . . And she knew why . . .

All day she looked forward to the evening walk with Colin. There was no more dressing up in the elaborate picture frocks now, no more lying on the sofa to be read to by Maman . . . Maman still prepared the elaborate evening meal and Ann-Marie ate it, but quickly (though quite heartily), waiting for the knock at the door that meant Colin's arrival. Then they would set off across the fields or woods for the walk that was to Ann-Marie the only real part of the day. The long light summer evenings, cool and fragrant, seemed to have been made for them. Looking back over her life, Ann-Marie didn't seem ever to have noticed the seasons before. It might have been the first summer she had ever known.

On Saturdays Colin called for her immediately after lunch and they went for a longer walk, ending up at Greenways for tea.

Mrs. Pollock had at first reacted to the situation by assuming an air of suffering so intense as to be almost embarrassing. Madness had seized her Little Flower, but, Mrs. Pollock assured herself, it would be short-lived. She was too fastidious to be deceived for long by such a—even Mrs. Pollock, whose vocabulary so seldom failed her, was hard put to it to find words adequately to express her opinion of Colin. Last night her pent-up emotions had suddenly burst forth in a stream of eloquence.

"I cannot stand by to watch it in silence any longer, my little one. This man—this *cad*, this *lout*, this *boor*—he is coarsening you. Body and mind, he is coarsening you. I see you change before my eyes and I cannot endure it. To see my Little Flower lose her bloom, her fragrance, her delicacy of soul, her——"

"Please don't talk like that, Maman," said Ann-Marie.

"I must," said Mrs. Pollock, her voice rising hysterically. "You are wilfully deceiving yourself, wilfully blinding yourself. To let this man of no manners, no breeding, no sensitiveness of mind, make a plaything of you . . ."

Ann-Marie had flushed.

"He isn't making a plaything of me."

"What is he doing then?" asked Mrs. Pollock, gesticulating wildly. "What is he doing?" Her voice sank to a note of tenderness and the fluttering of her hands ceased. "Darling, you know . . . you surely know . . ."

"What?" said Ann-Marie, her heart beginning to beat unevenly.

"I do not like to say it, but I must. This man would never marry you. No man would wish a cripple for his wife."

Ann-Marie's flush faded, and her cheeks paled beneath their sunburn.

"There's no question of that," she said. "We're just friends."

Mrs. Pollock laughed mirthlessly.

"Friends! Do you honestly believe that a man and a girl of your age can be *friends?* You are pretty and no doubt he is content to— play with you till some other attraction appears or your disability begins to weary him, as undoubtedly it soon will. Probably he pities you. He may, in spite of his boorishness, be kind-hearted. The English are like that. They love to what they call help lame dogs over stiles. But it means nothing, nothing . . . This lout is not bad-looking. He is, one presumes, a full-blooded young man, able in body, if imbecile in mind. Such a man will wish a wife, but, as I said before, he will not wish a cripple for a wife. It hurts me to speak thus openly to you, *chérie*, but it is my duty."

Ann-Marie's pallor had spread to her lips. Ice seemed to close around her heart.

"I'd rather not discuss the matter, please, Maman," she said with dignity.

"But it must be discussed," said Mrs. Pollock, returning to her normal vehemence of voice and gesticulations. "I am your mother. I have given up my life to you. I cannot stand by and see my little flower broken and dragged in the dust . . . Have you no dignity, no self-respect, *chérie?* Will you wait, hanging round this man's neck, till he throws you off?"

"*Don't*, Maman," said Ann-Marie, rising and putting her hands to her ears. "I can't listen to any more. I'm sorry. I'm going to bed. Good-night."

Mrs. Pollock, left alone, shut out from her Little Flower's *couché*, for Ann-Marie no longer allowed herself to be put to bed as if she were a child, walked up and down the room, her lips moving silently, her white hands flashing to and fro. So deeply was she moved by her own inaudible eloquence, that soon the tears were streaming down her cheeks . . .

And Ann-Marie, who of late had slept deeply, dreamlessly all night long, lay awake till the first streaks of dawn. The delicious carefree progress of her love for Colin had received a check. She must look, not at the flower-decked path she was treading, but at the end to which it led. And already something of the anguish of that inevitable end—as it seemed—pierced her heart . . . Reluctantly, painfully, she made up her mind what she must do . . . She must break this friendship while she was still able to do it. Every day that passed would make it more difficult. Even now she loved him so much that it would be like tearing out part of her own body to let him go.

But what Maman had said was true, and, now that she realized it, the old unclouded happiness could never again be possible.

"You're very quiet this afternoon," said Colin suddenly.

"It's all so lovely," she said. "I notice things I never used to notice before. Look! That's a woodchat, isn't it? It's just like the one we saw the other day."

"Yes. You're growing quite country-wise . . . But these woods are best in the autumn. They'll take your breath away then."

She was silent, thinking that they would hold no delight for her without him. She didn't know how she was going to break their friendship. She only knew that she must do it and do it to-day. If she let herself weaken, put it off, the pain of the final break would be unbearable.

They were walking along the field path that led to the gate of the little back garden of Greenways. It was downhill and rather difficult for her.

"Take it easy," said Colin, slackening his pace.

She thought how irksome it must be for him to walk in step with her uneven halting gait and remembered again what her mother had said. "Pity" . . "Kind-hearted" . . . "Helping lame dogs over stiles" . . . The weight at her heart grew so heavy that it was almost unbearable.

"Here we are," he said, opening the little green gate. "It's been grand, but you'll be glad to sit down."

He fetched two deck chairs and put them under the apple tree at the end of the lawn, then went into the house.

"The others haven't come in yet," he said when he returned. "Blanche has gone into Nettleford to do some shopping, Roger's at the rehearsal (it's the performance to-morrow, you know), Laura's out with Hubert Fielding and the Two are playing with a friend next door. I've put the kettle on."

"Can I do anything to help?"

"We'll all give a hand when the others come in."

She wondered whether to tell him now, but the peace of the moment was too precious to destroy . . .

"What is it that smells so lovely?" she said.

"It's the honeysuckle . . . Blanche brought it in from the woods and planted it there by the fence."

Suddenly Rachel came running round the side of the house, followed more slowly by Richard. Her face was tensely set and already crumpling up into tears. She flung herself upon Colin, clasped her arms round his neck and hid her face on his shoulder.

His arm closed round her protectively, and he looked at Richard for an explanation.

"It was the cat," said Richard, sitting down cross-legged at his feet. "It had got a bird and we tried to catch it. The bird was fluttering in its mouth. It was beastly. I threw a stone but it missed it. Then Peter caught it and got the bird out, but it was so badly hurt that he killed it. He wrung its neck."

"It was *cruel*," sobbed Rachel.

"No, it wasn't, Rachel," explained Richard patiently. "It couldn't have lived much longer and it was in pain. It was much kinder to kill it."

"It was a chaffinch," said Rachel in a choking voice, her face still hidden on Colin's shoulder, her arms strained tightly round his neck.

Richard looked at Colin in a man-to-man fashion.

"That sort of thing *does* upset girls," he said, "and, of course, it *is* beastly. And she wasn't a cry-baby, Colin. She didn't cry till she got to you."

"She's never a cry-baby," said Colin.

"I knew you'd come home, so I knew it would be all right," said Richard simply.

Colin was always Rachel's haven in the rare tempests that disturbed her usually serene life. He didn't offer the meaningless platitudes of sympathy that most grown-ups offered and that not only failed to console but added irritation to one's grief. He didn't insult one by offering treats or presents in compensation for what was beyond compensation. He seldom said anything . . . He was just there—and himself—and that, for Rachel, was enough . . .

"Well, this chicken I was telling you about," said Colin to Ann-Marie, as if continuing a conversation, "was made a pet of by the whole family, and it was all right as long as it stayed a chicken. They used to put it on the table and feed it from their plates. But, when it grew into a hen, they still let it fly on to the table at meals, even when they had guests, and it used to walk about the table, pecking first at one plate, then at another, just as the fancy took it. It must have been most disconcerting to be a guest at one of those dinner-parties and have an old hen putting its beak into your potatoes or walking off with your best bit of chicken."

"Or paddling in your gravy or laying eggs in your soup," shouted Richard, turning a somersault backwards on the grass.

Rachel raised her head. A smile was dawning behind her tears.

"Is it true?" she said.

"Yes."

"Where was it?"

"Somewhere in France. I read about it in a book the other day."

"It must have looked funny. I don't expect many people would want to go to dinner there. Still—I'm glad they let it keep on doing it. It would have felt so sad if they'd stopped it just because it was getting old. What was its name?"

"I don't know. What do you think?"

"Greedy Gladys," shouted Richard.

"Pecking Polly," said Rachel.

"Paddling Pamela."

"Cackling Kathleen."

"Egg-laying Edith."

Both children were laughing . . .

Richard sprang up and held out his hand to Rachel.

"Come on," he said. "Let's go back."

Rachel looked anxiously at Colin.

"Could anyone tell I've been crying?"

Colin took out his handkerchief and wiped her cheeks, then handed her the handkerchief.

"Have a good blow," he said, "then you'll be all right."

She had a good blow, returned the handkerchief to Colin and ran off round the house again with Richard. The tragedy of the chaffinch was now a memory. It was an unhappy memory, but it was no longer an ever-present horror, darkening the sunshine, shutting out all the kindliness of life.

"Poor little Rachel!" smiled Ann-Marie.

"She's a grand kid," said Colin. "They're both grand kids. I often think how proud my father would have been of them."

And of you, thought Ann-Marie.

"Look here," went on Colin, "I wonder if you'd find it too much next Saturday to take the train to Doveton and go on the river there. It's a lovely stretch of river and it's never crowded."

She looked away. Here was her chance . . .

"I don't think I can come, Colin," she said, in a small far-away voice.

"Why not?"

"I—don't think I ought to go out with you any more."

"Why not?"

She didn't answer.

"Has your mother been talking to you?"

She nodded.

"What has she said?"

"Nothing that—isn't true, that I oughtn't to have seen for myself."

"That's no answer. I asked what she'd said."

"That you're—sorry for me, that I'm letting myself get too fond of you and that—that no man could marry a cripple. *Oh!*" she gasped, "I didn't know how dreadful it would sound till I said it."

"What sounds dreadful?"

"Telling you that I've got fond of you. That's why I can't—go on."

His mouth was serious, but his eyes were full of laughter.

"I was going to ask you to marry me this evening," he said. "You've thrown out my whole time-table by proposing first."

She put her hands to her flaming cheeks.

"*Colin!*"

"Darling," he said, taking her hands away, "you must have known I was in love with you. I've been in love with you ever since I first saw you in Chapman's car."

"Then—what Maman said——"

"What Maman said was a lot of damned rot."

"You—want to marry me?"

"You bet I do."

"Oh, Colin! I can't believe it."

He kissed her.

"Do you believe it now?"

"Almost . . . You didn't love me at first, did you, Colin?"

He nodded.

"But you were so unkind."

"Unkind?"

"You snubbed me."

"There was a spoilt child in you and though I loved you I don't like spoilt children."

"Has it gone?"

"I think so."

"If it comes back, will you be kind to it?"

"I shall probably be as bad as Maman."

"I hope you won't," she said severely. "I don't want to get like *that* again . . . Oh, Colin, I *can't* believe it. I love you so and I was so unhappy."

"It's terribly difficult kissing people in deck chairs, isn't it? Let's go indoors . . ."

"Colin."

"Yes?"

"There's—Maman."

"I know."

"She'll be—difficult."

"I know."

"Colin, let's not tell people yet—till I've found out about her. I may be able to get her to agree to it quite easily, but, if people knew about it, she might take up some sort of—dramatic attitude and stick to it through thick and thin. Let it be just between ourselves, till I've—managed her."

"Well—for the present," he agreed. "Blanche knew I was going to ask you to-day, but we can tell her to keep quiet and, if you find your mother difficult to manage, I'll give a hand."

"I think you'd better stay out of it, darling. She calls you such dreadful names."

"Such as?"

"Lout and cad and boor and things like that."

He gave a shout of laughter.

"I had an idea she didn't like me."

"She says you've coarsened me."

"I hope I have . . . Happy?"

"When you kiss me like that I could die of happiness."

He looked out of the window.

"Here's Blanche."

Mrs. Gideon, a laden shopping-basket on her arm, was at the garden gate. Her gentle eyes went from one to the other as they approached.

"Now, you needn't tell me," she said, raising her hands to put her hat straight. "It blew off in Nettleford—I can't think why, because there wasn't a breath of wind—and it's felt funny ever since I put it on again . . . You needn't tell me. I'm supposed to be so vague that I can never see what's going on beneath my nose, but I can see this."

She held out her arms and kissed first Ann-Marie, then Colin.

"Darlings, I'm so glad."

Colin took off her hat and tucked it under his arm.

"It was back to front," he said, "that's why it felt funny . . . We're going to keep it quiet till Ann's approached her mother."

Mrs. Gideon and Ann-Marie went indoors first, Mrs. Gideon's arm round Ann-Marie's waist, and Colin followed with the basket and the hat.

"Very well," smiled Mrs. Gideon, "but when she sees how happy you look, darling, she'll give you her blessing."

"Perhaps," said Ann-Marie uncertainly.

"Has Laura come in yet?"

"Not yet."

"Well, let's get tea . . . Oh, the kettle's boiling. Good! You make the tea, Colin, and you get out the cakes, Ann, darling—you know where they are, don't you?—and I'll make some sandwiches."

Ann-Marie limped happily about the kitchen, getting out the cakes, setting the tea-tray. This carefree family atmosphere, with its under-current of affection and loyalty, was new and beautiful to her, and her love for Colin threw a glamour over every detail of it. Will Colin and I ever have a home and be getting tea together like this?

she wondered, and a sudden chill invaded her heart, because such completeness didn't seem possible . . .

"Happy, darling?" said Mrs. Gideon, holding her face between her hands and kissing it.

Ann-Marie smiled tremulously.

"Don't!" she said. "You're making me cry."

They were having tea under the apple tree when Laura and Hubert arrived. Laura sat on a deck chair and Hubert on the grass beside her. His face looked pale and drawn in the sunshine.

He still felt dazed and bewildered by what had happened, but he knew that his love for Trixie had gone, and that he loved Laura with all his being. He had been attracted by Laura at their first meeting, but he had fought against the attraction. Trixie was his wife. He loved her and owed her loyalty . . . Then—it had begun the night of the picnic, when Trixie had made him demand an apology from Cynthia. Everything had been spoilt since then. Before then, Godfrey's affection had been the background of his life at Westover, giving him a feeling of security and contentment, despite Trixie's vagaries and the friction between her and Cynthia. His love for Godfrey had grown with him from childhood, was in some ways deeper even than his love for Trixie, and she had spoilt it. Never since that night had Godfrey looked at him with the old affection in his eyes. Trixie had come between them, and he couldn't forgive her for it. It seemed to free him from any bond of loyalty towards her, and he turned from her to the warm radiance of Laura's love that he had known was his from the beginning. He spent as little time at Westover now as he could. The atmosphere there was full of constraint and unhappiness. They were all miles away from each other—avoiding each other's eyes, each other's company. Even Godfrey had withdrawn into himself, Trixie was sullen and silent, Cynthia, when with them, was hard and scornful, but she wasn't often with them. She was going about with Adrian Maple, meeting him almost every day in London, going to dances, theatres, concerts with him. She had told Godfrey last night at dinner that she would be away for the week-end. Godfrey had made no comment and the silence had become more constrained even than usual. Two hard bright spots had burnt on Cynthia's cheeks. It was all hateful, and Hubert wanted to get away from it. He saw his marriage to Trixie as the foolish action of a lonely youth, so starved for companionship that like a lost dog he had followed the first friendly voice he heard.

And this afternoon he had declared his love to Laura, begging her to marry him.

"Trixie will divorce me. It was all a mistake."

"You loved her once."

"I don't know that I did . . . I was so desperately lonely over there . . . And when first she came here—yes, perhaps I loved her then, but it was purely physical. It's burnt itself out, and left—nothing."

"Didn't she love you?"

"I don't think so. She didn't want to come here. Her people had to make her. She'll be glad to go back to them."

"Have you told her about—us?"

"No. I wanted to ask you first, to make sure you loved me."

"You knew I loved you."

"I think I did, but—Laura, you will marry me, won't you? I know it will be all right. She'll divorce me. Even if she won't . . ."

"It's not as simple as that."

"It is as simple as that. We love each other. That's all that matters."

"It isn't, Hubert. There's Trixie and Blanche and Colin and—Father to be considered."

"Your father's dead."

"I know. That doesn't make as much difference as you'd think. I remember him quite well."

"Darling, don't complicate things so. This only concerns the two of us."

"Even so, I'm not sure . . . Oh, I know I love you. I knew that right from the beginning . . . I tried to hope that you wouldn't love me . . . though I couldn't really make myself hope that. But—however you look at it, Trixie's involved. And the others."

He glimpsed the bedrock of firmness beneath her gentleness and fragility.

"The trouble is that you don't really love me," he complained.

She gave him a faint smile.

"No, the trouble is that I *do* really love you . . ."

They had come to no decision when they reached Greenways. The strain of the situation showed in their troubled young faces and in the abstraction of their manner, though Laura tried to join in the casual inter-play of family conversation.

"Did you get your shopping done all right, Blanche?" she said.

"Yes, thank you, dear."

"She came home with her hat back to front," said Colin.

"You are a sneak, Colin," said Mrs. Gideon.

She was watching Laura covertly, her heart heavy with anxiety. Laura had been Humphrey's favourite child. Looking at her now, Mrs. Gideon saw her as a toddler, coming carefully downstairs, tense and solemn, holding the banisters with both hands, while Humphrey waited at the bottom smiling, his arms outspread for the final jump . . . as a slender barelegged child riding pick-a-back, her arms round Humphrey's neck, shouting with delight . . . as a girl of twelve, thirteen, setting off with Humphrey for the long walks they both loved . . . Humphrey's eyes had always softened when they rested on her. How he would have hated this! And she hated it too. There was a look of dewy innocence on the young face. She could not bear to think that she must watch the shadows closing over it. She wanted a happy normal married life for Laura, not this stealing of another woman's man, this building her home on the ruins of another woman's.

But it never occurred to her to speak to Laura of what was in her mind. She was an intensely reserved woman and found the discussion of serious subjects difficult even with her own children. But she had a simple childlike faith and a sincere conviction of the power of prayer, and had always believed that it did more good to pray for people than to reason with them. And, as she went about her household tasks these days, her soul was wrapt in fervent prayer for Laura . . .

Hubert made little attempt to join in the conversation. He sat, a pinched drawn look on his thin face, staring moodily at the grass. Suddenly he rose jerkily to his feet.

"Well, I ought to be getting on," he said. "Thanks so much, Mrs. Gideon. Good-bye, Colin . . ."

He looked at Laura but she did not move. It was Colin who saw him to the gate.

"And I ought to go, too," said Ann-Marie. "Don't come back with me, Colin."

"Sure you'll be all right?"

"Sure."

He took longer seeing her to the gate than he had taken with Hubert. When he returned, Mrs. Gideon had gone indoors and Laura was putting the cups and saucers on a tray.

"I'm glad things are all right with you and Ann, Colin," she said.

"Thanks," he said, lowering himself into his deck chair. He looked at her for a few moments, then said quietly, "Things aren't all right with you, are they?"

"No."

She put down the cup she was holding and came and sat down on the grass by his chair.

"What am I to do, Colin?"

He lit his pipe and threw away the match.

"No one can decide that for you," he said. "I can only tell you that, whatever you do and however much I hate it, I'll stand by you."

She was silent, then:

"You would hate it, wouldn't you?" she said.

"You know I would."

"But——" she began, and he interrupted her, smiling.

"Now don't say that your life's your own to do as you like with, because it isn't. No one's life is their own. We're all too closely linked to each other for that."

"I know," she sighed. "That's what I've been trying to make Hubert see."

He said nothing further, and she leant her head against his knee, finding peace and comfort in the silence.

XIV

THE performance of *Loyalties* had taken place and had been an immense success. At the last moment the young man who was to have taken the part of De Levis had developed a sore throat and become voiceless, and Roger, handing his own small part on to some-one else, had taken his place and given a fine sensitive performance, far outshining that of the original actor. He had been, in fact, the success of the evening.

Every seat in the Village Hall had been occupied, and people were standing at the back and down the sides, even sitting on the high window-sills. The Vicar and his sister sat together in the middle of the front row. The Vicar's sister had taken a good deal of trouble over the seating arrangements, seeing to it that her brother was surrounded by family parties or the less attractive of his parishioners. The few suspects—attractive women, "getting on" but not yet elderly, who might be expected to consider the Vicar better than nothing—were all seated several rows away from him. The Vicar was a man of blameless life, who had never shown any tendency to dalliance with the opposite sex, but his sister left nothing to chance. She was one of those women who love organization for its own sake, and her staff work was always perfect to the last detail.

Just behind the Vicar sat the Gideons—Mrs. Gideon, Colin, Laura, Richard and Rachel. Richard and Rachel were agog with excitement, greeting every movement behind the curtain with rapture, clapping at every opportunity.

"Roger!" they gasped ecstatically when he appeared, and pro-ceeded to discuss him in squeaky undertones till silenced by a glance from Colin.

Laura, alone of the Gideons, was distrait, her mind far away from what was happening on the stage. She had made her decision at last and was feeling the peace and weariness that accompanies any decision formed after days and nights of wavering. She felt at peace just because she had decided, because her mind need no longer thresh to and fro . . . round and round. Last night, because she had decided, she had slept soundly for the first time for weeks.

She had resolved to go with Hubert and let Trixie divorce him. She couldn't live without him and he couldn't live without her . . . and that was all that mattered. Other people didn't matter . . . Trixie, Colin, Blanche and the others . . . It wouldn't wreck their lives. They'd be angry or hurt or unhappy, but only for a time. They'd get over it. They'd come to accept it or ignore it, and it would make little difference to them in the long run. But she and Hubert would be maimed and broken for ever without each other.

Why should she put the happiness of these others before Hubert's?
She loved him more than any of them. Her duty was to him . . .
As to Trixie, the marriage had been a mistake. It was monstrous
that two people who did not love each other should be forced to live
together, if even one could find happiness elsewhere. She had made
the resolution in weariness of spirit, but was determined to uphold
it, to shut her mind to the other considerations should they try to
enter. And already they were trying . . . Colin, Blanche, even the
Two . . . It would be the first time in her life she had hurt them.
Don't, she cried desperately. I can't start all over again, twisting
and turning, going round and round, being torn in pieces . . . I can't
bear any more of it . . . I'm happy now . . . I've made up my
mind. I've done with thinking. She wanted to tell Hubert of her
decision, so as to make it irrevocable. Once she had told him, she
could not go back on it.

He was sitting a few rows behind her with Godfrey and Trixie
and Cynthia. The four of them were very silent and did a good deal
of studying their programmes as if to hide their lack of conversation.
Behind them were Lucy and Letitia and Miss Parsons. Cynthia
turned round during the interval to talk to Letitia.

"Rather a trial these affairs, aren't they?" smiled Letitia. "I've
always said that amateur theatricals should be forbidden by law."

But Lucy watched Roger, her eyes starry with pride, and Miss
Parsons, whose years of attendance on her mother had prevented her
going to theatres, was almost as much excited by the play as Richard
and Rachel.

Ann-Marie had arrived just before the performance and slipped
into the seat next Colin.

Mrs. Pollock shared Letitia's attitude to amateur theatricals, and
was without that wholehearted if malicious interest in her neighbours
that made it impossible for Letitia to keep away from any place where
she could have them under her eyes. Even though it meant sending
her lamb unprotected among those ravening wolves of Gideons, Mrs.
Pollock could not bring herself to face the ordeal.

"I am an artist," she said. "Not, I admit, a creative artist, but
an artist. I cannot endure these performances of the unprofessional.
The banality, the crudeness, of them . . . Even five minutes of it are
a crucifixion of my whole being. To sit for an hour, two hours, it
would keel me . . . You may go, my child. You have gone so far
from me in these few weeks that a leetle further will make no matter
. . . I will order the car."

"Oh, not the car, Maman," laughed Ann-Marie. "The Village
Hall isn't any distance. I can easily walk."

"Walk!" echoed Mrs. Pollock with a groan. "You will keel
yourself with this walkeeng."

So Ann-Marie, bareheaded, wearing a loose tweed coat, her fair
hair blown about by the wind, her face lit by its new glow of health
and happiness, limped briskly up the hall and into her seat next Colin,

slipping her hand for a second into his before she took off her coat. To be there with him, to meet his smile, was like coming into the warmth and sunshine out of the dark.

"Well?" he said. "Did you break the news?"

"Yes."

"And it was with you, the deluge, I suppose."

The curtain was going up.

"I'll tell you in the interval," she whispered.

She had chosen, as she thought, a propitious moment for breaking the news of her engagement to her mother. Mrs. Pollock had received by the morning post the copy of a book she had wanted and had believed to be out of print; she had been to London and had found at her favourite Italian shop in Soho various commodities that she had not been able to get since before the war; she had bought a new and extremely becoming *negligée* . . . But it was useless. Mrs. Pollock's horror burst forth in a torrential flood, overwhelming all Ann-Marie's pleading and self-justification. She called Colin a "blackguard" (which Mrs. Pollock pronounced as spelt), a "thief," even (for some reason not clear to Ann-Marie, or, probably, to Mrs. Pollock, either) a "cut-throat." Her Little Flower was "a poor deluded one," a "victeem," dragged in the dust and debauched by this goat-satyr in human form that was Colin.

"Maman," expostulated Ann-Marie, "we've hardly kissed each other."

"I speak of things of the soul, of the mind," said Mrs. Pollock, throwing out her arms. "It is thus he has debauched you. You are no longer the Little Flower you were. Everything fine in you has been made coarse, everything high dragged down to his beast's level."

"I'm going to marry him," said Ann-Marie firmly.

"Nevair with my permeesion," said Mrs. Pollock dramatically.

"Then I shall marry him without."

Mrs. Pollock replied by a stream of French so incoherent that even Ann-Marie could not follow it.

"Ann-Marie," said Mrs. Pollock suddenly the next morning, "I will agree to this marriage on one condition."

"Yes, Maman?"

"That you continue to live here. That I can still look after you. You are fragile and delicate. Even if you marry this Colleen" (she always pronounced Colin's name as if he were one of the female inhabitants of Ireland) "you will need a mother's care. There is room here for three of us. I will—accept this man, make him welcome. I will share you with him. But I will not give you up. I know my duty too well for that. It would be murder. You take all I do for granted. That is natural. I do not complain. You do not realize that it is my care that keeps you alive. I watch over you . . . tend you . . . guard you from ill . . . You will give up your work if you marry?"

"Yes."

"And you will live here with me. This Colleen will live here too. I will look after you both. It is a great sacrifice I am making. I do it only because I put your happiness before my own."

The curtain fell to a fury of applause at the end of the first act. The hall was inadequately ventilated and most of the audience went into the lane outside for a breath of air during the interval. Colin and Ann made their way out with the others . . .

Laura turned round to see if the Fieldings were going out. She must see Hubert to-night. He was watching her, and, meeting his gaze, she tried to tell him by her eyes what she had decided. Then, glancing away, she met Letitia's eyes, bright with malice, and turned back, her heart beating quickly. When she turned round again, they had gone out. She half rose to follow them, then sat down. With Trixie and Cynthia and the others there, she would not get a chance to speak to him alone and she could not bear to talk to all of them as if—nothing were happening. She must wait till to-morrow night. They had arranged to meet to-morrow night . . .

Derek Frame came down from the stage and leant over the seats in front to talk to the Gideons.

"Roger's jolly good, isn't he?" he said.

"*Isn't* he!" said Mrs. Gideon proudly.

"May we go behind the curtain and see him?" said Richard.

"No, darling," said Mrs. Gideon.

"*Please!*" said Rachel. "Well, may we go behind the curtain and just stand and watch. We won't be a nuisance. We won't speak to anyone."

"We'll hardly breathe," said Richard.

"Come on," smiled Derek. "It's all right, Mrs. Gideon. They won't be in anyone's way. I'll keep an eye on them."

"Thanks *frightfully*," said the Two.

He went off with the two of them towards the steps that led up to the platform.

Mrs. Gideon glanced at Laura's pale profile bent over her programme.

"I think the way they've managed the scenery is so clever," she said.

"Yes," agreed Laura, "and the dresses."

They talked about dresses and scenery, but their thoughts were far away. Laura was thinking of Hubert, and Mrs. Gideon was praying: "Please, God take care of her . . . and if Humphrey can help, please let him . . . She's so young . . ."

Colin and Ann-Marie joined the procession of couples and groups promenading up and down the country lane.

"Well?" he said, stopping to light a cigarette.

"She says she'll agree to the marriage if we live with her."

Colin threw her a half-smile.

"I'm not marrying you on those terms, my girl, so don't you think it."

"But, Colin, it might be the thin edge of the wedge."

"It'll be that, all right."

"*Listen!*" she laughed. "I mean, for *us*. We can start there with her . . . and gradually accustom her to the idea of our going and finding a place of our own."

"Now you listen to me," said Colin. "I've known dozens of young married couples who've started life with the girl's mother, and, even when the mother's well-intentioned, it's seldom been a success. I don't think that your mother is well-intentioned. In fact, I know perfectly well that she'll be out to wreck our marriage from the start."

"She couldn't do that."

"Don't be too sure."

"We love each other."

"That's the trouble."

"What shall we do then?"

"We'll have to think again."

Cynthia and Letitia passed, Letitia looking tall and elegant in a black velvet cloak lined with white satin. They were followed by Godfrey and Trixie, Hubert and Lucy bringing up the rear. Miss Parsons had gone behind the scenes to mend one of the actresses' dresses that had been torn in the first act.

"Aunt Letitia looks very grand to-night," said Colin.

Ann-Marie pressed closer to him.

"She's got snake's eyes," she said.

"Rubbish! She's supposed to be a very handsome woman."

Derek Frame came to the door of the Village Hall and rang a bell to show that the actors were ready for the second act.

As Colin went in, Derek said:

"You ought to be proud of young Roger."

"I am."

"I've had the Two behind on the stage helping with the scene shifting. They're tickled to death with themselves."

Colin laughed.

"I bet they are. There'll be no holding them."

The next day Roger was suffering the inevitable reaction. He had not slept the night before the performance or the night after it, and he was moody, difficult and on edge. Over-sensitive at the best of times, swinging always between one extreme and the other, he was at one moment thrilled by the certainty of his success and at the next convinced that he had made a dismal failure of the whole thing and exposed himself to the ridicule of everyone present. The one occasion on which he had forgotten his lines was magnified in his mind into a catastrophe damning the whole performance. Looking through the curtain just before the second act, he had seen Colin and Derek Frame laughing together at the back of the hall and was so certain they were laughing at his performance that his whole body had turned

hot with humiliation. The sincerity of Colin's congratulations afterwards had reassured him, but he was still touchy and suspicious and
ready to take offence.

Mrs. Gideon had tried to make him stay in bed this morning—
he looked pale and exhausted, with dark shadows beneath his eyes—
but he refused. He must go and help clear up the Village Hall.
They had promised to have everything out by three o'clock, because
it was wanted for a whist drive.

"But surely, Roger, they can do it without you."

"I've said I'm going and I'm going," said Roger, looking so tense
and speaking with such barely concealed impatience that she said no
more.

He did not come in to lunch, sending a message that there was so
much still to do that he couldn't spare the time. Mrs. Gideon sent
him back some sandwiches by the boy who had brought the message,
but about a quarter of an hour later she saw the boy pass down the
road, eating the sandwiches himself.

Quite apart from Roger, there was a shadow over the house.
Laura had withdrawn herself from them. There was a far-away look
in her eyes, and she, who had once been the soul of the home, seemed
now to have no concern in it. She did her tasks absently and half-
heartedly, ignored the Two, avoided her mother's eyes. She was so
far away from them that not one of them could reach her. She's
terribly unhappy, thought Mrs. Gideon. She's persuaded herself
that she's happy, but she knows in her heart that she isn't. I think
I could bear it, whatever she did, if she were happy . . .

Laura went into the village to do some shopping after lunch, and
Mrs. Gideon sat in the garden, knitting a pair of socks for Richard.
She had forgotten that it was Miss Parsons' "afternoon off" till she
saw the neat little figure at the gate. The sight seemed to lift something of the weight from her spirit.

"Oh, this *is* nice!" she said. "Come in and talk to me. I'm all
alone."

"Get me some mending then," said Miss Parsons. "I've brought
my own thimble."

"Isn't it dreadful of me to let you do it!" said Mrs. Gideon. She
went into the house and came back with her mending-basket.

"There's masses," she said.

"Any priority?" said Miss Parsons.

"Well, Rachel will need that Liberty bodice on Monday."

"Right. I'll start on that . . . Now let's talk about the play. I
was so thrilled I lay awake all night thinking about it. Wasn't
Roger grand! I'm certain no professional could have done it
as well!"

"Oh, I don't know . . ." said Mrs. Gideon, then, giving up the
attempt to be modest about it, "Well, frankly, I don't think anyone
could, but I'm their mother, and I think they're all wonderful . . .
And now tell me about your plans, dear. Have you decided?"

"Yes. I'm going. After all, if I make a hopeless mess of it, they can only send me home, and I'm back where I was before, with no great harm done. It seems rather an adventure at my age, of course, but one has to start adventuring sometime. At least, if I don't now, I never will. It's my last chance, and I'm going to take it. I don't really want to go on being a companion to old ladies for the rest of my life."

"I expect you find Aunt Letitia rather trying."

Miss Parsons looked up from the Liberty bodice with a twinkle.

"You said it, not me," she said.

Laura came in by the garden gate and went straight into the house without looking at them. Upstairs, in her bedroom, she sat on the bed, staring dazedly in front of her . . . So sudden and short had been the encounter that it seemed she must have dreamed it. She had been leaving the post office when she came face to face with Trixie. They had stood motionless, looking at each other in the sunny village street. Trixie's hair fell from its red ribbon snood on to her shoulders. Her cotton dress reached her knees and she wore red sandals on her bare feet. She looked like a little girl . . . Her eyes were fixed on Laura's, not in anger or sulkiness or defiance, but with a curious earnestness. Suddenly she spoke in a low level voice.

"Laura," she said, "you can't do it. I'm going to have a baby."

Laura's hand flew to her throat. Her voice came in a whisper.

"He never told me."

"He doesn't know. Don't tell him . . . please."

Again they looked at each other with that strange silent intensity, then Trixie turned on her heel and went in the direction of Westover.

Laura had come back to Greenways, walking blindly, hardly aware of what she was doing. If Trixie were going to have a baby, Hubert must stay with her. Or must he? Did it make all that difference?

She dropped her head into her hands. Oh God! Was it all to start over again—the wondering, the indecision, the being torn in two?

She heard Roger come in, heard Miss Parsons' eager congratulations and his pleased boyish laugh. She glanced at her watch and, rising wearily, went downstairs to put the kettle on. They had just settled down to tea ("Let's have it in peace before the Two come in," Mrs. Gideon had said) when James arrived. His arrival flurried the little party.

"Oh dear, I wasn't expecting you, James," said Mrs. Gideon, adding hastily, "but it's *lovely* to see you. You must stay and have some tea."

"No tea, thanks," said James. "Got to get back for an engagement in town. Just brought some papers for you to sign, Julia."

"Oh dear! . . . Have you put a pencil mark where I sign? I always seem to sign in the wrong place."

"Yes, you signed all the last lot on the date line and the ones before that on the witnesses' line."

"That's the sort of thing I do," explained Mrs. Gideon. "Documents fluster me. They make me feel that I've done something criminal that has to be covered up."

"Here they are," said James, a little impatiently.

"Come and be a witness, Laura," said Mrs. Gideon, and the two went indoors.

"Sorry I've been so long," said Mrs. Gideon when they returned. "I'd lost my spectacles. At least I hadn't lost them, I'd put them away in a safe place."

"When Blanche just loses anything, it's all right," said Laura. "We soon find it. But when she puts it away in a safe place, it's hopeless. It takes *hours*."

"They *are* safe places," said Mrs. Gideon. "but I forget where they are." She handed the papers to James. "I've signed them, James. What are they about?"

"Good Lord!" exploded James. "Haven't you even read them?"

"No, I just found the pencil marks and signed there."

"Surely you remember that when last I saw you we decided to re-invest——"

"It doesn't matter, James," said Mrs. Gideon placidly, sitting down and taking up her knitting. "I don't really want to know. I shall have forgotten five minutes after you've told me. Besides, I'm not terribly interested in money . . . There! I thought I'd dropped a stitch. It's gone down five rows."

"Give it to me," said Miss Parsons.

"Actually I like being poor," confessed Mrs. Gideon.

James shook his head in sorrowful bewilderment.

" 'The rich have butlers and no friends; we have friends and no butlers,' " quoted Roger. There was a sardonic half-smile on his dark good-looking young face.

James turned his gaze slowly on his nephew, and the two looked at each other in mutual animosity. In both their minds the drop of poison, so carefully instilled by Letitia, had been working for some time. James saw Roger mimicking him, making fun of him, thinking how cleverly he had fooled him by destroying the evidence of his "unsteadiness." Roger saw James grumbling to everyone he knew about his school fees, grudging every penny, regretting the passing impulse of generosity that had induced him to offer to pay them—for Letitia had not failed to repeat to Roger, with the few necessary additions, what James had said when he had lunch with her.

"Hope you've been doing some studying these holidays," said James gruffly.

"I've not had much time for studying," said Roger.

"He's been getting up this play . . ." said Mrs. Gideon uneasily, aware of the tension in the atmosphere.

"Roger took De Levis," said Laura, "and he was splendid."

James looked at Roger again, and the contempt in the dark eyes stung him.

"Maybe," he said dryly, "but I don't pay two hundred a year for that sort of tomfoolery."

Roger sprang to his feet. His face was white.

"You can keep your damned two hundred a year," he said, "I don't want it."

James had flushed a dusky red. For the first time since his childhood he lost his temper.

"I'll do that without your advice," he rasped. "If this is the sort of thing your education teaches you, you impudent young puppy, you can do without it as far as I'm concerned."

Then, without another word, he pocketed the documents and stumped off down the path to the gate.

Miss Parsons, feeling that the crisis was one best left to the family to deal with alone, took a murmured farewell of them and followed James.

Seeing her, he held the gate open.

"Coming my way?" he muttered.

"No, I'm *not* coming your way," said Miss Parsons. "I'm going in the other direction, but before I go I'd like to tell you what I think of you. You're a mean, conceited, pompous fool. You ought to be proud of the privilege of educating a fine boy like Roger. Instead of which, you goad the boy into saying what he doesn't mean and then turn on him. You ought to be ashamed of yourself. And I wish you joy of the two hundred a year you've saved this afternoon."

She turned and walked away. He stood staring after her for a few moments, still brick-red and breathing heavily, then stumped on in the direction of the station.

He looked a very angry man, but he was feeling hurt and bewildered and intensely mortified . . .

The Gideons looked at each other in silent dismay.

"Oh Roger!" said Mrs. Gideon at last, reproachfully.

"What are we going to do now?" said Laura. "He meant it, you know. He won't pay a penny more."

"We'll have to wait till Colin comes home," said Mrs. Gideon, "and talk it over with him."

"And do you expect me to sit here," said Roger hysterically, "and wait for Colin to come home and bully me?"

"Colin's never bullied any of us in his life," flashed Laura.

"And he's not going to get the chance to start with me."

"Now, Roger, don't work yourself into a state like that," said Mrs. Gideon. "If Uncle James won't go on paying your fees, we can manage somehow. There are other schools. I must find out exactly what I can afford——"

"I don't want anything from any of you," said Roger, his voice coming in shrill sobbing breaths. "I can look after myself. I can earn my own living . . . I——"

He turned and went indoors. They heard the slamming of his bedroom door.

When Colin came home they told him the story over his tea. He looked worried but said little.

"I've been upstairs several times," said Mrs. Gideon. "He won't answer and he's locked his door."

"Leave him alone," said Colin. "He'll have come to his senses by the morning."

But in the morning Roger was nowhere to be found. His room was empty and his bed had not been slept in . . . He had taken his night things, and a small attaché case.

XV

It was four days before Roger was found, and it was Colin who found him. The police traced him as far as Camberwell, and there the trail ended. A lorry-driver had given him a lift so far, and Roger had told him that he was making his way to Liverpool, but further enquiries had proved fruitless. Mrs. Gideon went about, white-faced and desperate, secretly blaming herself for what had happened. In her dreams she seemed to see Humphrey looking at her sadly, reproachfully . . . He had always said that Roger would need careful handling as he grew older, and she hadn't handled him carefully, she hadn't troubled to understand him. She had failed them both—Roger and Humphrey. Outwardly she was as quiet and gentle and self-contained as ever, but Colin could not bear to see the look of torment on her face.

"He'll be all right, darling," he said. "Don't worry so much."

"If I could be sure!" she said. "If . . ." she broke down suddenly. It was the first time in his life that Colin had ever seen her cry. "If I could be sure he hadn't——"

"Listen," said Colin, "I'll go up to London to-morrow—it seems the best place to start from—and, God helping me, I won't come back without him."

She looked up at him, her eyes still heavy with tears, but full of a wild unreasonable hope.

"Oh, Colin!" she said.

Colin set off the next morning and went to the spot where the lorry-driver had put Roger down. The police had taken for granted that Roger had made his way from there towards the North, but Colin wasn't sure. The police didn't know Roger and he did . . . Standing there, he imagined himself to be Roger . . . Roger's temperament was mercurial. He was full of a nervous energy that would impel him to fantastic effort, then suddenly desert him . . . He was physically and mentally exhausted when he started on his enterprise. Standing there, as Roger, looking round at the dreary little streets, Colin felt his courage fail. He was secretly aghast by what he had done, terrified at the thought of facing the world alone, upheld only by a sensitive pride that would not admit defeat or accept humiliation . . . . He would instinctively make for the nearest shelter. Colin spent the rest of the day threading his way through the maze of dingy streets, going from door to door asking for news of Roger. He was met sometimes by sympathy, but more often by suspicion or open hostility . . . and his enquiries had no result.

He found a room for the night and started again first thing the next morning. It was about mid-day when, passing the end of a side street, he saw a boy going into a house, carrying some newspapers under his arm. He was Roger's height and Roger's build, but he had vanished so quickly that Colin could not be certain. He waited a few moments, then went to the house and knocked at the door. A blowsy, harsh-featured woman answered his knock. She wore a dirty overall, pinned across her chest by a rusty safety-pin, and shapeless felt slippers from which her bare toes protruded. She held the door open a few inches and regarded him with hard eyes and grimly-pursed mouth, waiting for him to speak.

"Have you a boy lodging with you?" he said.

"What business is it of yours?" she answered.

"I think he's my young brother," said Colin. "I'd like to speak to him."

She opened the door wider, still scowling suspiciously.

"So that's it. He's run off, has he? Thought there was something fishy . . . He's in the room at the top of the stairs."

She stepped aside to let him pass, then stood watching him as he went up the filthy uncarpeted stairs. A smell compounded of dirt, dust and decay hung over the place. The walls were thick with grease. Colin opened the door at the top of the stairs and entered the room.

Roger sat at a table, surrounded by newspapers open at "Situations Vacant" column.

So great was Colin's relief that a rush of anger, as unexpected as it was uncontrollable, surged over him.

"You crazy young fool," he shouted, "what the devil d'you think you're doing?"

Roger looked at him, his eyes big and startled in his white face.

The past days had been a nightmare . . . He had started off on the adventure, upheld by a certainty that he could "make good." He could go on the stage, get a job on a newspaper . . . anything. He would return rich and famous, and his family would realize how badly they had treated him. He had taken with him his fountain pen, watch, and stamp album, thinking that the proceeds would keep him till he had found work. He had sold them all for a good deal less than they were worth and had spent the last penny on the newspapers he had bought this morning. He had been to theatrical agencies and newspaper offices and been impatiently turned away. He had told the theatrical agent of his performance of De Levis in *Loyalties*, and the man had laughed. It was quite a kindly laugh, but Roger could still hear it.

"Won't you try me with something," he had pleaded. "Let me read a part . . . Honestly, I *can* act."

"I haven't any more time to waste," said the man. "Clear out and don't come back."

Yesterday he had applied for several clerks' jobs in the City—walking there and back because he dared not spend money on the bus fare, only to be met with the same impatient refusal.

"Job's filled . . . No, there's nothing else. Sorry."

He had lain awake most of the night, thinking of his father. His father seemed now to be his only hope. He still clung to the certainty that his father had not been killed and that he would return unexpectedly. Light-headed with lack of food and sleep, he began to imagine his father's coming to this house. He was vague as to how it would happen, but it would happen. The door would open, and his father would come in and—all his troubles would be at an end.

Sitting at the table, the newspaper in front of him, he had shut his eyes and was desperately willing that his father should come to him . . . I'll kill myself if he doesn't . . . I'll throw myself into the river . . . I won't go back . . .

And then the door opened and Colin stood in the doorway. Strain and anxiety had deepened the lines on Colin's face, and, for a moment, it might have been his father standing there. Roger turned ice cold and his heart raced . . .

Colin was still shouting at him, but he was so dazed that only a few words reached him. "Selfishness" . . . "stupidity" . . . "mother's anxiety" . . .

Suddenly Colin stopped and they looked at each other in silence.

"I'm sorry," stammered Roger.

Colin tried to retain his anger, but the stony look on the boy's face melted it.

"All right, Roger," he said quietly. "I won't say anything more . . . No great harm done, after all, I suppose. You'll come back with me?"

Roger nodded. Colin saw that he was fighting back his tears and went to stand at the window, his hands in his pockets, looking down at the street, till he had recovered himself. He knew that Roger would never forgive anyone who had seen him cry. When he turned round, Roger was still sitting at the table, his head resting on his hands.

"Get your things together," said Colin, "and have a wash. I'll go out and telephone Mother and find a taxi." He glanced round the room. It was furnished with a camp bed, a wooden table and a

chair with a broken back. It was as filthy as the rest of the house.
"How much do you owe this woman?"

Roger raised his face—a child's face, marked by tears, hunger and
sleeplessness.

"Nothing. She made me pay in advance."

"Right. I'll be as quick as I can."

Roger was on the doorstep with his attaché case when Colin came
back in the taxi. In the sunlight the shadows under his eyes looked
startlingly black.

"Had any breakfast?" said Colin.

Roger shook his head.

"When did you last have anything to eat?"

"I don't know."

Colin looked at him . . . He wanted to wipe that look of defeat
from the young face, to wipe from the young mind the memory of
the squalor and dreariness in which he had spent those days.

"We'd better have some lunch . . . The Savoy," he said to the
taxi-man.

They were fortunate in getting a table, and it happened that
several parties of gay young people were lunching near them. Roger,
always sensitive to atmosphere, responded instinctively to the festivity
in the air. His eyes brightened, the tight line of his lips relaxed, the
set strained look left his face.

"What shall we have?" said Colin, studying the menu. "Beef,
braised ham, veal . . ."

"Veal seems appropriate," said Roger, and they both laughed.

"Let's celebrate by a bottle of champagne and damn the expense,"
said Colin. "We don't come here every day."

They talked of superficial things—of the people around them, and
even, ignoring what had happened in the interval, the play. Colin
told him that a rumour of the Vicar's engagement to the postmistress
had flown round the village, only to be at once contradicted. It had
been said that he had hummed his proposal to her over the counter,
when buying a book of stamps, with his sister standing by. Once
Roger tried stammeringly to express his contrition for the anxiety he
had caused, but Colin cut him short.

"We'll talk about that when we get home. Not that there's much
to talk about. You've been a prize idiot and you'll do all you can
to put it right, won't you?"

"I'll do anything you want me to."

"That's all there is to be said then, so let's forget it."

Though their conversation was trivial and flippant (each made a
good many rather poor jokes that the other much appreciated), both
were aware of a new relationship between them. In spite of the
failure of his gesture of independence, Roger was happy. He had
stopped fighting against Colin. That moment when Colin stood in
the doorway and he had identified him with his father remained and
would remain. He was willing at last to yield Colin his father's place,

and he realized that it was what he had longed to do from the beginning. The end of the struggle was like the cessation of some physical pain. He felt tired but utterly at peace.

Colin, too, was happy in their new relation without understanding how it had come about . . . They hadn't had enough patience with the kid. They'd let him get on their nerves. They must all be more careful in future. For, in spite of everything, he was a grand kid . . .

He took out his watch.

"Well," he said, "we ought to be getting on . . . Enjoyed your lunch?"

"It's been—marvellous. Thanks awfully, Colin. You're—frightfully decent."

Colin looked at him with a twinkle.

"I'm a darn fool," he said. "What I ought to do with you is give you a damn good hiding."

"I know," grinned Roger with unprecedented humility.

He went with Colin out into the sunshine of the Strand.

He was going back, but, thanks to Colin, not in disgrace or humiliation.

Colin certainly was (despite his literary bent, Roger's vocabulary was in moments of deepest emotion still that of a schoolboy) frightfully decent . . .

XVI

CYNTHIA stood on the platform of the London station with Adrian Maple, waiting for the train that would take her back to Nettleford.

She looked tired and bored, he sulky and resentful.

"You've not played the game with me, Cynthia."

"I promised you nothing."

"Not in words, perhaps, but——"

"I wanted a change from an atmosphere that was getting on my nerves. That's the only reason I went away."

"But——"

"You insisted on coming with me. If you chose to misunderstand the situation that's your affair."

"I don't think I did misunderstand the situation," he said.

She tapped her toe impatiently on the platform and looked away from him. Despite the cold aloofness of her manner, she was feeling guilty and a little ashamed. Adrian had been in love with her since he was a boy and, before she met Godfrey, she had almost persuaded herself that she was in love with him. He was kind, good-tempered, amusing and very well off. If she hadn't met Godfrey that night, she would have been engaged to Adrian the next day. She had received in the afternoon one of the letters Adrian wrote at regular intervals, begging her to marry him, and she had decided—finally as it seemed to her—to accept his proposal. So it was to Adrian that her mind turned when she felt that Godfrey had humiliated her beyond forgiveness.

Adrian had continued to write to her since her marriage, though, for the most part, she had ignored his letters. The first few meetings in London had been quite successful. Lunch or dinner in smart restaurants—a welcome change of food and atmosphere from the *ménage* of Westover—a play or concert that gave them something to talk about . . . a few quick crowded hours . . . then back to Westover with the bitter exultant feeling in her heart that she was punishing Godfrey for the slight he had put on her. She always told Godfrey when she had been out with Adrian, and he accepted the information in his usual pleasant unemotional manner, sometimes without comment, sometimes with a few amiable questions about what they had seen. She could almost hear him saying to himself, "It'll blow over . ."

Her contempt of him increased, and with it a baffled feeling (as though she were hurling herself against some impregnable rock) that changed gradually to recklessness. She'd *make* him fight or show him up as the coward he was . . .

She mentioned the week-end to Adrian on impulse, but, once it was suggested, he gave her no peace, and, the more she thought about it, the more it seemed a solution of her problem. She couldn't go on living with a man she despised. There were no children to complicate the situation. And Adrian . . . she had loved him—or nearly loved him—once. It should not be difficult to learn to love him again now that she no longer loved Godfrey. At any rate, he would be the means of gaining her freedom . . .

She had stipulated for single rooms and he had agreed. Women had, he knew, their whims and fancies even on such occasions as these. He had not the slightest doubt that she intended to sleep with him, and he had every confidence in his own ability to break down any show of reluctance she might think proper to put up. Both of them, when they set out to the hotel in Sussex, took it for granted that they would return with their future settled and their boats burnt behind them.

Adrian was physically and mentally a complete contrast to Godfrey. He was small and dark and vivacious, with the reputation of being witty and charming. Cynthia was fully prepared to surrender to his charm . . . but somehow, in the years that had elapsed since she had last felt its effect, it seemed to have lost its potency. He was the same, she knew. It was she who had changed . . . Before the end of the first evening he was badly on her nerves. He was restless and fidgety, jerking forward in his chair whenever he spoke, crossing and uncrossing his legs, playing with his tie, drumming his fingers on the edge of his chair. Though she tried not to, she couldn't help contrasting his manner with the restfulness of Godfrey. In his excitement, he joked too much with the waiters and again she couldn't help contrasting Godfrey's quiet, pleasant dignified manner with such people . . . She was out of tune with his "wit." His jokes seemed puerile to her, his anecdotes long and pointless. Had he always been like this, she wondered despairingly, or had she grown up in the meantime? His laugh—and he laughed frequently—was high-pitched and a little shrill. There was something faintly girlish, she decided, about his whole personality. He remained full of high spirits on the second day, but, when her door was still locked against him, a faint sulkiness invaded his manner.

The inn they had chosen was set in a countryside that would have been lovely, had it not rained throughout the week-end. They played billiards, two-handed bridge, did crossword puzzles, read books. Her boredom was a physical oppression. He still joked and laughed gallantly, without respite, becoming each moment more hopelessly on her nerves. Only on the last morning (having knocked in vain at intervals throughout the night on her door) did he become silent and morose, feeling that he had been made a fool of. She, too, was resentful, as though he had deliberately failed her and closed her only way of escape. They breakfasted without speaking . . .

The train came in, and, looking at each other with disillusioned eyes, they took their leave of each other. She's changed, he thought. There's no fun in her any longer. Gosh! how she snapped at me last night! She's getting—shrewish. She's played me a dirty trick, but I'm well out of it.

"Good-bye, Adrian," she said, and thought: It's seemed more like a month than a week-end. It's going to be heaven to-night not to have to listen to his silly jokes. I think I'd have murdered him if I'd married him . . .

But her new dislike of Adrian did not lessen her anger against Godfrey. It rather increased it, for this week-end seemed a further humiliation inflicted on her by him.

Adrian raised his hat, and the train slid out of the station.

Cynthia leant back in her seat, and her lips curled into a little twisted smile. The week-end hadn't been altogether wasted. She had the hotel bill in her handbag made out to Mr. and Mrs. Adrian Maple. Upon investigation, of course, it would not furnish grounds for divorce, but Godfrey could not know that—yet. The week-end had done what she wanted of it—given her a weapon that would force Godfrey to fight or own himself a coward.

No one was in the flat when she reached Westover, but when, after bathing and changing, she went into the sitting-room, Godfrey had come home and was in his usual chair by the window, reading the evening paper. He looked up at her with his slow smile.

"I didn't know you were back," he said. "Had a good time?"

"I spent the week-end with Adrian, Godfrey."

He looked at her, and his expression, pleasant, mildly interested, did not change. Her eyes met his with a long cruel stare. The silence stretched a full minute. She thought, I'll *make* you do something. If you never faced an unpleasant fact in your life before, you shall face this . . . I'll *make* you . . . She opened her bag.

"Here's the hotel bill."

He made no movement to take it.

"You can show me as many hotel bills as you like, my dear," he said. "You've not slept with Adrian Maple."

"How do you know?"

"Because I know you."

Her lip curled.

"So that's to be your attitude, is it? Your wife is, in the very nature of things, too noble to be capable of such an action."

"Not at all," he said, still in that level good-humoured voice, "but I know you so well that if you'd slept with Adrian Maple I'd have known it the second you came into the room . . . And, by God, if you had——" He stopped and the sudden steely glint in his eyes faded again into his lazy smile. "It's Mrs. Grimes' evening off, isn't it? Can I help you at all?"

"No, thank you."

She went into the kitchen, closed the door and sat down on the nearest chair, because her knees were too unsteady to support her any longer. She hadn't forced him to fight, but she'd forced him to show that he could fight, if he thought it worth his while. Or had she? Had she imagined that sudden hardening of his pleasant face, that steely glint in his eye? Was she romanticising him into a sort of Sir Percy Blakeney, because she had to love him, whatever he was? She'd proved that to herself, at any rate. She'd fought desperately against her love, but she'd been beaten by it . . . Adrian giggling in the hotel lounge . . . whining on the station platform . . . Well, she knew it now. For better or worse, she was Godfrey's woman. Right at the bottom, she'd known it all the time.

Only Godfrey, Cynthia and Trixie sat down at dinner.

"Where's Hubert?" said Godfrey.

"I don't know," replied Trixie casually.

"He's probably at Greenways," said Cynthia.

She spoke quite innocently. So absorbed had she been by her own troubles that Trixie's had escaped her notice. She had taken for granted that Hubert's frequent visits to Greenways meant only a friendship with the Gideons in general and Colin in particular. Trixie understood the words as a taunt. Her eyes smouldered angrily.

"Nothing of much moment has happened while you've been away, my dear," said Godfrey, instinctively tiding over the awkward moment. "Young Roger has returned, Mrs. Pollock seems to have hysterics every night and the butcher sent us an amazing joint. None of us could make out what part of what animal it was."

"Oh yes, you've been away, haven't you?" said Trixie with quiet insolence. "How's the boy friend? Did he come up to scratch?"

For answer Cynthia leant across the table and slapped her face.

There was a sudden tense silence, then Cynthia said unsteadily:

"You've made me do something I shall be ashamed of for the rest of my life."

Trixie sat with a half-smile on her face, one cheek pale, the other red from Cynthia's palm.

"You should have done it before," she said. "I often wondered why you didn't."

"I'll go and dish up the pudding," said Cynthia shortly, and retreated to the kitchen.

A moment later they heard her voice.

"Will you come and give me a hand for a moment, Trixie?"

Trixie rose and joined her.

"Will you take up the pudding while I see to the sauce?"

There was a friendliness in her voice that Trixie had never heard before.

Trixie turned the pudding out into a dish, then said:

"Cynthia."

"Yes?"

"Did you know that Hubert was in love with Laura Gideon?"

Cynthia turned round from the gas stove.

"No."

"It's my own fault, I suppose. I asked for it, just as I asked for what I got from you in there. I didn't really love him till I found that he was in love with Laura and then I began to love him so terribly that I don't know how to bear it."

"I'm—sorry, Trixie . . . What's going to happen?"

"I don't know . . . Hubert wants me to divorce him so that he can marry her, but Laura can't make up her mind about it. I'm—just waiting."

"Will you divorce him?"

"If he wants me to."

Hubert was in the dining-room when they got back. He looked pale and dispirited.

"I'm terribly sorry I'm late, Cynthia. I'd have rung you but I thought I'd just make it . . . Some blasted firm wanted their stuff in by to-morrow."

He went out again immediately after dinner, without saying where he was going. Watching from the window, Trixie saw him turn in the direction of Greenways. She yawned ostentatiously.

"I'll go and mend some stockings," she said. "My ladders would stretch from here to Heaven. I haven't any of the right coloured mending silk. I never have."

"Take what you like from my work-box," said Cynthia.

"Thanks."

Alone with Godfrey, Cynthia relaxed wearily in her chair and closed her eyes.

"I'm so tired I could die," she said.

"Poor kid!" said Godfrey, standing on the hearthrug and filling his pipe.

She opened her eyes. The week-end with Adrian had given her a strange disturbing sense of precariousness. She wanted to feel secure, to feel tied to Godfrey for ever . . .

"Godfrey, this isn't a home," she said suddenly. "Let's have a home—we can find one if we try hard enough. A home and children."

He was silent for a few moments, then said:

"I thought you didn't want children."

She answered dreamily, her eyes fixed on the fireplace: "I shouldn't mind a little boy with grey eyes and fair hair."

He looked down at her with a twinkle as he lit his pipe.

"Or a little girl with dark hair and the devil of a temper."

Her eyes met his and returned his smile.

"She'd be better than nothing."

"All right . . . Let's chance our luck."

Trixie came in with an armful of stockings.

"The damn things are all holes," she said.

"Don't bother with them to-night, Trixie," said Cynthia. "You look all in. Go to bed, and I'll get you some hot milk."

"I'd rather have a nice cup of tea," grinned Trixie, flopping into a chair.

"You shall. We'll all have one," said Cynthia.

XVII

COLIN leant against the apple tree directing a boxing match between the Two. The gloves were on the big size, but, on the whole, they were making satisfactory progress. They wore grey flannel shorts and green blouses. Their faces were grimly set . . .

Occasionally Colin's eyes wandered to the gate, for he was expecting Ann, and they had a good deal to discuss.

Roger came out of the house, his cricket bat under his arm. He was playing in the village cricket team against Nettleford—the most important match of the season.

"Good luck!" said Colin.

"Thanks," said Roger. "I shall need it."

The combatants ceased hostilities.

"Don't get a duck," shouted Richard.

"May I go with him to the bus stop, and carry his bat?" said Rachel.

"No, you mayn't," said Colin. "People don't go to cricket matches hung round with kids."

"Cheerio," said Roger from the gate.

There had been a new suggestion of stability about Roger since his escapade. He was less touchy, felt himself less isolated from the others, thought less about Westover and his father. Though he was ashamed of his flight, the distress and anxiety it had caused had shown that they *did* care, that he *was* one of them. And his new relations with Colin gave him a feeling of family responsibility, a desire to "pull his weight."

James had come over the day after Roger's return, and the interview between them had been not without a certain dignity. Both had prepared stately well-worded apologies, which they delivered almost simultaneously in the manner of a Greek chorus, each of them far more taken up with the apology he was delivering than the one he was receiving. The atmosphere was somewhat constrained for the remainder of James' visit, but the foundation of a better understanding had been laid and, on taking his leave, James had looked at Roger with something of the old pride . . .

"That's enough for to-day," said Colin, seeing Ann approaching the gate with Trixie Fielding.

The Two ran down to open the gate for them.

"We met on the way," said Trixie with her gamin grin. "I wasn't asked. I just came."

"Gate-crasher!" said Richard.

"You don't *need* to be asked," said Rachel. "If you did you'd be asked every minute of every day, because we love you . . ."

"Where are the others?" said Trixie, looking round.

"Roger's gone to a cricket match, and Mummy and Laura are doing the shopping in Nettleford. Colin's been giving us another boxing lesson. Richard made my nose bleed in the one we had yesterday, and I didn't cry."

"You nearly did," said Richard.

"I never said I nearly didn't," said Rachel. "Can't we go on a bit longer, Colin?"

"Not to-day."

"Let's go to the stream and sail the boats then."

"Put the gloves away first . . . Come and sit down, Trixie."

"No, Trixie's coming to sail boats with us. You will, won't you, darling? It's always more fun when you're there. And we won't ask Richard."

"I'm coming whether you ask me or not."

"Gate-crasher!"

"Whose boats are they, anyway?"

"They're only bits of paper—envelopes and letters and things."

Richard brought out the box which contained the paper boats he had made that morning—large, medium-sized and tiny ones, fashioned from newspapers, old letters and envelopes.

"Here! Where did you get all that stuff?" said Colin.

"It's waste paper," said Richard virtuously. "It's what we used to give to salvage in the war."

"Don't you *dare* touch anything on my desk!"

"We don't touch things on people's desks," said Richard with dignity.

"All right. Keep your hair on," said Colin, rumpling it as he spoke. Richard did a couple of cart-wheels on the lawn.

"Don't show off," said Rachel, who couldn't do them. "Come on. Let's get cracking . . ."

"Well?" said Colin to Ann when they had gone.

"Colin, it's hopeless. We had the most frightful scene last night . . ."

Mrs. Pollock was determined not to be parted from her Little Flower. She admitted that she could not force them to live with her at Westover, but, wherever they went, she said, she would follow . . . The hysterical accusations she flung at Ann-Marie night after night had an extensive range, but to this decision she held firm. Wherever Ann-Marie went, she would go, whether she was wanted or not. Even against Ann-Marie's will, she would save Ann-Marie from the horrors of a motherless life. At first she had pleaded her case with a certain show of reason.

"You cannot cook, my darleeng, or do the housework. You are too delicate, too—handicapped. You shall have your own rooms. I will not obtrude myself. I will keep to my own room. You and your Colleen shall almost think you are alone in the house, except that there will be what you call a Brownee, so that your meals will appear as by magic——"

"I'm sorry, Maman. Colin won't agree."

Then Mrs. Pollock abandoned her show of reason.

"Wherever you go I go. This is a free country. Where you take a house, there I take a house—and next door to you if possible. If you go to a hotel, I take a room there, too, in the same hotel, next door to yours. Not to be with you would send me to my grave. And you will need me, *chérie*, though you do not think so now. This Colleen of yours is cruel. You must have a friend to turn to when his cruelty reveals itself, and who should that friend be but your own mother? He will not be faithful. No man would be faithful to a cripple wife. You are not as other women. He will soon tire of you and turn to girls who can dance with him, play games with him, swim with him, walk fast as he likes to walk fast. When that happens I must be there. I will never leave you. You cannot escape me. However far you go, I will follow. I will be there next door, two doors off. You will open your door each morning and—*voila!*—there will I be on your doorstep."

And when Ann-Marie still refused to agree, she would work

herself up into a state of hysterical anger and distress, so that all the other inmates of Westover heard the torrent of shrill expostulation ending in high-pitched sobs. Ann-Marie lost sleep and appetite. The cloud darkened her new-found happiness, began to affect even her love for Colin. She shrank from all this noise and turmoil, and, though she would not have acknowledged it, something in her looked back with nostalgia to the sterile days of peace before this disturbing element had entered her life.

Colin watched her, his mouth set grimly, as she described last night's scene. Mrs. Pollock was fast ceasing to be funny.

". . . and when I told her that really we didn't want her—I said all the things you'd told me to say—she just got up and went to her bedroom, and then I heard the most frightful scream, and I ran in to her, and she was lying there on the floor in a sort of fit—all stiff and unconscious—holding one of the shoes I'd worn when I was a baby to her breast. I had to get brandy . . ."

"Good Lord, Ann!" said Colin, contemptuously. "Don't you realize it's all play-acting?"

"I don't think it is."

"Well, let's call her bluff. Let's get married and go as far as we can from her and see what she does. I'm probably going to Uncle James' office in the autumn, so we're not tied to Nettleford . . ."

"I can't face it, Colin. She'd follow us, I know she would. She'd come to the door and make scenes. She'd make scenes in the street. It would kill me . . . And even if she didn't——"

"Yes?"

"I'd feel miserable. I can't help it. I'd be thinking of her, lonely and unhappy, and it would spoil everything. After all, Colin, she has given up her whole life to me. Every minute of it. She's *slaved* for me. I've never spent a night away from her since I was born. Even my work with Mr. Chapman didn't take me from her——"

"I bet it didn't."

"I mean, I just went there and back in the car. I never really *left* her."

"But she's got other interests, hasn't she? She reads a lot, she's fond of music. She goes to theatres and concerts . . ."

"But only with me, Colin. I—said that to her and she said——" she hesitated.

"Well, what did she say?"

"Don't laugh, Colin. It sounds theatrical, but—in a way it's true. She said that they were all flowers on the altar of her love for me."

He gave a harsh shout of laughter, and she withdrew her hand from his.

"I asked you not to laugh."

"Well, I can't help it. It's so damn funny. At least it would be if it weren't so devilish."

She turned to him and fixed her eyes on him imploringly.

"Colin—for my sake, won't you agree to living at Westover with

5

her? I'll see she doesn't—worry you. She does run the house well,
and—we'd have the boudoir for our own sitting-room. In the evenings when you came home, you needn't see her at all if you didn't
want to."

"I've already told you that I won't agree to that in any circumstances whatsoever."

She looked away from him.

"You'd rather we—didn't get married?"

"I refuse to see that as the alternative."

"I can't be—cruel to her," she said.

"Well, you've got to be cruel to her or me. That's what it boils
down to."

"It doesn't," she cried despairingly. "I won't see it like that.
Other girls don't have to give up their mothers when they marry and
I don't see why I should."

"Other girls' mothers aren't like yours and other girls——"

"Aren't like me?"

"Yes. They haven't been brought up in that foul atmosphere,
shut away from every healthy outside influence. When first I saw you,
you looked as if you'd been reared in a cellar without light or air."

"I know, but—Colin, you can't take me away from her altogether."

"I can have a damn good try."

Her eyes hardened.

"You don't even want to understand. She's my mother and I
love her." She looked away again and he saw the colour flood her
cheeks. "She says——" she stopped.

"Yes? Let's have it."

"She says that I'm so—unlike other girls that you'll soon get
tired of me. She says that a man wants a girl he can dance with
and play games with and swim with . . . She says I'll be a drag and
you'll come to hate me. That's why she wants to be there to—help."

"And you listened to all that poisonous rot?"

"I didn't really believe it."

"No?" He spoke bitterly. "It seems to me that she's made a
pretty good start in messing up our marriage."

"Colin, *don't* . . . I do love you."

"Yes, but not quite enough, it seems."

"It's you who don't love me enough."

Desperately she wondered what had happened since the days of
her first radiant love for Colin. Then, her mother had not seemed
to exist. She did not love him less, but her love for her mother and the
thousand little memories that bound them to each other, had gradually emerged from the mist that had seemed to hide them, forging
chains from which she could not escape. Every memory of her life
till she met Colin had included her mother. Her mother's tenderness
and devotion and self-sacrifice were woven into the very tissues of
her being. And Colin wanted her to disown it, and to behave as if
it had never been . . .

"You can't build your happiness on someone else's unhappiness," she said.

"You can't in every case, I admit," he said, "but in this particular case, you can. And she won't be as unhappy as you think. She'll raise hell, but she'll get a kick out of it."

"You don't understand," she said again. "You only see her as she is on the surface. I've lived with her all my life——"

"Yes, that's the trouble."

Mrs. Gideon and Laura came in by the side gate. Mrs. Gideon kissed Ann affectionately.

"I'm going to make some scones for tea," she said. "You said you wanted to know how to make them. Come along to the kitchen and watch me."

"Don't take her too seriously, Ann," said Laura. "When Blanche makes anything she generally forgets the vital ingredient."

"If she's making ginger biscuits she forgets the ginger," said Colin.

"And if she's making currant cake she forgets the currants."

"She once made a treacle tart without treacle."

"Don't take any notice of them, darling," said Mrs. Gideon with dignity. "I have my little tragedies like everyone else, but I'm really an excellent cook."

They went indoors, leaving Colin and Laura together.

"Anything settled between you and Ann?" said Laura.

She avoided being alone with Colin now, and, when she was, began quickly to talk about his affairs, before he could mention hers.

"No," he said. "She doesn't want to leave her mother, and I won't marry her unless she does."

"A deadlock?"

He nodded.

She sat down by him.

"There must be some way out."

"It's difficult to see it."

"You seem to be leaving Ann to do all the fighting."

"What can I do?"

"Do it yourself."

He shrugged.

"I tried to. The woman screamed in my face. Now she pretends to be out when I go. She's hopeless. One can't deal with her."

"Yet you expect Ann to."

"It's Ann's job, surely."

"No, it's your job. And there *must* be a way. Something that will appeal to her. Something wildly theatrical. That's the only sort of thing that could appeal to her. I know!"

"What?"

"Blackmail."

"Don't be silly."

"It's not silly. I'm certain she's got a past. She's just the sort of woman to have one."

"She may have, but I don't know anything about it."

"I don't think you need," she said slowly. "In films and books they just throw out dark hints that might mean anything, and then the person flees the country or commits suicide."

He grinned.

"I shouldn't mind which she did."

They heard the sound of the children's voices outside in the lane.

"Trixie's here," he said.

"Is she?"

A mask seemed to close down over her face. She picked up her things and went indoors.

Richard appeared first, wet and muddy, carrying the remains of his paper fleet.

"The thin ones sink almost at once," he announced, "but the thick ones last quite a long time."

Rachel followed, wetter and muddier, but much concerned for Richard's appearance. She was suffering one of her periodic excesses of maternal solicitude towards him.

"You *are* in a state!" she said. "Come upstairs and I'll get you tidy for tea."

"All right," said Richard absently, his mind still occupied by naval affairs. "I'll make some more to-morrow. It was fun sending them down the waterfall, wasn't it?"

He allowed himself to be led indoors.

"Sorry I let them get so wet," said Trixie, "but you can't race boats on a stream and keep dry."

"You don't look much better yourself," said Colin.

"I had to do a bit of lifeboat work. It's all right. I came in old things on purpose."

Mrs. Gideon and Ann brought out the tea. Trixie looked at the door but Laura did not appear.

"Somehow I'd never have thought of putting potatoes in scones," said Ann, setting down the tray.

"You see, Colin," said Mrs. Gideon triumphantly, "I remembered the potatoes."

Colin's eyes followed Ann as she moved about with the tea-things.

Mrs. Gideon thought, they love each other terribly, but they've been hurting each other.

Richard and Rachel came out into the garden. Rachel, in her fit of maternal fervour, had cleaned Richard till he shone but had forgotten to apply the same process to herself.

"He looks a bit better now, doesn't he?" she said with pride.

"Here!" said Richard indignantly, suddenly realizing the ignominy to which he had been subjected, "who d'you think you are? You jolly well leave me alone and mind your own business."

"I put iodine on where he'd cut his knee," said Rachel complacently.

"You leave my knees alone, too," growled Richard, trying to re-establish his male supremacy. "They don't want *you* messing about with them, thanks."

"Can we take our tea to the tree?" said Rachel. "We want to be the crew of a shot-down Lancaster in a rubber dinghy with only our iron rations."

"Very well," said Mrs. Gideon, "but I wish you'd stop these dreadful war games."

"They're much more fun than peace games," said Rachel. "Oh, Laura told us to tell you that she won't be coming down for tea. She's got some stuff to get ready for her babies. May we take three scones each and four sandwiches? Come on, Richard. May I be the pilot?"

"Yes," said Richard, as they ran off to the tree, "because I want to be the rear gunner."

"All right. You're badly wounded and I'll look after you."

"I'm jolly well not, and I'm jolly well not having *you* looking after me even if I am."

"All right. The navigator's wounded. We can pretend him."

"I'd hoped Mary would come in the afternoon," said Mrs. Gideon. "Have you seen her to-day, Trixie?"

"Miss Parsons? I saw her this morning. She's very busy. She's going to Italy next week, you know."

"Yes. We shall miss her terribly."

Trixie stood up.

"May I take a cup of tea into Laura?" she said, trying to speak casually.

"Yes, dear . . ."

Laura was sitting at her writing-table, arranging some coloured raffia to be plaited into mats or baskets by tiny fingers.

"I've brought you a cup of tea," said Trixie, putting it down on the table.

Laura's eyes met hers levelly.

"What have you come for?"

"I wanted to speak to you," said Trixie. "What I told you the other day isn't true. I'm not going to have a baby. I told you I was because I thought it would make you give Hubert up, but it was a lie."

"Why are you telling me this now?"

"Because I think you'd make him happier than I could. I don't want to—force him to stay with me against his will. You're much more—his sort than I am, and—you love each other. You didn't tell him what I told you, did you?"

"No."

"It's all right, then."

She went abruptly from the room.

Laura took up her work again, but her fingers were trembling so much that she could not hold the strands of raffia. She dropped her face into her hands and sat there motionless . . .

When she came downstairs, the garden was empty. Through the leaves of the tree at the bottom of the garden could be seen the gleam of Richard's bare torso and the flutter of green as the abandoned crew waved their shirts in an attempt to attract the notice of passing aircraft.

She went into the kitchen, where Mrs. Gideon was washing-up.

"Let me give a hand," said Laura. "Where is everyone?"

"Trixie went home some time ago, and Colin's taking Ann home. Laura . . ."

"Yes?"

"What did Trixie want to say to you?"

"She'd told me—last week—that she was going to have a baby and to-day she said—it wasn't true. She said she'd told me because she thought it might make me give up Hubert."

"She is going to have a baby, Laura."

"Did she tell you so?"

"No. She may not even know it herself. But I could tell by her eyes. I knew as soon as I saw her this afternoon."

Laura stood motionless, staring in front of her.

"Can you tell by their eyes?"

"Not always, but you can sometimes. I'm sure about Trixie."

Laura's motionless form was suddenly galvanized into activity. She gave a choking sob and snatched at her coat that lay over the back of a chair.

"I'm going to Hubert," she said, wildly.

"Laura!"

She pushed Mrs. Gideon aside.

"He's waiting," she said. "I can't bear it . . ."

She was gone. Mrs. Gideon turned back to her washing-up. Her face was very white.

Please God, take care of her . . . take care of her. Let Humphrey be there with them. Let him help them. The plate slipped into the sink and was smashed . . . Oh dear, thought Mrs. Gideon, I am careless . . .

Richard and Rachel came running into the kitchen.

"We were rescued by an Air-Sea Rescue launch," said Richard.

"Too late for the navigator, poor chap!" said Rachel with morbid relish. "We buried him at sea. Only just in time for the rear gunner. He was almost dead."

"I was *not!* said Richard indignantly.

"Go and put your shirt on, dear," said Mrs. Gideon.

Colin and Ann walked slowly down the road to Westover. Ann limped slowly. Something of the gallant bravery of her swinging uneven step had left it . . . They walked in silence, both unhappily aware of the barrier between them and not knowing how to break it down. When they reached the avenue they turned by tacit consent into the belt of trees at the side.

"Colin," said Ann suddenly, "I can't fight her. She's so strong." Her voice broke.

"Darling," said Colin, taking her in his arms.

She clung to him and he kissed her eyes and lips and tear-stained cheeks.

"Don't, darling . . . It'll be all right. We'll find a way."

She broke from him abruptly and ran to the house.

Back at Greenways, he heard his mother's account of Laura's departure. The muscles of his face tightened as he listened.

"Don't you think you ought to go after them, Colin?"

He shook his head with a faint smile.

"One doesn't do that outside Victorian novels," he said.

"What can we do?"

"Only stand by her, whatever comes of it."

"If she doesn't come home to-night——"

But she came. Colin was sitting at his desk writing, and Mrs. Gideon was upstairs superintending the children's baths.

Colin saw her pass the window and went into the hall. She was going past him to the stairs without speaking, but he caught her by the arm and pulled her roughly round. They stood looking at each other in silence, tense, unsmiling. He could see that she had been crying, but her eyes were calm and steadfast.

"Well?" he said at last.

"I've said good-bye to Hubert."

"Thank God," he said, releasing her and turning back to the sitting-room.

Soon she came down and sat by him. He went on writing for a minute, then leant back in his chair and laid his hand, palm upward, on the desk. She slipped hers into it, and his fingers closed round hers tightly. He looked at her.

"You're a grand kid, Laura," he said.

She smiled tremulously.

"I still think blackmail," she said.

XVIII

COLIN walked slowly up the drive to the front door of Westover. It was, he felt, the most fantastic expedition he had ever embarked upon. Only Laura's persistence could have driven him to it . . .

"I shall make an almighty fool of myself," he had said, "and probably land up in jail."

"I don't think you will," she said, "and it's worth trying."

Mrs. Pollock opened the door of her flat to him. She drew herself up, eyes flashing, nostrils dilated, reminding him of a rocking-horse he had had when he was a child.

"May I speak to you for a moment, please, Mrs. Pollock?" he said.

Despite himself, he assumed the sinister air of the conventional villain. Had he had a moustache he would have twirled it. Had he had a cloak he would have flung one end over his shoulder.

"There is nothing further for you to say to me or for me to say to you, Meestair Gideon," said Mrs. Pollock, registering so acute a distaste as to border on physical nausea.

"I think there is," said Colin.

He heard himself speaking in a low threatening voice, quite unlike his own. He felt his features drawn into a sneer . . .

"Will you kindlee go?" said Mrs. Pollock through clenched teeth.

For answer Colin stepped into the sitting-room. She followed him. He closed the door.

"And now——" said Mrs. Pollock.

Having said that there was nothing further for her to say to him, she proceeded to talk fluently for the next quarter of an hour. She accused him once again of poisoning her Little Flower's mind, of dragging her Little Flower in the mud, of harbouring the most unspeakable designs against her Little Flower's purity . . . She thrust her face so close to his and flung her arms about so wildly that Colin was forced slowly back against the wall.

"But you have me to deal with, me to answer to," she said, her voice rising shrilly. "I do not meekly surrender my child, as you think. I follow her . . . I am there always to defend her. You cannot escape me. I weel not betray my trust. Go to the ends of the earth, and I follow. I have no ties to bind me. I am free as air. Already you make her unhappy. Already you break and crush her. I feel it. I know it. It weel become worse and worse. But always I will be there, to help, to solace, to protect . . ."

She paused for breath.

"Mrs. Pollock," said Colin, deciding to give reason a chance in this preposterous interview, "why do you take for granted that I want to make your daughter unhappy? I love her——"

"Ah!" said Mrs. Pollock, pointing a finger at him dramatically as if she had scored a point. "If you love her why not come here and let me give her a mother's care? In the evenings, when you are at home, you need not even see me if the sight of me causes you distress. But in the day I could give her the care and tenderness that she needs . . . But no!" flinging her hands out. "You will not have it so. You fear my love because your designs on her are evil. You wish to possess, to break her . . . She must be your prisoner. She must know no happiness but what you choose to give her. You prove yourself cruel, monstrous. I will nevair agree. If this is all you have come to say to me—*Go!*" She flung out her arm towards the door in dismissal.

"It is not all I have come to say to you."

"What else have you to say?"

Colin drew a deep breath and took the plunge.

"I think there is something in your past life, Mrs. Pollock, that you would not wish your daughter to know."

He felt his villain's manner returning to him. His voice was low and silky. His lips took a sinister curl.

"There ees nothing in my life I would not wish my daughter to know," said Mrs. Pollock, throwing back her head.

But she said it just too late. The second before she said it, Colin clearly discerned a flicker of dismay in her eyes. His spirits rose. He was encouraged to proceed.

"I think there is, Mrs. Pollock," he said. "May I—refresh your memory?"

As soon as he'd said it, he realized that it was a rash offer, but fortunately she refused it.

"*Stop!*" she cried. "You have said enough. Theese ees blackmail."

Colin shrugged. It was a good shrug.

"Call it," he said, "what you will."

"Blackmail, Meestair Gideon, is an ugly thing."

"Other things are—uglier," said Colin.

That, he thought complacently, was a pretty good line. He could almost hear the applause of an imaginary audience.

"I have only one answer," said Mrs. Pollock with dignity. She went to the telephone and took up the receiver. "I call the police."

"I don't think you do, Mrs. Pollock," said Colin, a good deal less sure of himself than he sounded.

She hesitated, then replaced the receiver.

"You are right, Meestair Gideon. I do not . . . Let us be frank with each other. You refer to something that took place before Ann-Marie was born?"

"Yes," said Colin gratefully. "I refer to that."

"And how, may I ask, deed you deescover it?"

Colin did his shrug again. He was getting fond of his shrug.

"I prefer not to tell you that."

"You have been spying on me, nosing on my past. That alone shows you are the blackguard I have always said you were . . . Well?"

"Well?" said Colin, playing for safety.

She flung him a glance of devastating contempt.

"What is the price of your silence?"

"I want you to keep away from Ann for two years."

"Ah!" she screamed. "So that is it. You want a wife without friends or relations or protectors. I have heard of such cases, of such men——"

5A

"Mrs. Pollock," he said patiently, "I don't think you're quite as silly as you're pretending to be. I love Ann more than anyone or anything else on earth, but, as long as you're within reach, she'll be torn between us. Two years will give me my chance."

A slow smile curved Mrs. Pollock's lips.

"You are—jealous of my eenfluence—is it not?"

"Put it that way if you like."

She was silent for a moment or two, then turned to him with a frank, rather pathetic little smile.

"Let us be friends, Meestair Gideon. If I have said or thought hard of you, I apologize. Why should we not share our Little Flower? You have nothing to fear from me. Why not all three be happy together? I will fight against you no longer, if you will no longer fight against me. There is no need of this—nosing, this—blackmailing into the past. Let us all be at peace. I am a lonely woman. I have few friends. You shall be one of them. We will all be happy together."

He shook his head.

"It's no use, Mrs. Pollock. Either you accept my conditions or I tell Ann-Marie."

"I can explain everything," she said, raising her shoulders and throwing out her hands. "Everything."

"You can explain to Ann-Marie."

Her shoulders and arms fell dispiritedly.

"No, you are right. She would not understand. She is too young . . . What do you propose, Meestair Gideon?"

"You have relations in France?"

She nodded.

"You could arrange to go to them?"

"Yes . . ."

"If you stay away from England for two years, Ann-Marie will know nothing."

"And if I go what surety have I that you still will not tell her?"

Colin thought that she had a pretty good one, but it wasn't one he felt inclined to give her.

"Only my word," he said.

"Ees that enough?"

"It is enough," said Colin.

Again her hands performed a series of amazing revolutions.

"So it is you, you, who win."

"It is me, me," said Colin simply.

Something else seeemd to strike her.

"But how can you ask me to go back there—where it happened?"

"You will find they have forgotten," said Colin. "Such things are —less regarded in France."

"You are right, Meestair Gideon. You are, I believe, a man of broad mind. Perhaps in the future we may agree well together. Y-yes, to return, to see the old scenes again it will not be unpleasant.

You have probably heard what you say a garbled version of the story. I admit, it does not sound pretty, but the manager's sister was not in the hotel at the time and what the waiter said was untrue. He brought no omelet to my room, as he said, so he could have seen nothing and, as for the poodle, it was not clipped till the next day."

"Yes," said Colin, dazedly. "May I rely on you, then, Mrs. Pollock?"

But Mrs. Pollock was caught up on the current of her memories and could not be stopped.

"Lies, lies, *lies*. All of it. They were jealous of me. *She* was jealous of me. Beauty? No, I was never beautiful, but I had charm and that is more than beauty. And I had *chic*. While she . . . like a walking rag-bag, she was, in spite of her beauty. Though, mind you, I nevair granted her beauty. If they told you she was beautiful they lied. Like a doll she was, with flat breasts. No one could say of me that my breasts were flat . . . I shall nevair forget her face that morning . . . Oh, la, la!" Mrs. Pollock uttered a sudden peal of hearty laughter." How it all comes back! I had almost forgotten it till you nosed it up again . . . I hope she is still there. Yes, I should like to see her again. Women of that type age quickly. I am sure she weel have grey hair and the pouches under the eyes. No one can say of me that I have the pouches under the eyes . . . Meestair Gideon, when they told you the story, deed they tell you how the trapdoor came to be open?"

"I'd rather not discuss the details of the incident," said Colin stiffly.

Mrs. Pollock sighed.

"Ah, no, you are young, you are English, you are shocked. You are right to be shocked. It was—Oh la, la!" Again her laughter pealed out. "It was very shocking." She grew serious. "And Ann-Marie would be shocked. I should not like her to be told. When I came to England I decided to devote myself to things of the mind. I thought it wiser. And always there has been a serious side to me . . . Well, Meestair Gideon, I bear you no eel weel. When Fate put such a weapon in your hand you would have been hardly human perhaps if you had resisted the temptation to use it. Yes, the more I think of it, the more interesting it will be to go back there. I can trust my Ann-Marie to you, yes?"

"Yes," said Colin.

"And if I keep my part of the bargain, you will keep yours?"

"I will," said Colin.

"You swear by all you hold sacred?"

"I swear by all I hold sacred," said Colin.

"We will be good friends, perhaps, in the future?"

"I hope so," said Colin.

Mrs. Pollock seemed to be much more amicably inclined to him since he had blackmailed her. He supposed that it gave him his entrée into the world of intrigue which had once so evidently been her native element.

She went to the door with him.

"I will get in touch with my relations. They have influence. It can be arranged. Good-bye, Mistair Gideon. Or, Au revoir."

"Au revoir, Mrs. Pollock," said Colin.

As soon as he reached the shelter of the trees he stopped to take out his handkerchief to mop his brow.

"Gosh!" he said to himself. "I'd give anything to know what it was."

XIX

LETITIA walked up the avenue, carrying an elegant string bag in which reposed a few purchases that she had made in the village. (Letitia always refused to do any of the household shopping, but occasionally she bought digestive biscuits to eat when she woke in the night or a pot of Patum Peperium for her own use.) Her brows were drawn into a frown, and her lips were tight. People who only saw Letitia during her social triumphs would hardly have recognized her when she was, as now, absorbed in her own thoughts. Letitia's thoughts were seldom pleasant ones, and she had several reasons at present for being annoyed.

First, there was James. After shilly-shallying for weeks about the flat, he had at last decided to take it, but was now talking of sub-letting it and had, she believed, even made tentative arrangements to go into rooms kept by a friend of his present landlady. He was like a snail . . . At one minute he would poke his head out of his shell and ask, almost eagerly, if the hot water system of the flat was all right because he knew that to a woman it was most important, and the next he would draw in his head and begin to talk about rooms . . . Sometimes she wondered despairingly if he were really as stupid as he seemed.

Short of putting it into actual words, she could hardly have offered her services as housekeeper more plainly. Sometimes he seemed to understand what she meant and sometimes he didn't. Sometimes he seemed tacitly to accept her suggestion. Sometimes he looked as if he didn't know what she was talking about.

'I could shake him,' she muttered savagely to herself.

She hadn't, of course, given up hope. She still saw herself sitting at the head of James' table, entertaining select dinner-parties, shopping in her pet exclusive shops, meeting her friends at restaurants . . . theatres . . . living a life that would give her sophisticated charm the scope it needed, her good looks the admiration that was their due.

'Buried alive in this God-forsaken hole!' she muttered.

Then there was Roger . . . Roger's insolence to James, his shocking behaviour in running away, should by all the laws of what was just and reasonable have caused a permanent breach between them, instead of which it seemed to have drawn them closer together. When she had tried to point out to James that it completely justified him in refusing to continue to pay the fees, James had said: "The boy's all right, Aunt Letitia," and gone on to talk of something else.

Then there was Miss Parsons . . . Letitia disliked Miss Parsons and often tried to persuade Lucy to dismiss her, but, when Miss Parsons gave notice of her own accord, she felt affronted and indignant. Her indignation was increased by the knowledge that Miss Parsons had been offered a good post in a good firm abroad. She laughed shrilly on first hearing it.

"*That* woman!" she said. "They must be mad."

She had accosted Miss Parsons, when next she met her, with a mocking little smile.

"I didn't know that you were one of the leading lights of the world of commerce, Miss Parsons," she said.

"I have a pretty sound knowledge of foreign languages, Mrs. Drummond," said Miss Parsons tranquilly, "and I think that's all that will be required of me."

"It will be an interesting experience," said Letitia, "and, after all, you can always return to domestic service."

"Of course I can," said Miss Parsons, as if pleased by a happy suggestion.

Lucy had decided not to engage another companion. Instead, she had engaged a girl from the village, who had just left school, and was going to train her as a maid. Letitia smiled wryly when she heard this. She remembered the maids whom Lucy had "trained" in her Midland home.

"I hope you'll discourage familiarity from the beginning," she said.

"Oh, I don't know," said Lucy. "I rather like them chatty."

Letitia had raised her eyes heavenwards in silent eloquence.

She glanced at her watch. Sally, the new maid, was starting her duties to-morrow and was coming this afternoon to have the work explained to her. Letitia had offered to conduct the interview herself, but Lucy had refused the offer.

"I know you know more about maids than I do, Letitia," she said, "but I think I can put the little thing at her ease and make her feel at home."

Again Letitia's eyes went heavenwards . . .

"Well," she said with a shrug, "don't blame me afterwards."

"No, Letitia," Lucy assured her, "I won't do that."

Julia and the children were coming to tea, too. Letitia couldn't think why Lucy had them to tea so often. It wasn't very considerate of her, for Letitia had often told her that she found children tiring—

and Julia's particularly so. They were badly behaved and undisciplined.

"I know it sounds old-fashioned," she said, "but I think that when children are with grown-ups they should be taught to speak only when spoken to. They talk such nonsense."

"I expect they think the same about grown-ups," said Lucy mildly.

She saw Hubert and Trixie Fielding approaching and composed her features into an expression of graciousness, that changed by natural gradations into a charming smile as they met.

"It really does begin to look like autumn, doesn't it?" she said. "I should think this place is quite too terrible in the winter."

"I rather like the country in winter," said Trixie. "I think people miss a lot who never see it then."

"I'm quite willing to miss a lot," smiled Letitia.

"She's always very sweet to me," said Trixie, as they walked on, "but I don't like her, do you?"

"Oh, she's quite a pleasant old thing," said Hubert.

"How she'd hate to hear you say that!"

They reached the road, and stood for a minute in the gateway.

"Where shall we go?" said Trixie. "Through the wood or up to the hill?"

"Up to the hill," said Hubert.

He didn't want to go into the wood, because it was there he had said good-bye to Laura last Saturday. Already it seemed to belong to another life . . . He had begged her to meet him by the stream.

"I don't think I can, Hubert," she had said. "It's Saturday, you know, and everyone's at home, and Blanche needs me."

"I'll be there," he said. "Come if you can. I shall wait."

And she had come, running breathlessly down the little path that wound through the trees. Her face was white as paper and she was trembling. She held him off as he tried to take her in his arms.

"Don't, Hubert . . . We mustn't . . . When I started I didn't know what I was going to do, but suddenly—just now—I knew. Hubert, you must go back to Trixie. She needs you . . . She's going to have a baby. You didn't know, did you?"

He shook his head.

"You must go back to her."

"I can't."

"You must . . . Hubert, she's sound and sweet and she loves you. You loved her once."

"Never as I love you."

"You'll love her again. We could never be happy now. You know we couldn't. Let's say good-bye. Quickly."

He caught her to him, and she clung to him for a few moments, her slender body tense and quivering, then freed herself.

"Don't . . . I can't bear it . . . We can't either of us bear it . . . Go now, Hubert . . . Leave me here . . ."

"Laura!"

"Nothing can make any difference. I know what I must do now. I didn't know before . . . Please, Hubert."

He looked into her eyes and read her inflexible resolve.

"It's cruel of you to stay," she went on. "It's hurting both of us so terribly . . . Please go."

So he had gone . . . walking with unsteady steps along the little path. At the last bend in the path he looked back. She was still standing there where he had left her, her head turned rigidly away.

There was no one in the flat when he reached home. He sat down in the armchair by the bedroom window, his long thin figure slumped wearily, his eyes staring bleakly before him. Then Trixie came in. She started on seeing him and stood irresolute.

"Trixie," he said. "Are you——? Laura says——"

"Yes."

"Why didn't you tell me?"

"I told Laura when I knew and then I told her it wasn't true."

"Why?"

"I didn't want to make you stay—that way."

"I'm staying anyway."

She crossed the room and knelt by his chair, looking up at him earnestly.

"Hubert, don't stay—just for that," she whispered. "It'll be all right. I'll go to Mum."

"Do you want to?"

She shook her head.

"I've made you very unhappy, Trixie," he said. "Will you forgive me?"

Her eyes filled with tears, but she smiled tremulously.

"It was my fault," she said. "I've taken a terribly long time to grow up, but I am grown up now, Hubert. I'll try—I've learnt a lot since I came here. I will try . . ."

He put his hand on her hair and looked at her, his heart aching.

"Let's—make the best of things, then, shall we? Try to rub along . . ."

"Oh, Hubert!"

She put her arm across his knee, hiding her face in it. Tenderness and pity swept over him. For all her talk of growing up, she was a child—so sweet and honest that one could not help but love her. It was not the love he could have given to Laura, but it held the seeds from which something strong and beautiful might grow.

She raised her head suddenly.

"Hubert . . . let's get away from here."

"How do you mean? Have a home of our own?"

"No, I mean—let's go abroad to one of the Colonies. You hate your job, don't you, and I hate all this . . . Let's start fresh somewhere . . . I shouldn't mind how hard I worked, would you? Would you like it?"

"Yes, I think I would," he said slowly. His lips took on a firmer line. He squared his shoulders. "Yes, Trixie, it's an idea. Let's try it."

Peace had descended on the household. It was a peace of exhaustion but it was peace. Godfrey's eyes met Hubert's with the old candid affection. Cynthia and Trixie talked together in a new intimacy. The four discussed their plans.

"We want a house of our own," said Cynthia, "not a bit of some-one else's house. I don't know why it makes such a difference, but it does."

"Trixie's got Canada on the brain," said Hubert, "but I have a hankering after New Zealand. We shall probably end by going to Kenya."

"Anyway, it's been grand to have been here together," said Godfrey, "and we'll be your first visitors in the great open spaces."

Letitia sensed the new atmosphere of harmony that had descended upon the family, and it depressed her, as other people's happiness always did. 'I thought I liked them at first,' she said to herself, 'but they're—terribly ordinary. Suburban, in fact.' No more damning adjective could be applied by Letitia to anyone than "suburban."

Just inside the hall she met Ann-Marie—Ann-Marie radiant, starry-eyed. She was to be married to Colin in two months' time. Her mother was going on a long visit to her relations in France and was leaving England almost immediately after the wedding.

From inside the Pollocks' flat came the sound of Mrs. Pollock's voice upraised in a gay little snatch of song as she planned the wardrobe that was to turn the "rag-bag" green with envy.

Ann-Marie's happiness in her marriage and her mother's happiness in her visit, increased the weight at Letitia's breast. Impossible people, all of them. What a tragedy that she, with her gifts and charm and experience of a wider world, should be condemned to live among them!

She entered the flat. On the floor, just inside the door, lay a letter. She picked it up. It was addressed to Miss Parsons, and it was in James' handwriting. Her heart quickened, and the clouds gathered more darkly on her brow. What could James have to say to Miss Parsons? She hesitated a moment, then slipped the letter into the pocket of her coat. No one else could have seen it. Lucy would have picked it up and put it on the table. Miss Parsons would have taken it. She remembered that she had met the postman in the drive. It must have been delivered only a few minutes ago.

She went to her bedroom, took off her hat and coat, and again examined the letter. The postmark was London and it was certainly in James' handwriting. She tried the flap, but it was securely fastened down. She went into the sitting-room. No one was there. A kettle was singing on the hob of the fire. That was one of Lucy's middle-class habits—boiling kettles on the sitting-room fire. She knelt down on the hearthrug and held the envelope in the steam till the flap could be eased up, then she went to the writing-table by the window, moved a pile of books to shield her from view should anyone come into the room, and drew the sheet of note-paper from its envelope.

Dear Miss Parsons (she read),

I am writing to ask you if you will do me the honour of becoming my wife. I have had the matter in mind for some time, but did not know that you had decided to go to Italy till I received a letter from Aunt Lucy this morning. I hope I am not too late.

My regard and affection for you have increased with every meeting. If I do not use the word "love" it is because I am neither young nor romantic, but I am convinced that the feeling I have for you would outlive any more ebullient emotion.

I need hardly say that if you are good enough to accept this proposal, I shall do everything in my power to make you happy. Aunt Letitia assures me that the flat in Chelsea (which I have now definitely taken) is easily run and in a good neighbourhood.

I shall be coming over to Westover to-morrow to transact some business for Aunt Lucy, and I hope to receive your answer then.

I remain,
Yours very sincerely,
JAMES PETTIGREW.

P.S.—All you said to me about Roger was true. I can only add that I deeply regret my own part in that incident.

Letitia was breathing noisily. Her lips were tight, her eyes steely, her face a mask of fury. So *that* was what the sly, two-faced, crawling creature had been up to! She'd disliked her from the beginning, and this proved how right her instinct had been.

Her mind worked quickly. James—poor simple James—must be saved from this unscrupulous designing woman . . . Miss Parsons was spending to-morrow afternoon at Julia's and on the next day she was leaving Westover, to sail for Italy at the end of the week. James was coming over to-morrow afternoon, bringing with him some income tax papers for Lucy to sign. Miss Parsons would not be there, but James would receive her answer. Oh yes—Letitia's lips moved with a little smile of triumph—James would receive her answer . . .

Lucy's bedroom door opened, and, on sudden impulse of panic, Letitia crumpled up the letter and dropped it into the wastepaper basket.

"Oh, there you are, dear!" said Lucy. "I've been resting for a moment, but I see that Julia and the children are just coming."

She went to the door to admit Julia with Richard and Rachel . . . There was a black streak down Richard's face and his knickers were torn.

"The little wretch has been climbing trees on the way," said Julia mildly. "May he go and wash his hands and face, Aunt Lucy?"

"I got to the top anyway. I had to because I'd dared myself," said Richard as he departed.

"One would hardly think, to look at him, that he was coming out to tea," said Letitia acidly.

"I'd have taken him home to clean up, but I knew Aunt Lucy wouldn't mind," said Julia.

"Of course I don't," smiled Lucy. "Now, Julia, you must come and look at the bit of garden that Mary's been working on. She's made it look so nice. Come with us, Letitia."

Letitia hesitated, unable for the moment to think of any excuse for not accompanying them, guiltily anxious not to do anything that might draw suspicion on herself. The letter was safe enough for the present in the wastepaper basket. Better wait till the coast was quite clear before dealing further with it . . .

They went out into the garden and inspected the plot. Richard and Rachel galloped round like a couple of frisky ponies.

"What *are* they doing?" said Letitia irritably.

"I don't know," said Julia. "It's just youngness."

"You mean youth," said Letitia with a superior smile.

"No, youngness. They get youth later."

She glanced up at the Fieldings' windows and thought of Laura . . . Laura, quiet, pale but tranquil and resolute, spending all her time on work for the crêche, making golliwogs, teddy bears, painting pictures . . . anything to fill up the long hours of the long day . . . She'll get over it, of course, but I'm sorry it had to happen.

The church clock struck four.

"We'd better go in, now," said Lucy. "It's later than I thought. Sally should be here."

Sure enough, Sally stood on the doorstep—a round-faced rosy-cheeked little girl, shy but important.

"There you are, dear," said Lucy. "I hope we haven't kept you waiting."

"Dear," echoed Letitia to herself despairingly.

"Now if you'll all just excuse me," went on Lucy, "I'll explain to Sally what she has to do and then she can run away home till to-morrow. Here's the sitting-room, Sally. You'll get here by half-past seven, won't you? Then you can make yourself a cup of tea and take one up to Mrs. Drummond. Do this room first of all. Sweep it and dust it and tidy up anything that's left about and shake up the cushions."

"I can do that now, can't I?" said Sally, who was evidently longing to enter upon her new career. She pounced on the cushions, shook them, smoothed them and replaced them.

"That's right," said Lucy. "And remember to empty the waste-paper basket. It's under the writing-table."

Sally looked into the basket.

"I can do that now, too, can't I?" she said.   "It's got quite a lot in."

Letitia had turned pale, but Lucy's smiling eyes were fixed on the child's face.

"Yes . . ." said Lucy.   "I'll show you what to do with it.   Bring it into the kitchen.   We needn't bother about salvage now, so you can just tip it into the boiler."

Letitia followed them, her heart beating violently.   She went over to the kitchen window and stood looking out as if bored by the whole proceeding, her ears strained for any comment or query from the two who were tipping the paper into the furnace.   None came.

"There!   That's all gone," said Lucy.

Letitia turned round.   They were just replacing the boiler lid. The flames roared furiously.   The wastepaper basket was empty. Not a shred of paper had escaped on to the floor.

She drew a breath of relief . . .

XX

"So that's what she asked me to say to you, James dear," said Letitia.   "She'd arranged to go to Julia's this afternoon, anyway, and she thought it would give you less pain if I gave you her message than if she saw you yourself."

"Yes," said James, "Yes, of course.   That was—very considerate of her."

There was a tight look on his face—the look of a man who has received a blow and has need of all his fortitude to bear it without flinching.

"She asked me particularly to tell you how deeply she felt the honour of your proposal, and how much she regretted that she was unable to accept it.   She has never thought of you except as a casual acquaintance, and, naturally, her whole interest is now set on this work she has been offered in Italy."

"Of course," said James.   "Naturally."

"She asked me to give you a further message, James," said Letitia, still speaking in a voice of sympathetic solicitude.   "It isn't likely that you'll ever meet her again.   She's staying at Julia's for dinner, and I don't suppose you'll be staying here as long as that——"

"No, no," said James hastily.   "I have a dinner engagement in town."

"And she leaves us to-morrow, you know.   But if ever, through any unlikely chance, you should meet her again, she begs you not to refer to it.   She thinks it would be best if both of you behaved as if it had never happened."

"Yes, yes," said James, "I understand.   The arrangement will save us both embarrassment. Proof, if one were needed, of her delicate feeling and womanly understanding."

"Need I tell you, James, dear," went on Letitia, "how deeply I sympathise with your disappointment?"

"Yes . . . it *is* a disappointment," admitted James. "One might almost say a bitter disappointment—though I don't know how I could have expected any woman——"

"Oh, don't say that, James," said Letitia, wondering whether the moment were ripe to offer the consolation of her presence in the Chelsea flat and deciding that it wasn't. It might spoil everything to be too precipitate. Better wait a week, at least . . .

"Miss Parsons is unlike any other woman I have ever met," said James. "Her good sense and even temper, her humour and strong principles and—but you know her even better than I do, don't you?"

"Yes," said Letitia, unable to keep the dryness out of her voice. "Oh, and James—one more thing——"

"Yes?"

"Lucy knows nothing of this, and neither does Julia, and Miss Parsons doesn't want them to know. She thinks that——"

"It's enough for me, Aunt Letitia, that Miss Parsons doesn't want them to know. Naturally, I myself would prefer that as few people as possible knew of it. It is not exactly—er—a humiliating or ridiculous position, but it is not a position in which one feels at one's ease. One cannot but be aware that people might think it strange that one should have ever hoped that such a woman as Miss Parsons——" He cleared his throat to cover his embarrassment, and went on quickly, "I can only express my deep gratitude to you, Aunt Letitia, for the kindness you have shown me and for the sympathetic and tactful manner in which you have delivered her message. I am not surprised that Miss Parsons, knowing you, should choose you as her messenger."

"Thank you, James . . . Well, we'd better be going indoors or Lucy will be wondering what's happened to us," said Letitia. She had taken James out of doors, on the pretext of showing him Miss Parsons' garden, in order to deliver her "message," leaving Lucy to get the tea ready. "And, James, don't be too much depressed by it. You have so many other friends, and I'm sure that you have a pleasant happy life before you, in spite of it."

James cleared his throat again and said, "Thank you, Aunt Letitia."

Lucy was just putting the tea-tray on the table.

"You'll stay and have a cup of tea, won't you, James?" she said.

James consulted his watch and sat down.

"Thank you, if you don't mind my going immediately afterwards. I have an engagement and mustn't be late for it."

"You must have one of these delicious scones. Mary made them."

James took one with an air of solemnity, gazing at it in reverent silence for some moments before he bit it.

"They are good, aren't they?" said Lucy.

"Delicious!" said James sorrowfully.

"She's an excellent cook and *such* a dear. I shall miss her terribly . . . though Sally's a nice little thing."

James finished his scone and rose, brushing the crumbs off his waistcoat with a certain reluctance, as if loath to part from them.

"Well, if you'll excuse me now, Aunt Lucy . . ."

"It's so kind of you to have come over, James dear," said Lucy, "and to bother about my income tax. I do find it so bewildering. George, of course, always used to see to it." She glanced out of the window. "Why, here's Mary," she said in surprise.

Miss Parsons had arrived at Greenways about three o'clock.

"You told me to come early," she said. "Is this too early? I'll go back if it is."

"Of course not," smiled Mrs. Gideon. "I've been expecting you for ages. Let's make the most of the sunshine, and sit in the garden. I don't suppose we shall have it much longer. It's October next week, isn't it? . . . I ought to have taken the washing in before you came," she glanced apologetically at the line of washing hanging at the bottom of the garden, "but they're not really dry yet. It was so misty this morning."

"Leave it there," said Miss Parsons. "I like it . . . Are those saucy knickers yours?"

"No, they're Laura's. Mine are those depressingly respectable ones with the darns."

"Which reminds me. Have you any socks for me to darn?"

"Not on your last visit, Mary. I oughtn't to let you."

She spoke in the tone of one ready to be persuaded against her will.

"Go and fetch them or I'll rout them out for myself . . . It would spoil the whole visit for me if you didn't let me darn socks."

"Well . . . they do seem to have accumulated again, I don't know how it is."

She went into the house and returned with a basket full of socks, which she put on the grass between their chairs.

"I'll do Colin's if you'll do Richard's . . ." She threaded a needle and ran her hand down the sock. "Don't let me forget to take the rice pudding out of the oven. It should be nearly done . . . I'd meant to have it for lunch, but the milk didn't come in time, so we had fried bread and syrup. The children love it. I thought if I made the rice pudding this afternoon, we could have it cold this evening. They like it cold with fruit."

"My *goodness!*" said Miss Parsons, putting her whole fist through the heel of a sock of Richard's.

"Yes, that's why I suggested that you did Richard's," said Mrs. Gideon demurely. "I hope you don't bear me any malice."

"On the contrary," said Miss Parsons, "I feel touched and flattered by your confidence . . . Where are the Two?"

"Playing soldiers on the rockery."

"Hello, Aunt Mary," said Rachel, standing upright. "I hadn't time to say it before. My men are defending the rockery against Richard's, and I was rather hard pressed."

"Roger gave them his pre-war collection of soldiers before he went back to school," explained Mrs. Gideon, "so they've been playing soldiers ever since . . . I hope you're being careful of the rockery plants, children. Colin took such a lot of trouble over them in the spring."

"Well, the top growth is getting a little battered," admitted Rachel, "because I've had to adopt the scorched earth policy, but the *roots* are all right, I think, and it's the *roots* that matter, isn't it?"

"Don't you dare hurt his lithosperum."

"It was dying, anyway. At least, it was after Richard took the height where it lives."

"I risked my best men taking it," said Richard. "I couldn't afford to consider vegetation."

His freckled face was tense and earnest, brows frowning, mouth set.

"Things are always life or death to Richard," said Mrs. Gideon. "He's going to be like Roger."

"Have you heard from Roger since he went back to school?"

"Yes, I heard the next day and there's a letter for Laura by the mid-day post. He doesn't usually write to Laura . . . Did I tell you that Colin gave him Humphrey's watch the night before he went back? It was sent to us from Africa with his other things, you know."

"I thought you'd given it to Colin."

"Yes, but he's never used it. He said at the time he was going to hand it on to Roger when he was old enough to appreciate it. I suppose he thinks he is now. Poor Roger! He was so pleased that it was all he could do not to cry."

"I've ambushed your general!" shouted Richard.

"Yes . . . all right, you have," agreed Rachel. "He was a rotten one, anyway. He never wanted to be a soldier, but his mother made him be one . . . He wanted to be a taxi driver. I shall promote the major. He comes of a real soldier family. All his brothers are generals. He felt frightfully out of it at their last Christmas party, not being one . . ."

"Rachel's always more interested in the families and characters of her soldiers than in the campaign," said Mrs. Gideon.

They darned for some moments in silence then Mrs. Gideon said: "We're going to miss you terribly, Mary."

"I shall miss you. It's been an—oasis, coming here."

"I'm afraid it's sometimes a bit of a muddle. I never seem to have things as straight as I'd like."

"You're—all so fond of each other," said Miss Parsons slowly. "It—gives one a nice feeling, being with you—the sort of feeling one doesn't get anywhere else. I've come to the conclusion that family life is the highest form of life that civilization has to offer."

"Not *this* sort, surely," said Mrs. Gideon. "Washing on the line, and toys all over the place and all the socks wanting mending and wondering if the milk will come in time to make a rice pudding for lunch . . ."

"Yes, *that* sort," said Miss Parsons firmly.

"Then, if you like it, you mustn't complain when tea-time comes and you find that the cake's sat down in the middle. Rachel was skipping in the kitchen, and she jogged my elbow when I was putting in the baking powder, and I put in too much."

"I didn't mean to," said Rachel from the rockery. "Richard, that man can't defend the pass. He's been dead for hours."

"I never complain when cakes sit down in the middle," said Miss Parsons. "I like it. I can't think why people don't always make them that way."

"Neither can I, Aunt Mary," said Rachel. "Mummy often does."

"Oh, Rachel!" said Mrs. Gideon reproachfully.

"But we *like* them, darling . . . How did these soldiers get here, Richard?"

"Air-borne."

"I never saw them."

"I did it when you were talking."

"Oh dear!" said Rachel.

"Here's Laura!" said Mrs. Gideon. "I hope she won't notice that I've got my old knitted suit on. I'd meant to change."

Laura entered by the gate at the back of the garden, smiled a greeting at them as she passed and went on to the house. She stood for a moment in the doorway.

"What a smell of rice pudding!" she said.

"Oh darling!" said Mrs. Gideon. "Turn it out . . . I quite forgot it."

Laura went in and returned, reading Roger's letter. She handed it to Mrs. Gideon and sat down by her while she read it. It was quite a casual letter with nothing in it beyond a few items of school news, but it held a tentative note of affection. It was as if he realized that Colin's marriage would leave her rather lonely and were shyly offering his own friendship.

"Nice of him to write," said Laura lightly.

"Yes, isn't it?" said Mrs. Gideon. Colin will be pleased, she thought . . . "Did you have lunch with Colin?" she went on.

Laura nodded.

"Ann met us, too. Her mother had gone to London to do some shopping. She's buying stacks of clothes for her visit to France. She's determined to startle the natives."

And Laura smiled to herself, remembering the day when Ann had arrived at Greenways, bright-eyed with excitement to tell Colin that her mother had received an invitation from her relations in France to stay with them for an indefinite period.

"She says that she thinks she'll go there for the next two years,

Colin," she said, "till you and I have got settled down. She seems quite pleased about it. Darling, it—solves the whole problem, doesn't it?"

"I think I carried it off rather well," said Colin to Laura afterwards. "I seemed quite surprised, didn't I?"

"Surprised?" said Laura severely. "You gave the most outrageous exhibition of over-acting I've ever seen in my life."

"My men hold the heights all round yours," shouted Richard. "Will you surrender?"

"All right," said Rachel, "if you'll care for my wounded and bury my dead."

"I'll care for your wounded but you can jolly well bury your dead yourself."

"Very well."

"We'd better not bury them really, Rachel. It might spoil the paint, and Colin said we'd got to take great care of them."

"We could bury them in a box."

"Yes, but—I've had enough of it, haven't you? Let's put them away . . ."

They took the soldiers indoors and came down carrying the cardboard box in which Richard kept his paper fleet.

"Aunt Mary, will you come to the stream with us and help sail our boats?" pleaded Rachel. "It's the last time and we do want you, don't we, Richard?"

"Yes, *please*," said Richard.

"Is there time before tea?" said Miss Parsons.

"We thought we'd wait tea till Colin came in," said Mrs. Gideon, "and all have it together as it's your last visit."

"That would be lovely."

"But don't go with them unless you really want to."

"I'd *love* to go with them," said Miss Parsons. "I *adore* sailing boats on streams."

"Come on, darling," said Rachel, holding out both hands to pull her to her feet.

Down by the stream Richard opened his box and took out his paper boats.

"I've made some new ones," he said. "Look, these three are about the same size. Let's have one each and race them. We'll start here and we can each have a stick to guide them till they come to the waterfall and the one that gets to the bottom of the waterfall first has won. You mustn't *push* them with the stick, you know— only keep them out of the way of stones and things, and loosen them if they get stuck . . . Here's yours, Rachel, and here's yours, Aunt Mary, and here's mine. Now, let's start. Ready! Steady! *Go!*"

Miss Parsons was guiding her boat with her stick, when suddenly her eyes opened wide in incredulous amazement, for there on the side of her boat, were inscribed the astounding words, "Dear Miss Parsons, I am writing to ask you if you will do me the honour of becoming my wife."

She gave a scream and snatched her boat out of the water.

"Richard!" she said, "where did you get this?"

"It's all right, Aunt Mary," he said, patiently, "they're all waste-paper."

"Yes, but this particular one . . . Where did you get it?"

"Oh that!" Richard glanced at it. "I got that one out of Aunt Letitia's wastepaper basket."

"*What?*"

"Yes, it's *quite* all right," Richard assured her again. "Honestly, she doesn't want it. I saw her put it into the wastepaper basket. I wouldn't have taken it if I hadn't *known* it was wastepaper . . . Let's get on with the race, Aunt Mary."

"Have you—have you read it, Richard?" Miss Parsons had now reached the end of the letter.

"No," said Richard carelessly. "It's only an old letter, isn't it? Can't we go on with the race, Aunt Mary?"

"I want you to tell me exactly how you got this letter, Richard."

"Oh, very well," sighed Richard, "but honestly, Aunt Mary, I haven't done anything naughty. It honestly *is* a wastepaper letter . . . We were going to tea to Aunt Lucy's yesterday and I was ready first and Mummy said that I could run on and play in the garden till she and Rachel came, but I mustn't worry Aunt Letitia and Aunt Lucy, and I *didn't*. I climbed the tree I'd dared myself to climb, and, when I got to the top, I looked round and I could see right into Aunt Lucy's sitting-room, and I saw Aunt Letitia opening the letter and reading it and putting it into the wastepaper basket, and I could see that it was a nice *thick* sort of a letter that would make a good boat, and wouldn't get wet too quickly, and, when we got in, they made me go and have a wash, and, when I'd finished, they'd all gone out into the garden, so I got the letter out of the wastepaper basket and put it in my pocket and then went out into the garden, too . . . I never thought of *asking* anybody if I could take it, because I thought that, if it was in the wastepaper basket, it was all right . . ." He paused and added ruminatively, "She opened it in a funny way."

"How did she open it?" said Miss Parsons grimly.

"She put it in the steam of the kettle. I expect she wanted to keep the envelope to use again . . . *Do* let's get on with the race."

But Miss Parsons was already speeding down the path towards the main road.

The three of them stood and looked at her enquiringly as she entered.

"I've come to tell you that I'll marry you, James," she announced.

Lucy looked from one to the other in helpless amazement; Letitia turned a greyish-green.

"This is the letter you wrote me, isn't it?" went on Miss Parsons, taking the sodden paper boat out of her pocket.

"B—but Aunt Letitia's just told me——" began James.

"I've no doubt what she told you," said Miss Parsons dryly. "Are you asking her or me?"

"Whatever's happened, Mary?" said Lucy faintly.

"James wrote to ask me to marry him, and Mrs. Drummond intercepted the letter and thought she'd destroyed it. Richard took it out of the wastepaper basket to make a paper boat and—I've only just found it."

"But I don't understand," said James to Letitia. "It was *you* who first put it into my head."

"Me?" screamed Letitia.

"Surely, when you suggested the flat and told me how easily a woman could run it and how comfortable she could be in it, you were thinking of Miss Parsons. I took it for granted you were."

"Well, you know now she wasn't," said Miss Parsons. "Come along to Julia's, James. I've left the two children in the wood and a sock of Richard's half darned, and if I'm going to marry you I must send a cable to Italy."

He followed her from the room.

"As a matter of fact," she said, as soon as they got outside, "the whole question needs a good deal more consideration than I've so far had time to give it. I accepted you simply because I was so furious with Mrs. Drummond. Do you think that's a sound foundation for a happy married life?"

James looked at her with a faint and unfamiliar twinkle.

"I think it'll do for a start," he said.

"Well, if you'll take the risk . . ."

"But, Miss Parsons," said James, still a little bewildered, "why on *earth* should Aunt Letitia——"

"James, if I'm going to marry you, you really must stop calling me Miss Parsons. You know quite well that my name's Mary."

"Yes, yes, of course—Mary," said James.

Upstairs in the sitting-room Lucy turned to Letitia with a dignity and severity that no one had ever seen in her before.

"Letitia," she said, "you must understand that after what has happened this afternoon I can't have you living here with me any longer. I'll give you a small income and you must manage as best you can."

Letitia flung herself on the settee, sobbing wildly.

"Oh, don't, Lucy . . . don't send me away . . . I do love you . . I've been so unhappy . . ."

Lucy stood, looking down at her.

"You're bad, Letitia," she said slowly. "You're bad all through. I've only realized it since you came here. You were bad to your husband, weren't you? You've been bad to me . . . I think you've been bad to everyone in this house."

"Don't send me away, Lucy."

It's been partly my fault, thought Lucy. I've been too soft with her. Father used to say, "Letty's all right, as long as you don't give her her head."

The trouble was they'd all given her her head . . .

Letitia sat up. Her tear-filled eyes were fixed imploringly on Lucy. "You won't, Lucy, will you? . . . You're all I've got. . . ."

Lucy looked down into the aging face and saw only the lovely headstrong girl of thirty years ago.

"Will you try to be better, Letitia?" she said.

"I'll try . . . I will try."

"You've been extravagant—and I'm not a rich woman, you know—and you've been unkind and you've made mischief."

"Lucy, I'll be different . . ."

Lucy patted her shoulder. There was a little twisted smile on her lips.

"I don't think you will," she said, "but I will . . ."

XXI

"It's an offer that we're never likely to get again," said James.

He and Julia and Mary stood in the drive of Westover, looking up at the house. The trees had lost most of their leaves now, and the grey mist of the autumn afternoon made the place look bare and bleak.

James and Mary had been married three weeks ago and had dispensed with a honeymoon.

"We're past the honeymoon age," Mary had said firmly. "Besides, if we'd nothing to do but sit about and look at each other we might begin to wonder if we hadn't done something foolish."

"I shouldn't," said James gallantly.

"Well, I'm not going to risk it. In any case, I want to get down to work in the flat, and I've no doubt you've got quite a lot to do at the office."

"As a matter of fact," James admitted, "it would be a bit awkward to leave the office just now. I have several rather important pieces of work on hand."

"Then you'd be far better employed doing them than sitting on the banks of Windermere or wherever it should happen to be and wishing you were. It's a marvel to me that any marriage survives the honeymoon. The very word is enough to damn it."

"I believe that the custom owes its origin to the excessive modesty of the Victorian age," said James. "They did not wish the intimate relations of the married state to be inaugurated under the eyes, as it were, of their neighbours. It did not occur to the cruder Georgians to leave their homes for that purpose. They preferred to be sniggered at by their neighbours rather than by strangers in a hotel."

"We'll be cruder Georgians, then," said Mary. "Though I'm afraid that our neighbours are so completely uninterested in us that they won't even snigger. I'd love to be sniggered at."

Julia was watching her sister-in-law with approval. Even in the three weeks of their marriage Mary had acquired an air of matronly content, a *settled* look, as Julia put it to herself. She was plumper. The new serenity of her brown eyes had perhaps a little dulled their sharpness, but they were shrewd enough still. She was dressed in a trim neat tailor-made fashion and wore an extremely becoming hat. James' pride in her was rather touching. I believe the old darling's head over heels in love, bless him, thought Julia.

"But why on earth should they want to buy it?" she asked.

"I've explained, my dear," said James mildly. "This new road by-passing Nettleford will pass the gate and they want it for a road-house."

"But, James," said Julia aghast, "think of all the money we spent turning it into flats."

"My dear girl, they'll pay for that ten times over. They don't seem to mind *what* they pay."

Julia looked at the house, head on one side . . . The peeling stucco, the broken balustrade and pediment gave it a squalid look, and it wore its squalor without dignity or regret, seeming to revel in it. She saw it behind a line of petrol pumps, with cars and motor cycles, perhaps even charabancs, parked in the drive. They would paint it up and mend the pediment and balustrade, but it would still look shoddy. It's an ugly house, she thought. It's got an ugly soul. It hasn't made any of them happy.

"It'll like that . . ." she said.

"Yes, I believe it will," agreed Mary.

"Whatever are you talking about?" said James, but he spoke without the irritation that would have shown in his voice a month or so ago. There was, instead, a new amused interest.

She's making him human, thought Julia . . . She had noticed each time she met him lately that his smile was a little less frosty, his laugh more spontaneous.

"You wouldn't see through it, James," said Mary. "You probably believe everything it tells you."

"I probably should if it told me anything," said James, "but to return to the matter in hand. By a curious coincidence all the tenants want to give up their leases just as we get this offer. Godfrey Fielding has been lucky enough to get a little gem of a Georgian house not far from Westerham, the other Fieldings are going to emigrate, Miss Pollock——"

"Ann, James dear," said Mary. "You really must try to shed a little of this Victorian formality. She's going to be Colin's wife, you know."

"Ann, then," conceded James. "I was going to say that she's marrying Colin and her mother's going back to France, while Aunt Letitia—well, I think she feels a certain delicacy about living near Julia, where she would so often be meeting us, after what happened. She's a very sensitive woman."

"*James!*" expostulated Julia. "How *can* you say that after what she did to Mary?"

"She explained that, Julia," said James. "It was one of those strange impulses that come over women of a certain age and force them to do things quite alien to their usual characters. She says that she remembers seeing the letter on the mat and after that remembers nothing about it till Mary brought it into the room."

"How simple you are, my sweet!" said Mary serenely, "but I think I like you that way. I can be catty enough for two should the need arise."

"Where are they going?" said Julia. "I haven't seen much of them lately."

"There again," said James, "Fate seems to have stepped in. They've heard of a cottage on the outskirts of Exeter that seems just what they want."

"Poor Aunt Lucy!" said Julia.

"I don't know," said Mary slowly. "I have an idea that she's got the whip hand and doesn't mean to let it go. She'll be kind but firm. She'll keep Letitia busy, which is what the woman needs."

"She'll probably marry some unsuspecting widower—Letitia, I mean."

"She might . . . and make him quite a good wife. She's had a salutary shock. She's no fool . . . I dislike her intensely, but I must admit she's no fool. She may quite possibly have learnt her lesson."

"Well, about the house," said James patiently, bringing them back once more to the matter in hand. "You'll accept the offer, Julia?"

"Yes, if you think so, James," said Julia.

She looked at the house again and said:

"You're going to be a road-house."

The westering sun caught the windows, making them shine as if with malicious glee. The crack in the stucco across the front increased the effect of a smile.

"It's pleased," went on Julia. "Did you see it smirk?"

"Really," said James helplessly, "you're too foolish for words. It's quite impossible to talk business with you."

"I know I am and I know it is," agreed Julia. "Let's go back to Greenways and have tea . . . You needn't talk business with me,

James. Just decide what I ought to do and bring the papers and put a mark where I sign."

"Hopeless!" shrugged James.

"But she has possibilities, surely, as a client, James," said Mary. "She'd sign anything. Couldn't we malversate her funds or haven't you the courage?"

"It would be too easy," said James. "She wouldn't even wonder where the money had gone to. I should like a certain element of danger and adventure if I ever took to that sort of thing."

"We shall probably find someone with just the right degree of gullibility if we look round," said Mary hopefully.

"Come along to tea," said Julia. "I have a ghastly idea that I forgot to turn off the oven. If I did, a semolina pudding will be burnt to a cinder." She sniffed the air. "I believe I can smell it from here."

Laura had got the tea ready when they reached Greenways. She had also turned off the gas in the oven.

"And not a *second* too soon," she said, looking severely at Julia.

"I couldn't remember whether I'd turned it off or not," said Julia, as if furnishing an excuse that completely exonerated her from blame.

"I lit the fire, too," said Laura. "It's quite cold to-day. The summer's really over at last . . ."

"Yes," said James, going to look out of the window at the little lawn with its golden carpet of fallen leaves. "Messy things, those leaves. You ought to get them swept, Julia."

"Colin's going to do it at the week-end."

"And don't forget to have the gutters cleared as soon as the last one's down. If they get choked up, you'll be having the water coming in through the ceilings."

"Westover's going to be a road-house, Laura," said Mary.

"Poor old Westover!" said Laura.

"It'll like it," said Julia.

"It's just told her so," said Mary. "So none of us need feel any qualms about it."

"I suppose they'll call it Ye Olde English Hostelry and have a parking attendant in a smock."

"It's only just over three months since that day James came over to meet the Fieldings," said Julia. "How quickly the time's gone!" And what a lot's happened! she thought . . . Colin and Ann . . . Laura and Hubert . . . Mary and James . . .

"It was rather a waste of time and money and effort turning it into flats at all," said Laura.

"Here James should say something chivalrous," said Mary, "but he's always slow on his cues."

"Eh, what?" said James, who was examining the tiled surround of the fireplace. "Several of these tiles are loose, Julia. They'll be falling out before you know where you are. You ought to have it seen to."

"Stop *roaming*, James, and come and have some tea," said Mary.

They sat round the fire and Laura poured out tea. Julia watched her with a sudden contraction of her heart . . . The three months had left their mark on Laura. She was thinner. Her eyes had lost something of their child-like serenity. The lines of her young mouth had—ever so slightly—hardened. Life and suffering had already set their seal on her youth.

Life and suffering would claim them all, one by one. Colin was leaving her, Roger was growing up, Richard must go to his prep. school soon. Her thoughts hovered over them all in aching tenderness, with that deep pity that is somehow so inseparable a part of love . . . And suddenly there came to her a sense of Humphrey's presence—so strong and vivid that she could hardly believe he was not actually there. She closed her eyes . . . and it was as if she and Humphrey were sitting together, talking of the children, as they had so often done in the past.

"Tired, darling?" said Laura.

She opened her eyes and smiled, pushing back the strand of hair that had fallen over her forehead.

"No . . . Just day-dreaming . . . Were there any letters?"

"One to each of us from Roger. He's very clever the way he divides his news carefully into two and sends us half each . . . Here's yours . . . He wants us to go over for half-term."

"That would be nice," said Julia. She looked at James and Mary. "Will you two come with us?"

"We'd like to very much," said James, looking pleased. "Very much indeed."

The Two burst into the room.

"Mummy, may we have twopence for ice-cream? The man's coming down the road and, remember, you've got *all* the first years of the war to make up to us."

"Yes, darling," said Julia. She looked vaguely round. "I wonder where my purse is."

"Oh, Mummy, you've not lost it again?"

"No, not lost it, darling. I distinctly remember putting it away in a safe place before I went out."

With shouts of delight, the Two began the search . . .